AMBER STONE

ANGIE ANNETTS

Cockeyed Publishing

This edition first published in 2024

Cockeyed Publishing

ISBN (ebook): 978-1-8380151-2-1
ISBN (paperback): 978-1-8380151-3-8

Cover design by www.dissectdesigns.com
Typesetting by www.preparetopublish.com

1.

Dancing's All About...

I was remarkably hot and impressively drunk. And filled with the type of vodka-fuelled wisdom that made my spoken word the truth. I felt invincible, vivacious; a bit of a sauce bucket. I was ready to conquer the world!

But before all that, I had to impart some crucial and life-changing knowledge upon Andreas.

Whether he wanted it or not.

And more importantly; before I forgot what it was.

With his back ruthlessly towards me, Andreas stood at the far end of the bar, talking to some Cypriot men, who huddled conspiringly over their whiskies as they tapped cigarettes into heavy, clay ashtrays or blew out large plumes of smoke.

But I was having none of it.

I was on a deadline.

I cleared my throat and loudly called out for Andreas in a 'yoo-hoo' voice. When he turned and smiled at me in recognition, my fingers wiggled in greeting before flagging him over.

'Come here!' I mouthed to him.

Time was of the essence.

Andreas turned back to the men and said something that caused amused looks in my direction through curls of smoke. He then patted the bar twice and made his way over. I chose to ignore his weary smile – what I had in store for him was pure gold. And *then* we'd see who was a drunken pain in the arse.

When he reached my end of the bar, he leaned on it and looked me in the eye.

'Amber. What can I do for you – another drink?'

'No, no, no,' I said, flapping a hand about. 'I've still got this,' I added, indicating the near full glass in front of me. 'No, I've got something to tell you Andreas. It's *very* important.'

Andreas quickly checked over his shoulder for any waiting customers before giving me his undivided attention. As he smiled with thin-lipped, strained patience, I tried to ignore the nagging feeling that my 'very' had *very* possibly come out as 'verrrry'.

'Important, eh? You best tell me, then.'

'It *is* important. So I want you to listen verrr... *really* carefully. Okay?' I lightly touched his nearest forearm and threw in a few solemn nods to emphasis the gravity of the matter.

'Okay, Amber. I listen carefully.'

Progress.

I cleared my throat and leaned forward on my bar stool. This was it. The big banana.

'You see, dancing... ' I began. I looked at Andreas to make sure he was keeping up. A mini silence fell between us. My right hand made small, encouraging scooping actions towards him.

'Yes, yes, dancing,' he said. 'I understand what dancing is.'

I raised a finger in the air. 'Ah! But *do* you?'

He shrugged a Cypriot shrug. 'Course.' With an upwards tilt of his chin, he gestured towards the busy dance floor. 'Like them. Dancing.'

'Ah ha!' I cried. 'You'd think so – but here's the thing – so listen up.'

Another glance over his shoulder. And when he looked back at me, it was impossible to ignore the heavy sigh and defeated sag in his posture.

I was losing him.

With no time to hang about, I learned further across the bar.

'You see... *dancing...* is all about remembering the person you once *were... or* pretending to be someone *else.*'

There. I'd said it.

It was 'out there' now.

Andreas blinked at me steadily for a few moments. Doubtless in an attempt to absorb the enormity of what I'd just told him. I held his gaze with what I believed to be that of a kindred spirit basking in the wonder of enlightenment.

He took a few faltering stabs at speaking that failed to reach fruition. That was fine. And expected; Andreas had every right to feel blown away.

Indeed, were it not for hitting the sweet spot with my generously poured fifth vodka, it was entirely possible I may have failed to have seen the light myself. And now my eyes had been opened to whole new world of possibilities and understanding – not to mention, the inner workings of dancing like an idiot at a wedding reception.

No – Andreas was right to take a moment or two.

His eyes adjusted, as if I'd just snapped back into focus.

'This what you called me over for?' he asked.

'Yes,' I replied, with a squeeze of that forearm. 'I wanted to tell you first,' I added in a near whisper.

Andreas examined my face, as though seeing it for the first time. He pursed his lips and slowly wagged his head side-to-side in disbelief.

'I know it's a *lot* to take in,' I said, reassuringly. 'But once you see it – I mean, see it *out there... happening...* you can't unsee it.'

For dramatic purposes, I raised an arm and extended a quivering forefinger towards to the dance floor.

'Look,' I instructed.

But he wouldn't. And the wagging continued.

And just as I began to wonder if Andreas hadn't

understood *anything* I'd told him, or if he might be in dire need of some light slapping to make him see sense, his face abruptly creased into howls of raucous laughter.

'Amber! You crazy! You know that?' Then he shook his head, wiped away a lone tear of laughter, and did the worst thing a barman could ever do...

... he walked away from me.

I watched in disbelief as he sauntered back towards his chums. He obviously said something about me, as he cocked a thumb in my direction and caused hoots of laughter and animated cries of God-knows-what in Greek.

Hmm...

I lifted my glass, swilled its contents and gave Andreas and his lanky long hair a silent toast.

'Well, bollocks to you,' I thought with a lopsided smirk.

One of the older men at the end of the bar mistakenly thought I was raising my glass to him. He mirrored my actions, as his sun-ruined postcard face smiled at me through bad teeth.

'And bollocks to you, as well,' I murmured, before taking a mouthful.

I shifted on my bar stool and eagerly returned my attention to the dance floor. Tonight was SkaNite at Sonny's Bar, which ranked verrrrry highly on my Hoot-O-Meter for people watching and general mocking-forward-slash-piss-taking etcetera.

Marvellous.

My eyes scanned over the designated dance area, which was formed by a large semi-circle of white plastic tables and chairs filled with sweaty tourists. Behind, stood a small stage, flanked by sun-faded curtains that were probably sparkly once. And on the small stage, stood a small and pale DJ wearing a large baseball hat back to front.

Every 'Nite' was a different theme nite at Sonny's. It was like an al fresco version of The Captain's Table on heat-fuelled steroids – making it a magnet for Brits Abroad and other Europeans who fancied some pant-swinging and a favourably-priced gargle. And now, with the combination of sticky heat and alcohol, it looked like 'One Step Beyond' had galvanised the Dad Brigade into pretence or remembrance.

Dear, oh dear.

As I let out a half-snort at the sight of out-of-shape bodies enthusiastically hopping from foot to foot, a young Scandinavian-looking guy approached the bar and stood next to me.

Swivelling on my bar stool to face him, I nodded towards the dance floor.

'Look at those bad boys go!' I said cheerily.

He glanced at me with uncertainty, then over his shoulder.

'Yep, they sure seem to be enjoying themselves.'

'Enjoying themselves?' I laughed. 'Check out Calvin Klein – he's on the verge of a heart attack!' I gestured with my glass towards an extremely red-faced and overweight bloke, whose CK t-shirt of dubious origins was drenched in sweat and clinging to his jiggling belly. With each hop, his breathing became more laboured, his face redder and the leg lifts markedly lower.

'It doesn't look like he'll be lasting much longer,' my man politely agreed. As he gained Andreas' attention and ordered a couple of bottles of Keo, I silently congratulated myself on recognising his Scandinavian accent.

I pushed on.

'Of course, it's the women who have the right idea.'

As Mr Scandi turned to face me, the miniscule narrowing of his eyes revealed that I was beginning to get on his tits.

Pffffт! *Another* one.

No matter...

'You see, what the women do, is something I've christened 'economy dancing'.'

'Econ... sorry?' he asked absently, as he checked on the status of his drinks.

I lit up a cigarette and waved it around as I warmed to my topic.

'E-con-o-me dancing. It's when you expend as little energy as possible when dancing. I mean, in this fucking heat, you'd be mad not to. Right?'

I nudged his arm a little harder than intended.

'See for yourself,' I instructed, as I blew out smoke and pointed with my cigarette. With a sigh,

Mr Scandi looked across to a middle-aged woman on the edge of the dance floor.

'See? Her legs aren't *really* moving – they're just shuffling about on the spot. But she is, *however*, milking an imaginary cow that's hovering directly above her. Like this!'

With a slack face, Mr Scandi watched on in silence as I placed my cigarette in the ashtray and demonstrated by milking my own imaginary cow.

As the bottles of Keo arrived, Mr Scandi quickly gathered them up, took a half-step away from me and mumbled something about needing to get back to someone.

Not so fast, my old China...

'See? I'm doing it by not even getting off my bar stool. Genius, eh? I mean, what is it? 28 degrees? There or thereabouts? Why would *anyone* put themselves through normal dancing in this heat? I mean... *really*?'

I put a halt to the milking, retrieved my cigarette and leaned towards Mr Scandi.

'I think the whole concept of economy dancing is brilliant. And verrrry underrated. And I think that, when you get back to Norway or Finland – or is it Sweden you come from? – you need to spread the word. You never know, it could be the next big thing, and *you* will be the one who told them first. And if you think about it, you could even do it the other way round!"

I bounced off my stool, leaned against the bar

and hung my arms at my sides. 'Look!' I said, as I performed high kicks to the right and left with alternate legs. 'See what I mean?'

Mr Scandi edged another step away and nodded to the bottles in his hands.

'Yes, yes, I totally see what you mean. But I really need to get these back to my friend. And, don't worry, I'll make sure to tell everyone back home about economy dancing. Er... thank you.'

Well, that was good enough for me.

My work here was done.

'That's great!' I said, beaming with pleasure. I picked up my glass and clinked it against one of the Keo bottles. 'So, how do you say 'cheers' where you come from? Is it Skol?'

As I noted the sudden slump in Mr Scandi's posture, I wondered if the heat might be too much for him – what with Scandinavians not being used to it. And all that.

'No, it's not Skol,' he began, wearily. 'Where I come from, we say 'cheers'. Because where I come from is Clifton. In Bristol. Which is in a little-known place called England.'

And before I could say, 'blimey' or 'cheers' or start to tell him what a bastard it can be to park in Bristol, he was gone. And I was left to clamber back on my bar stool and briefly wonder why a lad from Bristol was trotting around impersonating a Scandinavian.

As I took a mouthful of vodka, I picked him

out, sitting with his friend at a table near the edge of the dance floor. Their heads were close together as they laughed and chatted over the loud music. For a moment I felt hopeful that Bristol was telling his mate all about the merits of economy dancing, but soon spotted their surreptitious nudges and snatched glances at a couple of large-breasted girls in tight boob tubes, who were sitting across the dance floor and determinedly sucking their cocktails through straws, as though auditioning for a career in adult entertainment.

I raised my glass once more. 'Skol! And good luck to the pair of you!'

And just as I was warming up to tag on another toast – that may or may not have made mention of leg overs and emergency clap clinics – my attention was drawn to the table next to the lads, where my old mate, Calvin Klein, had indeed found it all one step beyond.

Palms resting on his chunky thighs, he took in lungfuls of air as a middle-aged woman stood over him and offered words of encouragement or concern between dragging on a cigarette.

As she gave one of Calvin's meaty, sunburned shoulders a rub, she leaned forward and urged him to drink from the pint of lager she held before his gasping face.

'Ah, yes... ' I murmured with a grin. '... the time-honoured British tradition... never mind the oxygen mask, just give the bloke his pint.'

I drowned the remains of my drink, called across to Andreas and smiled sweetly as I indicated my empty glass. Message received, I checked back for a Calvin update: he was gargling down his pint, while the woman looked on in obvious approval. Once done, Calvin lifted his jumbo, sweating head to give a few reassuring nods as he lightly patted her shoulder-massaging hand.

Crisis over.

But just as I was thinking about 'lessons learned' and how he wouldn't be trying any of *that* again in the near future, the strains of 'Lip Up Fatty' filled the air, and fuck me – boof! Calvin was off again with his woman shuffling behind him and milking that pesky imaginary cow.

'No way!' I laughed.

Andreas arrived with my drink. 'You seem to be having a good time tonight,' he said as he leaned on the bar.

I looked at his smiling long face and longer hair, which was tied into its usual ponytail and coated with an oil that always made it appear a little greasy.

I held my glass aloft. 'Wherever I can. And whenever I can,' I said before giving him a wink and taking a dainty sip with a crooked finger.

'That's good, Amber. Maybe we'll see you dancing tonight?'

As the words left his lips, Andreas straightened and held his hands up in mock surrender. I took a playful swipe towards him that was never going to reach.

'You *know* I don't do dancing!' I cried with a laugh. 'Oh... hang on... have I ever told you my theory about dancing?'

Andreas threw his arms in the air.

'No more of this dancing madness! Enough! You're driving me crazy!'

Then he tapped the bar twice, smiled at me warmly, then made his way to a couple of waiting tourists.

Well, he's no fun, I thought, as I turned to get an update on proceedings.

Right then. What did we have?

It looked like Calvin had been introduced to the delights of economy dancing by his missus. So, no imminent heart attack there. Good, good, good.

Mr Scandi-forward-slash-Bristol and his mate were now sitting with the have-a-go porn stars... and from their hair-flicking and tit-bristling body language, it seemed the lads could be onto a dead cert. Good, good, good.

And everyone else looked pissed and happy. Albeit hot, pissed and happy.

As I twisted on my bar stool to check that the Cypriots at the end of the bar were still embroiled in their huddled discussion about world domination, I felt someone lightly bump into me as they approached the bar. I turned and looked into the face of a young woman.

'*Ooh*, hello!' I said, rather camply.

'Sorry. Bit pissed,' she said with a shrug. She

looked to be in her mid-to-late twenties and was attractive, despite wearing heavy make-up that was struggling with the heat. As she cocked her head and threw me a hardened glance, I immediately felt a palpable shift or prickle in the atmosphere.

Then she let me have it.

'You're that writer, aren't you? The one whose ex got murdered. Emma someone, isn't it?'

In an instant, I felt the effects of the vodka drain from me and I instinctively reached up to trace a finger over the scar that ran in a straight line from my right eyebrow to my hairline. As she stood looking at me with a scowled sense of entitlement, I briefly wondered how I had ever thought her to be pretty.

In a state of increasing panic, my mouth made a few soundless movements.

As she warmed to her subject, she edged closer with glittering eyes.

'No – it's not Emma, at all, is it?'

I'd fleetingly hoped she was a fan. But everything about her demeanour – including her obvious pleasure at making me uncomfortable – identified her as being an 'other'.

And still, I couldn't formulate a word.

She tapped a finger on her lower lip. 'It's not Angie, is it? Because, now I'm thinking it's something with an 'A'. I saw you on the local news, back home – you know, when you went to the trial in Exeter. Ooh... just what *is it*, now?'

This was the nightmare. Being played out in

front of me. I squeezed my eyes shut for a moment, in the vain hope she'd go away. But when I opened them, she clicked her fingers and pointed at me. With a flush of dread, I knew what was coming.

'I know! It's Amber! Amber Stone!' she triumphantly announced. 'I *knew* it was you!'

As she had doubtless known all along.

Her lips curled into a cruel smile of satisfaction. As I opened my mouth to try and speak, to try and tell her she was mistaken, she held up a 'hang on a minute' finger; Andreas was there to take her order. As she spoke to him, I looked at her smug, beaming profile; the false finger nails tapping on the bar in time to the music, matched by slight shoulder-rolling sways of her body. She seemed cocky, and it suddenly occurred that she might become difficult.

With a sense of detachment, I turned my gaze towards the dance floor and watched the bobbing bodies as Desmond Dekker sang about The Israelites.

It took me a moment to realise she'd begun talking to me again.

'... was saying to my friend over there, Tina – that's her in the yellow dress – that I thought it was you when I saw you in the toilet earlier. We were standing next to each other at the sinks. Remember?'

I kept my gaze on the dance floor. Calvin and his woman were laughing as they experimented with some shoulder-lifting moves as they held hands and shuffled on the spot. I suddenly wished I was with them. Or them.

'Remember?' she asked again, with more insistence.

I slowly turned on my bar stool and briefly studied her face. Upon closer inspection, there was less to admire about her appearance; too much foundation; big, heavily-pencilled eyebrows; almost comically large, false eyelashes; the look of too much lip filler. It was a shame – beneath it all, she was good-looking enough to get away with so much less.

All that aside, I'd hardly be analysing who was at the sinks when tackling the complexities of a drunken trip to the toilet.

I numbly shrugged my response.

Nonplussed, she flicked a few strands of her long, black glossy hair over her shoulder and continued. 'Anyway, Tina said, it couldn't be you because your hair should be dark, you know, like when you went to court for the trial and all that. But I told her, look – she's got a scar on her forehead – just like the woman we saw on the telly. And if you imagined her with blonde hair, rather than dark – then it'd be you.'

As I looked down at the glass in my hand, willing her to be quiet and wondering how best to get rid of her, I had a hazy recollection of someone beside me as I washed my hands and dabbed some water around my neck in an attempt to cool down.

'And then I remembered,' she continued, 'seeing an older photo of you in the newspaper – after the murder – and you had blonde hair. Bleached – like it is now. And that's when I told Tina. She didn't believe me. So I said I'd come over... '

I slowly lifted my head to meet her gaze. 'And pretend you didn't know it was me?'

It was her turn to shrug. 'So, what did you do? Dye it for the trial?'

She paused. Waiting for an answer I wasn't going to give. Instead, I placed my glass on the bar and watched my finger wipe away neat lines of condensation from the base to the rim.

These were the moments I lived in fear of; being recognised; the unwelcome intrusion; the unwanted questions, and the assumption that a total stranger 'knew' me. I had fled to Cyprus to avoid it all. Yet, here she was – expecting her personal scoop. And worse than that – for me to revisit those dark, dark days.

I looked her in the eye and mustered something resembling a friendly expression.

'I'd rather not talk about it,' I said, calmly. I did well. The voice in my head was screaming at her.

She let out a small, uncertain laugh of disbelief and examined my face for clues of a wind-up. It didn't go unnoticed that she let her eyes rest on my scar for a few moments.

'I didn't mean anything by it – I'm just curious,' she said with an unconvincing smile.

'Look... I'm very sorry,' I began, 'but I just don't want to talk about *any* of it. Okay?'

My words were measured but firm. I prayed she'd got the message loud and clear.

Instead, she let out an ugly scoff, took a step closer and leaned in towards me.

'What did that bloke get in the end? Life? Up for parole after 20 years? Or was it 25?

I jerked my head away from her. She worked her face into a sympathetic, 'you-can-tell-me-anything' expression, but her eyes sparkled in the greedy way I'd seen before from 'others' back in Exeter, who'd angled for some gossip under the pretence of concern or befriending me. Neighbours, total strangers – they all seemed to give it a go. Before I could respond, she elbowed my arm and added, 'You must feel *dreadful* about your ex-husband,' in a sickly-sweet, insincere voice.

'Get the fuck away from me,' I said, quietly.

Another scoff. A hardening of her face.

'Ha! And just who the fuck are *you* to be telling *me* to get away from you?' She rested her hands on her hips and looked me up and down with disgust.

'Look,' I said, 'I've told you nicely – I don't want to talk about it. So, *please*... just leave me alone.'

I could feel my hands begin to tremble through fear and rage.

'Just leave me alone,' she mimicked with an ugly expression. 'You should be grateful anyone's talking to you – no wonder you're sitting on your own – leading that poor man to his death. You should hang your head in shame. I mean, how on *earth* do you live with yourself, you murdering old slag?'

As she spat the last words in my face with a look

of triumph, it crossed my mind she could be itching for a fight. I circled a hand around my glass and wondered if I had it in me to smash it into her face.

Of course I didn't.

I released the glass and unsteadily got to my feet. Her words had catapulted me back to that hot summer night. Of my own face being smashed. And leading that poor man to his death. As she continued her rant, I felt a tremor of dizziness as her voice became white noise. I gripped the edge of the bar and became aware of Andreas pleading, 'Ladies! Please!' I wiped my forehead and incredulously inspected my sopping hand.

And she was still going strong.

I picked up strains of the original version of 'Red Red Wine' being played and lifted my head to gawp numbly at the figures on the dance floor. Whilst in front of me, she stood with her hands wildly gesticulating as her mouth formed distorted words.

As I felt myself sway; a flashback.

Of that poor, poor man.

Then in a beat, I was back to real time.

Red Red Wine. Oblivious dancers. A few curious onlookers. And one snarling bitch, eyeballing me with a challenging and expectant expression. I scooped up my phone, bag and cigarettes before throwing Andreas a half-shrug of apology and shouldered her out of the way.

As I passed, I hissed into her face, 'I don't live with myself. *Alright?*'

I managed to get a few steps away before her voice filled the air. 'Good for you, Frankenstein! Good for fucking you!'

I stopped in my tracks. Considered my options. Then continued walking away on legs that felt like jelly. As I felt conscious of heads turning my way, she screeched out her final offering. 'That's right! Fuck off, you monster!'

Gulping back sobs, I somehow reached the pavement and slowly weaved through the mass of milling tourists. Every unintentional bump or nudge I received felt like a personal attack. As if they *knew*. As if they *all* knew. Spotting a cruising taxi, I flagged it down and gave the driver directions before gratefully slumping into the back seat. Unable to stem the tears any longer, I let them run freely down my face.

The taxi made a tight turn in the road and slowly drove back past Sonny's. With my head leaning against the window, I numbly picked out Calvin on the dance floor; he looked as though he was having the time of his life.

With a familiar stab of self-hatred, I asked myself; what gave me the right to be taking the piss out of decent people?

Then I wiped away a tear and wondered how much I'd give to pretend I was someone else. Or remember the person I once was.

2.

Pebblemania

I took my breakfast to the poolside veranda and disinterestedly picked at the chunks of watermelon and olive bread. The events of the previous night still felt brutally raw and weighed heavily on my thoughts. And on top of everything, I'd walked out of Sonny's without paying, meaning I'd need to go back at some point and clear my bar bill. But not for a while; I'd be giving the place a wide berth until I was sure 'she' had buggered off back home after her week or two in the sun. And taken her disgusting mouth with her.

As I gazed into the distance, at the dazzling light that bounced off the Mediterranean, I struggled to stop replaying the exchange we had – knowing it would take me back to the places I fought so very hard to avoid on a daily, hourly or minute-by-minute basis. With her vile words still ringing clearly in my ears, I somehow managed to fast-forward past *that night* and instead settled on the months immediately after Spencer's murder. Of the jumbled, nonsensical and dazed days that passed achingly slowly, sped up, then merged into an everyday normality of madness and autopilot living. Of the time spent in hospital – unable to wail in grief when I missed Spencer's funeral as I recovered from the jaw and facial injuries and broken ribs.

And of the seemingly never-ending dental appointments, where I readily welcomed any discomfort or pain.

Let it be me, instead.

My eventual return to the flat was overwhelming and horrendous. The place had been half-trashed by Clarke. The Police almost managed the rest. If Elena hadn't been with me, taking control, gently guiding me towards the couch as she cleared up the mess and, more importantly, any traces of Clarke, I think I would have spiralled to new depths.

As I slowly convalesced, Elena arranged for painters to redecorate around me as I sat in cushion-hugging silence. Handymen arrived, as if out of the damaged woodwork, to replace the ruined doors, fittings and work surfaces that Clarke had gone to town on. And she'd patiently sit beside me with her tablet, offering gentle encouragement to pick out new furniture I wasn't interested in.

After all, money was no object.

I was Spencer's main beneficiary.

Obviously, I didn't feel entitled to take a penny. And as I repeatedly told Elena – if it wasn't for me, he'd still be alive. But his will – updated after our divorce – had been crystal clear; with no immediate family still alive, nor a long-term partner, he had chosen me. And the more I voiced my reluctance to Elena, the more she pushed back; it's what Spencer wanted; nothing was my fault or of my doing; he loved you. Then with her practical head, she reminded me that I'd be unable to earn for some time yet.

Still, I resisted. And still, Elena urged me take my inheritance. She wore me down and with more than a degree of discomfort, I finally agreed.

I gave away a fair-sized chunk to various charities Spencer liked to support, including an East London photography academy for the underprivileged.

And using Elena's words as a reminder – or permission of sorts, I kept the rest.

The ridiculous London prices meant Spencer's Camden flat had sold for a small fortune. I threw in the furniture as a goodwill or I-don't-know-what gesture, which suited the overseas buyer who bought it for his student son. The estate agents – after possibly helping themselves first – cleared out Spencer's personal effects, with instructions to give his cameras and equipment to the academy and clothes etc to charity. The rest, they boxed up and sent to me and deducted their costs from my proceeds.

Back in Exeter, two large and bulky cardboard boxes remain unopened in the depths of my wardrobe.

I just *couldn't.*

Aside from the flat, Spencer's growing success and glorious mentality of 'save half/piss the rest up the wall' meant he'd put away a tidy sum. And suddenly, I had the money to live pretty much where I liked. I could have and should have moved. But the flat offered me the daily punishment I deserved. Besides, at the time, I possessed neither the energy nor desire to cope with the upheaval of moving.

I whiled away the days doing nothing in particular, becoming a numb slave to daytime TV. Elena would pop in whenever she could. But after a while, her soothing tones changed. She wanted me doing something. Anything. What about my writing? It was the funniest thing I'd heard in ages, so I cruelly laughed in her face.

But she kept on at me.

Do something. You need to be doing something. Spencer wouldn't want you lounging around all day.

I told her it was time for her to go.

The self-loathing I felt as she walked out the door, stayed with me all night. I dwelled on her words and kicked them around. And remembered Spencer's unwavering support and enthusiasm for my writing; he'd *so* wanted me to do well. And achieve. I slept fitfully on the couch as I wrestled with my sleep demons, and when I woke, it was to the decision to brush the dust off of Susie. And take things from there.

With a rusty feeling of resolve, I made the pledge: I'd do it for Spencer.

But not before phoning Elena to whole-heartedly apologise and thank her.

With the darkest months fast approaching, and after a couple of teary false starts, I shook myself out of lethargy's grip and got my head down with Susie. I edited. Re-edited. Then threw in some more flouncy blouses, an asthmatic 3-legged cat called Brutus, and a surgery team building session in the moors, which literally went tits up when Susie and Nurse Simmonds ended up having a feisty and scantily clad wrestling match in the mud.

Hose me down, Doctor Rogers!...

Then I added a twist of this. Some sprinkles of that.

One up the Khyber from Dr Wellard.

An ill-fated – but well intended – séance, where Susie failed to hook up with her parents, but instead became rather chummy with a 1920's Parisian hairdresser called Bernard.

A bit of bish bash bong.

Then I edited again. And again.

And during the silent nights of Christmas, I submitted the opening chapters of 'Just Susie' to as many chick lit agents I could find, along with the handful of publishers who accepted direct submissions.

At a sudden loss as how to fill my time, I left my self-imposed prison and world of online grocery shopping and took to the streets in a wide-brimmed hat tugged down over my forehead. I'd wander about in a state of numb bewilderment – taking in the bright lights, cheery decorations and the world going about its serious business of celebration.

Oblivious to my heartbreak.

I moved about slowly in my impenetrable bubble, going a little further each day, almost relishing my feeling of isolation. And when the days rolled into the New Year and the world went back to work, I'd pace my flat and impatiently check for any Susie news.

Nothing.

As the days turned into weeks, rejections began to trickle through; standard letters offering no feedback and wishing me luck elsewhere. I began to question the crap I'd written, felt restless and heard mocking whispers of failure in my head. I took to walking again, and as I got stronger, my walks became longer and further. I even ventured to Gandy Street, where I defiantly stood outside The Grub Shack and took in its transformation to a trendy burger bar with a challenging stare.

When I'd had my fill and felt as though something had been resolved, my first instinct had been to pop into Elena's salon a few doors along and tell her about this landmark in my recovery. But after a few steps I changed my mind. What had happened, felt like a private exchange; a challenge to myself – which I'd met head-on. As, aside from the flat, The Grub Shack was the only place that held any meaningful 'Clarke connection' for me, and I felt chit-chatting about it would somehow dilute my achievement. The months of not seeing the place had turned its bricks and mortar into a Clarke-faced monster. But now, I just saw it as a burger bar.

With a half-smile and dismissive glance, I walked away.

Back at the flat, I checked my emails for anything Susie-related. When I saw there was nothing, I felt disappointed and fidgety. And for the first time 'since' I felt the need to be getting on with something – my life, I suppose – and was eager to take another step forward.

The days passed by.

Nothing.

Still nothing.

Then a bite.

And before I knew it, I had a publisher. And things to do.

I pushed my sunglasses past my forehead and squinted into the blazing sun as I picked up my phone. After a brief scan of the messages, I heavily sighed.

'Be careful what you wish for,' I murmured.

With a wince, I opened the latest email from my publisher, the mighty Eddie Hirst – who was one unhappy bunny and *really* pissed off with me. He was wanting – or to be more accurate – demanding, a progress update on the Susie sequel. But try as I might, I was doing nothing but hitting a brick wall.

I still found it inconceivable how quickly Susie rumbled into life, picked up a head of steam and was now like an out-of-control runaway train. Initially, she'd been signed up as a low risk 'digital first' novel. Simple concept; if she sold well as an eBook or 'print-on-demand' paperback, Eddie and his crew would take an overview and decide if it would be financially viable to do a lengthy print run, full marketing campaign, then shoehorn her into the major retail outlets.

After some speedy and collaborative editing, including a last-minute dedication to Spencer – using his occasional nickname of 'Shutterbug' in the hope of privacy – Susie donned her best blouse and went live. And against all the odds, she went apeshit mental. Eddie and his team worked hard and got Susie endorsed by other writers he represented, (including a couple of popular comediennes) and in front of prominent book reviewers, bloggers and social media influencers who, in turn, got Susie charging up the Amazon charts and capturing the imagination and approval of readers.

Or at least some of them.

Along the way, Susie picked up the dreaded 'Sticky Keyboard Award' – a badge of dishonour for dire literary offerings. I remember it really stung at the time and felt surprised at hearing Eddie's raucous laughter when I whined to him about it.

'It's brilliant!' he boomed down the phone. 'You'll see.'

As ever, he was right. Susie was totally unfazed and marched on, tits first, to even better sales and some weird form of cult status – with the consensus being; the book was so awful it was genius. Fans posed online with frilly blouses and bad wigs (one even went to the lengths of having the 'bastard perm' – and that was some bloke from Sheffield) or with a variety of outlandish homemade cakes. One particularly enthusiastic female even posed naked – but for three strategically placed pebbles, with the caption, 'TAKE ME NOW, DOCTOR WELLARD!'

The list goes on...

As do the partial nudity photos.

Or the ones of men or women dressed as Susie; mud wrestling, posing with a clipboard, a crystal ball or a cat with one of its hind legs poorly hidden. Nurse Simmons also got a look-in (mostly in garish Abba-type sparkly outfits), as did Doctor Rogers (some were humorous Doctor poses, whilst others bordered on obscene) and naturally, Christian Wellard (more often than not, fondling his pebbles with a dreamy expression... whilst others bordered on obscene...).

All that, along with some terrifying rumblings about a Susie Convention being arranged in Brighton.

Pebblemania erupted.

Susie keeps selling.

And I'm still trying to get my head around why she's loved so much.

I went through it all in numb disbelief. After the initial whirlwind of emails and phone calls, I finally came face-to-face with Eddie in his plush London office, where I met an attractive silver fox. All cufflinks, cologne, sharp suit and a sharper tongue. He told me I had 'a unique voice' and had given a new slant on traditional chick lit books – one that could capture a new and wide audience who were looking for something fresh.

To this day, he still has no idea my intention was for Susie to be as conventional as her supposed peers. And that I had dismally failed.

Yet, he spoke of a bright future for the pair of us. Got me to sign on the dotted line. Then set me off to work on more edits.

I travelled back to the West Country with my head spinning and a strong desire to get mildly shit-faced. And when I entered the flat, I remember feeling some kind of shift – as though its atmosphere had changed.

For the better.

I invited Elena over and we drank vodka and giggled and toasted one another.

And hugged.

It was a good day.

*

Shortly after Susie's online launch and meteoric rise, came a request for a trade press interview. I was reluctant from the start – the media already had pre-trial snippets about myself and Spencer – but Eddie convinced me that the only topic on the table would be Susie. In the end, it seemed I had no choice in the matter.

Despite my nervousness at the time, the female interviewer and her kind smile put me at ease. I was further relieved to learn she was happy to use the Eddie's black and white publicity photo he'd had taken of me wearing my wide-brimmed hat. The selected shot had been sympathetically taken in a subtle soft focus, with the brim covering or casting enough of a shadow over my still-healing scar and revealing as little as possible about my appearance. Eddie let me have my way with that, at least. Which made me wonder if it had suited him all along.

After some early innocuous questions about Susie – designed to settle and encourage – came a question about my writing habits. This included a reference to using a static caravan as a 'writing boot camp'. Told by Eddie to expect the question, I answered with honesty and trust about my writing regime for those 6 weeks – but omitted to tell her what kind of beach I wrote my notes on.

Looking up from her own notes, the reporter gave me a tight smile before asking, 'Was that the nudist beach? Was that where you got so much inspiration from?'

In shock, I looked at her blankly, and when it became evident I wasn't going to answer, she appeared completely unfazed and instead, jumped to her next question.

'Can you tell me what happened the night your ex-husband was murdered?'

I was caught completely off-guard and stuttered and stammered as she continued to fire a catalogue of increasingly prying and personal questions my way. And despite my garbled and repeated protests, they came harder, faster, and more intrusive.

Her face remained open and friendly throughout. Her tone soothing and concerned, as though asking whether I'd felt disappointed by a restaurant's menu. And when she finally realised I wouldn't answer her questions, she tried to prompt me by putting words in my mouth.

I recall shaking my head at her, willing her to stop – but she was relentless.

At the point she suggested I'd based Susie on myself and Doctor Rogers on Spencer, I found my voice, loudly told her to go fuck herself and walked out.

Eddie was wholly unimpressed when he found out. And of my subsequent decision to not partake in more interviews. He told me I had to be 'out there', selling myself and Susie. But I wasn't willing to deal with any rubbernecking ghouls. For anything. Or anyone. I was even prepared to walk away if it meant keeping what was left of my sanity.

After a frank and difficult conversation (that occasionally became heated), we made a compromise; Eddie's team would set up an account for me on X and post updates or whatever else they deemed fitting. They'd keep an eye on the followers and block anyone behaving inappropriately. The account would follow back those that didn't look like trouble, (Eddie had a thing about authors not following back as being "stuck up their own arse") and when the mood took me, all he asked was that I posted something or engaged with followers.

With TikTok and Instagram being visual, Eddie said we could park those for now. Likewise, Facebook – purely because he wasn't a fan.

All things considered, it was very generous of him, given his position and hard-nosed reputation. But he understood that videos or photos of me all over the internet could attract unwanted attention when I was still healing.

I had no desire to be on social media but understood its necessity. I told Eddie that sounded fair and thanked him.

In return, I was told to "fuck off and get my head straight", which he delivered with a trademark twinkle in his eyes. I remember laughing as I got up to leave. But when I closed the door to his office, I had a nagging feeling he was sizing me up to write 'my story' or maybe, get someone else to do it.

When my head was straight.

When the interview was published, most of

the emphasis was on my "petulant and arrogant behaviour" rather than anything particularly Susie-related. Soon after, (and beneath the screaming headline of "The Naked Writer") a tabloid reprinted parts of the interview and littered the rest of the piece with titillating semi-falsehoods. It ended with the revelation I was refusing to do anymore interviews – which apparently added to my 'mystique' and only served to fuel more interest in myself and Susie.

And when Clarke's trial began, the circus really came to town.

I remember thinking back at that time – amongst the utter madness of it all – to Eddie's twinkling eyes and wondering if, all along, he'd set me up with the interview, knowing what would happen.

I'll never know.

But if it hadn't been for my eagerness, ego, naivety and *total* stupidity, I should have told Eddie from the start, I wanted to use a pen name.

If only someone had suggested it.

But that someone should have been me.

I'm a fucking idiot.

And Eddie's no fool.

Missus Mouth Almighty from Sonny's had been right about one thing; Elena returned my hair to its natural near-black for the trial. I was hoping to be as unrecognisable as possible – which I couldn't achieve with a peroxide crop. As I dashed in and out of Exeter Crown Court with my head down, collar up, hat on and sporting big sunglasses despite the late spring clouds and chill, everything was fine, until one day, a sudden gust of wind temporarily dislodged my hat – resulting in a flash of cameras and my scar exposed. My standout feature.

As it turned out, the courtroom sketches glossed over the scar and didn't overly look like me.

But that was neither here nor there, when the photo Miss Mouth Almighty referred to was given to the press – courtesy of a so-called London 'friend'. It showed me in all my peroxide glory, included a smiling Spencer and was taken at our wedding reception. She also gave an 'insight' to our relationship, along with how Spencer and I met and, furthermore, how our romance 'blossomed'. She also described me as "flirty, fun and frisky".

The rage and betrayal I felt was total.

We've not been in touch since...

As the trial unfolded, and tales of nudey beach and booze and casual sex were revealed, Susie's sales went through the roof as I was depicted as a sex-mad femme fatale.

And when it was all over, Eddie was on my case. He was going to go hell-for-leather to get Susie into bookshops for the pre-Christmas rush. And whether I liked it or not, I would be attending a launch party, doing in-store book signings and maybe a 'carefully vetted' interview here and there.

Until then, as long as I was whacking out a much-demanded Susie sequel and occasionally dipping my toe into X, he'd leave me alone. But come early winter, it'd be time to toe the line.

My dream had happened too fast and too wrong. Reporters began to hang around the flat, waiting to ambush me with their cameras and questions whenever I took an increasingly infrequent step outside. But I wanted none of it. Only for Spencer to be alive again. And to be left the fuck alone.

My already-fragile mental health took a tumble.

And something had to give.

So, I ran away from the circus and ended up in Cyprus – picked for no other reasons than a liking for their food, it was hot, and 2,000 miles away. And after an online struggle to find an available villa for the time I wanted, I finally struck lucky when a letting agent came up with one about to go on the rental market. A price was negotiated and I snapped it up for the maximum 90-days my passport allowed.

In essence, I did exactly as Eddie suggested; I fucked off to get my head straight.

But not before seeing Elena to get my head straight. Peroxide again.

With a heavy sigh, I opened my laptop.

3.

Is This Progress?

Susie and Doctor Wellard have taken to hosting Wife Swap parties, and pull numbered pebbles from a lavishly embroidered pillowcase. Our Susie makes a gracious host as she mills amongst her expectant guests and lightly fingers her pearl necklace as she offers up a tray of homemade vol-au-vents.

Nah.

Bare-breasted and with her favourite blouse tied around her nut, Susie gallops over the fine sand of a West Cork beach. She whoop-woos at gawping holidaymakers as they rush to cover young eyes and relishes the throb-a-thon she receives from bouncing about on a ten-year old stallion called Craic.

If she gets a move on, she'll be more than ready to give her hunky shagmeister, Doctor Wellard, a well-earned treat when he gets home from work...

Worse.

Susie opens a frilly tea shop called 'Scrotes'. By day, she nips about in a 1950's housewife pinny. All homemade carrot cake, bone china crockery and her porcelain decolletage on view. 'I'll be Mother!' she says brightly, as she pours perfectly brewed tea for her gasping clientele.

But... by night... 'Scrotes' morphs into a massage parlour, with Susie sporting a 1950's pinny, a pair of patent slingbacks and nothing else.

'Shall I be Mother?' she asks the old scrotes as they lay naked and poised on the back-room massage table. Susie tells them what naughty boys they've been as she dishes out a firm rub down and slap about with a damp tea towel.

Maybe a cheeky jostle in the nether region... my, what gasping clientele...

For a few extra bob, they can get the House Special, which involves Doctor Wellard being wheeled-in on castors. Producing a freshly buffed stethoscope he'll ask, 'Tell me where it hurts,' before snapping on a pair of surgical gloves.

Dear Lord. Shite of the highest order.

Susie didn't get to go to Oireland with her hunky shagmeister.

And neither did I.

Of course, now I understand – or rather, have *adapted* to the fact 'Just Susie' is a load of old bollocks and viewed as a parody, I struggle to comprehend why anyone of sane mind would willingly swap their hard-earned pleasure vouchers to read it.

But swap they do.

I suppose I should mind – the way Susie's viewed – but it seems I've unwittingly stumbled over some kind of formula that gives pleasure to some people.

And sells.

It's strange... even after spending those dark (and darkest) months trying to improve it, beat it into shape and generally give Susie a good slapping around the chops – when I gave it a final read through, there remained a nagging concern it appeared as though a deranged, cat-loving bag lady had stumbled over a functioning laptop and whacked out a novel whilst steadily working her way through a healthy supply of Tennents Super.

But I was proud of Susie then. And still am.

I can't even imagine what'll happen when Susie hitches up her tights and hits the bookshops. But I suspect my friends in the press will have a field day.

And despite being careful about what I see online (including a complete swerve of those pesky hashtags) or Elena alerting me to anything deemed 'safe', it seems some commentators have despaired at Susie's success to date. One notable journalist even referred to my offering as "inane crap" beneath a roaring headline of, "IS THIS PROGRESS?"

And perhaps he's right.

Yet for every horrified reader who thinks I've committed a "crime against humanity" (a comment that nearly had me spraying a mouthful of coffee), there are a dozen avid fans – some of whom "identify with their inner Susie".

I dread to think what that might involve, but I wish them well.

But amongst the lovers, the haters, the indifferent, the feminists who want to set my tits on fire, Yours Outraged from Welwyn Garden City and a very strange follower called @ballbagderek, calls for a sequel have been impossible to ignore. Along with the rumbling demands for a film or Netflix series that have gradually picked up pace.

Which in turn, have fuelled Eddie's Jaws-like circling of my inbox, sniffing out pound signs as a shark would fresh blood.

I just wish I had it in me to write it.

God knows I've tried. And am still trying.

But given I wrote Susie's first draft when, mentally, I was more or less in a good place – what chance did I have now?

As I reached for a cigarette and gazed towards the twinkling Med, I was hit by the sudden memory of sitting in my Sophia Classique, head down and happily tackling my daily writing. I squeezed my eyes shut and shook the image away before it led elsewhere.

The sea was back again, along with a distant fishing boat.

I let out a half-laugh. 'Maybe I need a bigger boat!' I said aloud, as I was hit by the image of Eddie creeping up behind me to the theme music from Jaws. I shuddered away the thought, along with the brusque tone of his latest email and lit my cigarette.

As I blew out smoke, an unexpected surge of recklessness saw me reaching for my phone and opening X.

I scrolled about with the squinty-eyed wince reserved my occasional forays and hooted with laughter when I saw @ballbagderek had just had an "unsatisfactory flossing session". Quality.

Dipping into my feed, my first reaction was relief I hadn't posted any bollocks about economy dancing before the night went so badly downhill. I was already guilty of posting a couple of times whilst under the influence – only for one of Eddie's team to promptly take them down. The last made mention of the "sea being no one's mama". God knows what I was thinking... but it did cause Eddie to bare his shark teeth and have a few words with me.

Apparently, I was supposed to be posting stuff about my writing, with tantalising teasers about the sequel I wasn't writing or tips on my writing technique – the one I didn't have. Or, just general comments about 'stuff'. *However,* it appeared 'my' latest was a repost from another of Eddie's authors whose 'contemporary romance' had just been released, and I was urging my followers to check it out. Neat marketing.

Below that... ah... I was asking who would be up for a Susie Convention.

Dear Lord.

So. What did we have?

As ever, I didn't delve too far into the responses,

but from a brief scan, it appeared that aside from a few people who'd prefer to spend their time self-harming in some imaginative way, the majority were frighteningly eager for it to go ahead. And bewilderingly, it appeared that folk were looking forward to dressing up for the day, with @timtomready weighing up the merits of a pleated skirt versus a "nice pair of Doris Day slacks".

Jeez. If that ever rumbled into life, would that be something else I'd be expected to attend?

Maybe.

And somewhere down the line, after Susie hit the bookshops, the 'other' interviews would come. The ones Eddie would pressure me to undertake. As it was, human carcasses had already been thrashed about due to his reluctant rejection of offers.

I tried to imagine what my return to England would be like – to my 'literary dream' and struggled to imagine how I'd cope.

I switched off my phone, gave my pathetic writing attempts a dismissive glance, and slowly closed the laptop's lid.

Getting to my feet, I stubbed out the cigarette, stretched, and took in the view that never failed to mesmerise. From its elevated position, the villa overlooked a banana grove, and beyond, to the shimmering Mediterranean that hugged the sweeping coastline from Coral Bay towards Paphos. England and its bookshops and reporters felt a million miles away.

The familiar gratitude washed over me for having the opportunity and space to try and heal – something most other victims wouldn't be afforded.

Thank you, Spencer.

Beyond the grove, snatches of the main coastal road could be glimpsed. I enjoyed hearing the distant noise of passing traffic or occasional shrieks of pleasure as tourists rode by in a convoy of quad bikes. They served as a reminder that life went on. And people were out there. Having fun.

The villa itself, is white with a pitched, red-tiled roof and has glorious bougainvillea climbing its walls. Along the side of the villa that looks over the sea and grove, is a covered veranda with a table and chairs – home to my al fresco dining and unsuccessful writing sessions. And at the front end is a good-sized swimming pool with sun loungers. To the right of the pool is a cushioned seating area and hot tub, housed under drapes of white fabric and supported by ornate white and gold painted pillars. Bunched white curtains hang from each pillar, tied with a tasselled gold cord. It all looks a bit camp and 'Carry on Cleo' – but I love it.

There's a pool-side shower, along with a small outhouse full of inflatable toys and airbeds, and to my deepest of pleasures, a battered, but perfectly functioning, portable CD player/radio. This is little beauty is my sunbathing companion and dutifully plays the legend that is Radio Aphrodite – "All your favourite tunes on the sunshine island of *lurve*".

Said tunes are as cheesy as Club Tropicano fuck – but in the heat and the sun, it all sounds bang on and wonderful.

But what I love most about the villa is its privacy. As a detached white dot up a hill, I can wander about naked and partake in my cherished nudey sunbathing without bothering, or being bothered, by a soul.

Except Pool Man.

Who managed to scare the bejesus out of me when he rocked up the first time. Totally unannounced.

I'd been laying on a lounger, eyes shut and happily listening to the Isley Brothers telling me all about the Summer Breeze. I'd only been in the villa a few days and was fresh from groping my way around to find the essentials; decent bars and a good supermarket. And I recall feeling relaxed for the first time, in such a long time.

I didn't hear Pool Man pull up on the crunchy semi-dirt road on the far side of the villa, nor opening or closing any of his van doors. I didn't hear Pool Man pad down the access steps that led poolside in his flip flops. But at some point, I just became aware of *someone else.*

With a jolt, I had opened my eyes and found him on the far side of the pool, giving it a sweep with a long pole with a net on its end – the one which normally rested across some hooks behind the hot tub. Instinctively, I let out a squeal of surprise, rushed an arm across my breasts and began to tug at the towel beneath me to cover my lower parts.

He seemed oblivious to both me and my squeal; instead, his head was down and he appeared focused on the task at hand. Yet it was impossible to tell where his gaze was directed, as he wore a pair of black wraparound sunglasses with impenetrable lenses.

I lifted my backside and flapped a corner of towel across me, and with one arm still over my chest, I sat up straight and used my free hand to shield my eyes from the fierce sunshine. Almost immediately, I could see his hanging earphones.

I raised my voice to a loud, 'HELLO!!' then made big, sweeping arcs of a wave. 'HEL-LOOOO!! EXCUSE ME!!'

Success. He stopped. Pulled out an earphone. Looked my way, shrugged and said, 'Yes?'

I could have laughed at the pure comedy value.

'Sorry,' I said, 'but what are you *doing* here?'

'Every Friday.'

It seemed he didn't want to elaborate.

His accent could have been anything. And he wore tired-looking jeans and a polo shirt bearing the logo for a pub I'd seen in Coral Bay – aptly named, Coral Dreams. He had a dark, weathered tan, thick black hair and slightly pockmarked skin that brought Richard Burton or Philip Glenister to mind. He could have been in his 40's or early 50's. Either way, he assumed our conversation was over, as he reached for the dangling earphone.

'Sorry,' I repeated, and feeling a bit of an idiot,

added, 'but who sent you? You gave me a fright – I wasn't expecting you.'

As he faced me, one hand on his pole, the other wrapped around his earphone, I readjusted the arm across my breasts and tugged the towel further: I'd been wholly unprepared for a nudey ambush, and it'd been long time since having a conversation with no clothes on. An uncomfortable silence fell between us, and as the light bounced off his wraparound sunglasses, they seemingly grinned at me.

I finally broke the silence with, 'Well?' Then I loftily added, 'I *do actually* clean the pool with that thing.'

And just as I thought he didn't understand or wasn't going to respond, he suddenly said, 'Once a week. Friday morning. Pool. Hot tub.'

Christ. It was like pulling teeth.

'So, *who* sent you?' I asked, with an edge of irritation to my voice. Along with the car hire, I'd already paid a small fortune renting the villa during the peak period, and although I could afford it, I was always respectful of money – my chaotic and poor upbringing had seen to that. And particularly *this* money. I just didn't fancy getting lumbered with additional costs I wasn't expecting or hadn't budgeted for.

Pool Man lifted his earphone, ready to put it in.

'The owner. He pay me. Check water. Clean pool. Clean hot tub. Friday mornings.'

It was quite a speech and evidently heralded the

end of our conversation, as the earphone was back in place, and he continued his sweep of the pool with his head down. I remained upright and watched him, still clutching at myself as though under imminent attack as he worked his way ever closer. Without looking up, he unexpectedly spoke.

'Don't worry. I clean many pools. I've seen it all.'

It took me a few moments to process his words. He was more or less in front of me, taking turns to skim the net over the water's surface or run it along the pool's base. I picked up a faint tinny sound from his earphones and saw the water's reflection in his grinning sunglasses. And then, he'd passed me. I watched as he slowly moved along the pool's edge. Head down and retrieving small insects or stray leaves from bougainvillea or other plants from the gardens that flanked two sides of the pool.

As he moved further away, I let the hand over my breasts fall away and relaxed one of my legs so the towel only partially covered me. I guessed he had seen it all. And I *was* a seasoned nudey. Still, it would have been nice if the agent had warned me to expect him.

Pool Man completed his circuit, and stood, banging out the net over the back of a small bush to empty it. He returned the pole to its hooks, then went back to the pool, where he crouched to take a sample of the water. I wondered if he might glance my way and catch my more revealing stance – but the sunglasses remained fixed on his work. I couldn't quite see what he did to check the sample, but seemingly satisfied, he stood up and dipped into Chez Cleo, where he lifted the cover to the hot tub and took another sample. His eyes never strayed my way.

Hmm...

I glanced down at my body. Despite everything the past year had thrown at me, it was still in pretty good shape. For a 39-year-old. And I certainly hadn't heard any complaints.

Wiping a trickle of sweat from my stomach, I smiled as I thought, '*obviously* gay'.

As I idly traced a finger around my belly button, I decided I'd better get used to Pool Man seeing me naked as I certainly wasn't going to hide every Friday morning if I fancied some sun. Pushing the towel away, I reorganised it beneath me, and as I began to settle back into the sun lounger, I looked about to see what he was up to, only to find him gone. He was nowhere to be seen.

At first, I thought it was funny.

Fuck me, I thought, Daniel Craig's just sneaked in and out of here. Who knew his pole was so big?

And then...

Ah. He *must* have known this is a Bond girl's villa. Gotcha.

Then, just as I rested my head and closed my eyes...

... I seriously have no idea who that person is. He could be a random perv... a reporter... he could be *anyone*...

I sprung up from the sun lounger, dashed barefoot across the hot concrete to the veranda table, grabbed my phone and called the agents.

And… Pool Man turned out to be… the pool man. The woman I spoke to didn't know his name but, yes – every Friday. Just like he said. And while she had me on the phone, I could also expect a gardener every other week – but he'd be early evening, when it was bit cooler. An old man. Some relative of the owner. And like Pool Man, at no cost to me. Just general maintenance of the garden. Checking the sprinklers. Etc.

The drama was over. Stand down, Amber – there's nothing to see here.

So…

Each Friday. Pool Man. Broodingly silent. Disinterested. Of indeterminable nationality. And wearer of those fucking sunglasses.

And with all these private villas around, I wouldn't be surprised if he has seen it all. Particularly with those liberal, randy Scandies…

I looked at the pool and wondered if a swim would blow away the cobwebs of Missus Mouth Almighty or even, freshen me up enough to tackle some worthwhile writing. As I stood, undecided, two swallows plunged in quick succession to skim the water's surface in an attempt to cool down. They'd become an irresistible, daily joy to watch and never failed to put a smile on my face.

'Good idea,' I said.

I tightened my brightly coloured wrap around me, slipped my feet into my flip flops and made my way over to Chez Cleo, where I untied my wrap and threw it over the cushions. Then I made my way over to the poolside shower, kicked off my flip flops and let the icy cold water stream over me. Tilting my head back, I felt the full force of the water run over my face. Goosebumps prickled my flesh, my nipples hardened. And as I breathed in the heady scent of a nearby jasmine bush, I once again, thanked my lucky stars for being able to escape.

I swam for about twenty minutes, alternating between backstroke and breaststroke. As I swam on my front, I eyed one of the sun loungers as I neared it. With a mixture of feelings, I recalled the events from a couple of nights previous, when I'd picked up a bit of rough trade from Sonny's and brought him back to the villa.

He'd sidled up to me at the bar. 'You've got a nice smile,' he said.

'Thank you,' I'd replied, chirpily. 'They're nearly all my own teeth.'

He had no idea.

When we arrived at the villa, I put on the pool's night lights that were dotted beneath the water, cranked up Radio Aphrodite and went inside to fix some drinks. Upon my return, I found rough trade already in the pool and naked, with the lights distorting his body like an old-fashioned Hall of

Mirrors. I stood, watching him, as he grinned up at me, hair slicked back and inviting me to join him.

I hesitated.

Suddenly unsure.

I had already had sex. Since.

Once. And recently. It had been so long that, one night, when feeling drunk, summer randy, reckless, defiant – whatever you want to call it – I decided it was finally time to (literally) get back into the swing of things, and secured the services of two happy chappies who were part of a stag group.

On that occasion, the pool had come later. After they had come. Then we rinsed off in the shower before getting in for a 2am swim and lark around. But, before all that, we'd had our fun on Chez Cleo's cushions, with the obligatory cock in each end, swapping over and schoolboy, energetic pounding. We all played our part in a budget porn film with cries of, 'Ooh, yeah!' and ending with their synchronised ejaculation over me.

Any other time in my life, I would have chalked it down as a damn fine fuck, but something in me had felt robotic, as if I'd been going through the motions.

Or trying to fuck some normality back into my life.

Maybe it was that.

I didn't manage to come that night and put it down to the amount of drink I'd had. But now I think about it, I don't believe it was that at all.

In the pool, I had taken turns to kiss the two guys

as we had a three-way hug which allowed them to run their free hands over my body. We drunkenly laughed, sang along to some of Radio Aphrodite's tunes, and took breaks to drink from the bottles of beer resting poolside. Then, before I knew it, they were dressed and gone. And I was left floating on my back, staring up at the diamond-like stars that littered the sky.

Still. They'd been a welcome diversion at the time.

As I looked at rough trade flagging me to get in the pool, I suddenly couldn't be bothered. Instead, I carried our drinks over to a couple of sun loungers and placed them on the small, white plastic table in between. Then I sat down and stretched my legs out before me.

'Aren't you coming in?' rough trade asked, rubbing water from his eyes.

I half-remember thinking, if he wants it – he'll have to come and get it.

'I'm staying here!' I called out. I picked up my glass and playfully jiggled it in the air.

He smoothly swam towards me and hauled himself out the pool. I cast my eyes approvingly over his late 20's/early 30's body as he stood, hands on hips, watching me drink. Without a word, he walked towards me, leaned forward and yanked my ankles, so I slid down the lounger. Then, he knelt, pushed up my skirt to reveal my usual commando style, parted my legs and went down on me.

I watched him disinterestedly and took sips of my drink. He was being too *dithery*. And not getting stuck in. I sighed, put my glass down, and with some awkward adjustment, rested my feet on his shoulders and widened my bended knees.

More of the same timid, cat-like repetitive licks that did absolutely nothing for me: he was beginning to turn me off.

Either fucking do it or don't! I silently screamed.

Putting a hand to the back of his head, I pressed his face into me and felt a small, twinge of resistance. Obviously, this wasn't his forte. Or rather, his forte for someone like me. I kept my hand in place and silently urged rough trade to get rougher. But nothing. Just fannying around. Literally. And the slight but, unmistakable, withdrawal of his head into my palm.

Pressing my feet into his shoulder, I slowly eased him off me in increments as his mouth tried to remain engaged. For a few moments he stayed on his knees, blinking at me in confusion, with a sheen of wet around his mouth; his saliva, rather than me. Then his expression became unreadable, and just as I began wondering if I should worry or could be in danger, he stood and silently collected his nearby clothes. He quickly dressed, threw me a hostile glare and left.

I lay motionless on the sun lounger and listened to him start up the quad bike we'd ridden on. And when the last sounds of it disappeared down the hill, I kept still a while longer. My eyes darted about in search of any threat, then I glanced down at my hauled-up skirt and let out an unfamiliar laugh.

And as David Gray sang to me about Babylon and the crickets chirped their shrill chirps, I masturbated half-heartedly and unsatisfactorily until I gave up and reached for my drink.

At the end of my swim, I climbed out the pool and stood, letting the water run off my body. As I looked down towards Coral Bay and saw a couple of jet skis making circles in the turquoise water, I was hit by a glorious gust of breeze. I stretched my arms above my head to embrace it; I felt energised and alive.

'You would have loved it here, Spencer,' I whispered.

And in an instant, I once more felt my heart break into a million pieces.

I lowered my arms and blinked back tears.

Remember... one day at a time, Amber.

One day at a time.

4.

The Sexy Pirate

I spent the next week or so avoiding Sonny's, and when venturing into Coral Bay, I sought out quieter bars devoid of boisterous theme nites, and tentatively checked them out first for any sign of Missus Mouth Almighty. I felt a bit bad – still having an outstanding bar bill at Sonny's but, from my limited experience, it seemed the Cypriots exercised a fairly relaxed policy with locals and regulars. It could even be said, too relaxed – having already witnessed a few Cypriot-on-Cypriot exchanges about bar tabs that had gotten out of control – with one running into hundreds of Euros.

Add to that, the fact Cypriot A invariably gets offended when Cypriot B has the temerity to finally ask for payment, then it's all indignation, hand gestures, high-level shouting and on one occasion, a drunken (and markedly unsuccessful) attempt to vault the bar. At the end of it all, Cypriot A will toss a haggled-down amount of Euros on the bar, everyone's mates again and it seemingly starts all over the next night. "On my bill."

At least the piddling amount I owed wouldn't see Sonny's out of business.

Anyway. It wouldn't be long before I claimed back my bar stool.

Some nights, I just sat on my own. Content in my own company, drinking, smoking and happily watching the world go by. Other times, I'd end up chatting – under the guise of being on holiday for a week or two.

On one occasion, I got involved in a wonderful moan-a-thon with some English tourists as they sat around a bar. *Nothing* was like 'back home'. It was too hot. The food was shit. I eagerly chimed in and complained about the calibre of curries (I hadn't had one...) – which brought nods of agreement and a catalogue of unfavourable anecdotes about some place in a side street, called The Taste of Bengal.

Their moaning went on. Wrong ice cubes. Expensive sunbeds on the beach. Shoddy leather goods. Too much foam on a pint – and was it *really* a pint? Lashings of Germans around the pool. And breakfasts and roast dinners that were *nothing* like 'back home'.

When they finally ran out of steam, I threw my trump card into the arena and lit the touch paper.

'And what about not flushing your toilet paper and having to put it into one of those bins?'

Boom!

I sat back and admired my handiwork.

Oh, the hysteria! The *awfulness* of it all! It was *just* like being in a third world country! What was *wrong* with *these people?*

Bleurgh! Just... bleurgh!

Naturally, their bleurghs had no meaning, as each and every one of them fessed up to flushing the paper in any instance.

But *still*. Just the *thought* of it... bleurgh...

After a while, one of the more observant ones asked me, 'On your own?'

I had to fight an overwhelming urge to pat myself down and frantically check over each shoulder.

Instead, I regaled the sorry tale of my husband being back at the hotel and suffering from a robust bout of holiday shits.

'Could have been that meal at The Taste of Bengal... ' I offered with a rueful sigh.

Mutters of agreement.

I pressed a hand to my throat. '*And* I've given him strict instructions to flush *everything*.'

Nods of approval.

Well wishes for my husband.

Sympathies for being 'out on my own.'

A couple of free shots of Sambuca and a B52 to 'cheer me up'.

Marvellous.

*

One night, I wandered into Coral Dreams, curious to see if Pool Man was hanging out there in his polo shirt. Maybe catch him doing an Elvis impersonation on stage.

He wasn't there. There was no stage.

Instead, I found a number of glum-looking, sunburned tourists fixated on the bank of TV screens. Their attention was captivated by a rerun of Bayern Munich giving an unpronounceable team a bit of what for. To be honest, the place didn't look much cop, but the commentary was off, the music recognisable, and as there was a free table by the main drag, it looked ideal for a drink, smoke and watching the world go by.

I hadn't been there long when a lad strolled in, curious to see who was playing. When he realised it was an old game, his face registered disappointment. He looked around, as if surprised he was suddenly alone and caught me looking. He gave me a smile. I sent a small one back and returned my gaze to the busy road.

A couple of minutes later, he came and stood by my side, beer in hand, and brazenly asked if he could join me. He was a pup. About twenty – if that. And far too young to be sniffing around someone my age. Although I suspect he could have thought it was Grab-A-Granny Time.

He was cute, though. Magnificent brown eyes

and a dusting of freckles across his nose. Tall and lean, and with that thick, boyish hair you want to ruffle. And a killer smile. He should have been elsewhere, hitting on a girl his own age – he'd have no problem at all. But as he'd grown the balls to ask if he could sit with me, I let him: I was always in need of a laugh.

After a few rapid glugs from his bottle – which only served to emphasis his youth – he told me he recognised me from somewhere.

I felt the familiar jolt and stared at him coldly.

'Oh,' I drawled, sarcastically. 'And where do you think that might be from?'

I'd unsettled him. Give it a minute or two, and I'd be telling him to fuck off.

He nervously unleashed his smile, before creasing his face into confusion.

'I'm sorry,' he began. 'But aren't you an actress? I'm sure I've seen you in a film.'

'Actress?'

'Yes. I'm sure it's you,' he said, struggling to regain some composure. 'I mean, it's quite an old film.'

I studied the young face across the table and tried to spot if another Missus Mouth Almighty lurked within.

He filled my silence, taking it as offence.

'I'm sorry... I don't mean *old* as in, *you're* old... but it *was* an old film... ' He trailed off and chewed one side of his lower lip in puppy-like apology.

I took out a cigarette. 'Well, I *am* rather old.'

'Sorry. I didn't mean it that way... I meant to say...'

As I sparked my lighter, I raised my other hand to silence him from saying any more. Cigarette lit, I tilted back my head and blew a plume of smoke into the night's heat. And when I lowered my gaze, I looked laddo straight in the eye and let him have it.

'You're right. I *was* an actress. Once upon a time.'

His face beamed with delight. 'I *knew* it!'

'Well, allow me to expand on that. I used to be a Bond girl. A *long* time ago. Naturally.'

'A Bond girl? Wow!' Laddo leaned forward, his eyes on the verge of bulging out their sockets. 'What film was you in? Like... wow! I knew it was something like that I'd seen you in. Who was Bond?'

He had me stumped. I tried to calculate backwards with the Bond actors, but the drinks and being caught off guard made it a muddle. So, I figured 'old' just generally meant *old* to a youngster like him.

I decided to chance my luck.

'Sean Connery,' I said, as I tapped my cigarette over the ashtray, desperately avoiding his gaze in case I burst into laughter.

But he took it. Hook. Line. And sinker.

'Wow! He was just the best! Well... apart from Daniel Craig. Obviously. What was he like?'

I kept my head down. 'Oh, you know... he was a very talented actor. Funny. Caring... ' was I really going to do this? '... and the most generous lover.'

I raised my glass to my lips in the hope it'd disguise my broadening smile, then chanced a look. Laddo seemed as though his head was about to explode. 'No way!' he said a few times. I gave him a small nod of confirmation, then lightly touched one of his hands.

'Please,' I said quietly, 'please promise you won't tell *anyone*.' I threw a quick look over each shoulder for good measure. 'Listen... this has never got out. And I don't want it to. Particularly now... now he's... you know... *gone*. Family and all that.'

Laddo mustered a sincere expression.

'No, no – I wouldn't. Honest to God. I won't tell *anybody*. I swear.'

I looked at his young face and imagined him excitedly blurting about meeting a Bond girl who had shagged Sean Connery. Doubtless, sometime within the next half hour.

I gave his hand a squeeze. 'Thank you. And, sorry – but I don't know your name?'

He gave me his killer smile. 'It's Joshua. Or Josh. And... sorry... I know I recognised you, but I just can't remember yours at the moment.'

I took my hand away and drew on my cigarette. Dare I risk more?

I smiled sweetly. 'Why, I'm Susanna Wellard. Or, Susie, as I'm better known.'

Josh clicked his fingers. 'That's it! I remember now!'

Shifting on his seat, he adopted a serious expression. 'Listen, Susie... Susanna... can I ask you something – it's a bit personal... '

'I'm afraid I can't discuss *anything* that took place between myself and Sean,' I told Josh. Managing to keep a straight face, I twisted pressed fingers to the corner of my mouth in an indication that my lips were sealed.

'No, it's not that. It's to do with your scars.' Josh crooked a finger and pointed at my forehead, then gently touched beneath his chin. 'How did you get them – if you don't mind me asking. Sorry... I'm being personal.' Having asked the question, he immediately looked uncomfortable and took rushed gulps of his beer.

Well, that was a first. And the boldness of youth. As aside from Missus Mouth Almighty, Josh was the first person to mention my scars.

To my face.

And if you didn't count various consultants, hospital staff and Elena's unwavering support. Otherwise, people just stared or sneaked glances, but said nothing. Or let their eyes continually drift to my forehead when in conversation.

I took a final drag on my cigarette and crushed it in the clay ashtray in front of me. As I tilted my head upwards to exhale the smoke away from Josh, I realised how he'd spotted my jawline scar. I could sense his nervousness as I considered his audacious question, but after a quick mull, I decided I actually found it refreshing to be asked. Rather than be stared at. And wondered about. And would probably be happier if more people asked. They might not get the truth from me, but they'd at least get something to quell their curiosity.

I faced Josh. 'No, it's fine, I said, reassuringly. 'I don't mind talking about them. So... erm... an accident happened on set – a stunt that went wrong. There was the usual Bond car chase – Aston Martin and all that... '. Josh was goggle-eyed and hanging off my every word. '... and my stunt double had been taken ill... we were on a tight schedule, so I said, I was happy to be in the car. It was all pretty straight-forward – low risk and all that... and, well... it went wrong.' I paused and gave a 'C'est la vie' shrug. 'Of course, there had to be a huge script rewrite to kill me off, as I was so badly bashed up. Hence...'

I waved my hand around my face. 'I don't like to talk about it, really,' I added. 'And *obviously*, the scars meant the end of my acting career.'

I looked at Josh with a wistful expression.

'Oh, that's *terrible*,' he said. His young face crumpled into concern. 'So, how many Bond films did you do?'

'Oh, just the one,' I sighed.

'Which one was that?'

Christ. Now he had me. I wracked my brain for a plausible answer.

'From Nudey Beach with Love,' I told him, cringing inside.

Josh's deep frown told me I'd made a major miscalculation.

'Wasn't it called... ' he began.

'Oh, you're thinking of From Russia with Love,' I said, breezily. 'Yes, there was that one, but there was also one called From Nudey Beach with Love; there's a place in Australia called Nudey Beach. So, it was all bikini shots, sharks, boats – the ill-fated car chase – stuff like that.'

I could tell I didn't have him entirely onside, so I pushed on. 'Yes, stunning beaches there. In fact, that's where me and Sean... you know... before my accident. *Obviously*. So... *that's* the film you would have seen me in. And yes, it *was* a long time ago.'

'Yeah, I thought it was something like that,' he murmured, as though trying to convince himself.

'I'm afraid it wasn't the most popular Bond film,' I interjected. 'What with all the script changes that didn't really work. And after that... what with my face being scarred, no one wanted me... '

'Don't say that! You're bloody beautiful! You look like a sexy female pirate with those scars.'

I looked at Josh. All upright and indignant in his young, out-on-the-pull clothes, and felt a sudden well of tears behind my eyes. I liked the thought of being a sexy pirate. *Very* much. I blinked away the unwelcome memory of seeing my face for the first time. After. Compliments were cheap in a holiday resort but, bless his heart, Josh seemed sincere.

'Thank you,' was all I could say.

'I mean it,' Josh said. 'It's like the imperfections make you more perfect. You're well tasty.'

I had to laugh. 'Well, I'm not sure where you dragged that from, but it's very sweet of you. Now then… don't you have some mates or someone you should be getting pissed with?'

It was Josh's turn to laugh. 'Yeah, they'll be somewhere down the road, doing Depth Charges, probably. I only popped in to check out the footie. And then I saw you. Come and join us – it'll be a blast!'

I smiled at the invite.

'That's very kind of you but, no. You need to be with your mates, chatting up young girls, getting brutishly wankered and copping off at the end of it all. You don't need an oldie like me cramping your style.'

Josh leaned across the table and unleashed the smile. 'But suppose I want to cop off with you?'

I had to admire his spirit.

'Ah. Not going to happen, Josh. I might adopt you as the son I never had – but, no.'

He weighed this up for a moment.

'Well, how about an autograph, then?'

Once again, I laughed – he was delightfully incorrigible. I dipped into my handbag and plucked out the pen I redundantly carried around for any writing notes. Pulling a Carlsberg beer mat towards me, I wrote with some flourish: *To Josh, it was a Double O great to meet you. Be lucky. Susanna x*

Then I slid it towards him.

Josh's face beamed with delight. Downing the remains of his beer, he stood and rammed the beer mat into a pocket on the back of his shorts.

'Thanks, Susie... Susanna – that's awesome! Are you sure you don't want to join us? The lads are mental – Danny got smashed last night and accidentally punched himself in the balls.'

For a moment or two, I pressed my lips together to contain a snort of laughter.

'It's a good offer, Josh. And one I might regret not taking up. But, no. You crack on. Go forth. Be young. Have fun. Get laid.'

With a nod of understanding, Josh offered me a warm smile before stepping forwards and gently putting a hand on each of my shoulders. Then he bent and gave me a soft, little kiss on each cheek. It was the loveliest thing I'd felt for a long time. With his hands still on my shoulders, he gave them a shake.

'Only if you remember you're beautiful. You're a sexy pirate – right? And never forget that. Okay?'

With a lump in my throat, I looked at the face that would be breaking so many hearts.

'Okay,' I said, quietly.

Then he took one of my hands and gave it a smacker of a kiss.

'I won't forget you!' And off he went. I watched him as he joined the flow of tourists. Trendy shorts. Tanned limbs. With a night full of adventures ahead of him. And just as he was about to disappear from view, he suddenly turned, cupped his hands to his mouth, and bellowed, 'SUSIE!! SUSIE!! SUSANNA!!' I raised a hand and waved to him.

'WHO DID YOU PLAY IN THE FILM?'

I didn't miss a beat. 'FANNY BOUQUET!' I bellowed back.

'FANNY WHO?'

'FANNY BOOO KAAY!!'

That beautiful smile. A thumbs up. And then he was gone, gone.

And I was left with people staring at me.

I picked up my drink, shrugged and sipped away. Who cared? I was too busy, congratulating myself on plucking out that name so quickly. I would have hated to shatter the Double O illusion. So soon...

If only he knew it was a name I'd been bandying around for a Susie character...

As the gawpers wandered away, I took another sip. Farewell, young Josh, I silently toasted. I hope you'll forgive the pirate who told you so many lies.

I settled back in my chair. It had been great fun, being a Bond girl again – the lads in Flabby's would have been proud. I thought back to them all with genuine fondness and hoped that Jen was keeping them in check. I smiled as I wondered what Fucker Frank had broken recently. And if Stevie was still seeing the beautiful Freya. I hoped so. In some ways, Josh reminded me of an apprentice Stevie. Smiles, dazzle and charm.

I took a few deep breaths in and out. Then forced my thoughts away from Flabby's.

Instead, I revisited Josh's comments about my scars; if he'd seen them about a year ago, he certainly wouldn't be handing out any compliments.

I'd grown to live to them – no other choice, really – but found it impossible not to inspect them on a daily basis. They had come along nicely. Compared to how they were. And away from harsh lighting (and with some carefully applied make-up), the scar that ran from my eyebrow, didn't look too Frankenstein at all.

I ran a finger under my jawline, along the full length of the scar. The best part of four inches. Unlike my forehead, this one – although improved – was still bobbles and bumps and anger. And Frankenstein. The jaw that took so very long to heal. Tilt my head one way and you wouldn't know it was there. Tilted the other, and it looked as though someone had made a botch job of trying to cut my throat.

Maybe if Clarke had had the opportunity...

I shuddered off the thought and took my hand away.

My mouth was a different story. Full of shiny, new crowns. Well, six of them. And if anything, my teeth arguably looked better than before. They had cost a small fortune, and if it hadn't been for Spencer's money, I suspect the flat would have been sold to fund them.

But they were worth every solitary penny. And each ounce of discomfort and pain.

And in the days I still sobbed when I looked at my face – with all the injuries that seemingly took forever to heal – at least the gaps and the broken teeth that sliced my tongue and made it difficult to eat and speak, were replaced by things of beauty.

'Excuse me. I asked if you wanted another drink?'

I looked up at the waiter, surprised to see him standing beside me, wearing a familiar-looking polo shirt; I'd been miles away.

He pointed to my empty glass. 'Same?'

'Sorry. Yes please. Same.'

He looked at me appraisingly as he swapped my ashtray for a clean one, then picked up my empty glass. He threw me a smile. I sent one back. And gave him the most perfect smile in the whole wide world.

Us sexy female pirates can be fuckers like that.

Thank you, Josh.

Be lucky.

And I won't forget you, either.

5.

Mack the Knife

Eddie's phoned a couple of times and @ballbagderek has *'fashioned his eyelashes into a comb-over'*. And I'm not sure what disturbs me the most.

I was in the large, local supermarket when the first of Eddie's calls came through. Shorts, vest and sandals. And enjoying some respite from the blazing heat; courtesy of the store's powerful air conditioning. At the time, I'd been inspecting the jumbo bunches of coriander and marvelling at both their aroma and price of 40 cents. Back home, a few wheezing stalks were the best part of a pound, making what I had in my hand worth about £8 or so.

Just as I was weighing up the viability of becoming a coriander dealer, my phone rang. I plucked it from the bag in my trolley and was shocked to see Eddie's name. Aside from a couple of calls prior to meeting, Eddie was the King of Emails – as if building up an accusatory log of the times he'd asked, "How far have you got with the sequel?"

I had nothing to tell him on that front. My most recent, pathetic effort had seen Susie, heartbroken from her split with Doctor Wellard, and spending an inordinate amount of time snotting and wailing and hugging a resistant Brutus to her heaving bosom. Jeez...

He had caught me off guard – which I guess had been his intention. I left it to ring out to voicemail, but no message was left. I didn't like the sound of that.

I quickly buried the phone back in my handbag and carried on with my shopping. Eddie would be back. That much I knew. And he'd tearing a strip off me with his shark's teeth. I threw a bunch of coriander in my trolley and slowly pushed it towards the fruit section, all the while humming 'Mack the Knife' with a small smile on my face.

I thought back to my shopping expeditions back home and how they'd become a tedious chore to be endured once or twice a week. Even in the West Country, supermarkets got busy, tempers frayed, fruit and veg could look knackered and as though gasping for air. Then you had the customers who behaved as if their shopping trip was a life event; blocking your access while laboriously mulling over similar items with seemingly, all the time in the world. And when you finally dragged your weary backside to the till, you'd be confronted by a chirpy cashier asking, 'Is that what you're having for your tea tonight?'

Add to that, the self-service tills that were more ball ache than they were worth, it was no small wonder I switched to online shopping during my convalescence, and continually marvelled as to why I hadn't thought to do it sooner.

Here – and taking into account the novelty factor – the fresh goods were lush and abundant. Watermelons like small boulders. Grapes you could visualise on their vines. Fish that looked like they could muster a flap. And fresh bread and pastries that had you thinking 'fuck it' to the carbs.

I hummed my way along aisles, made my selections, then headed towards one of the tills. Once there, I couldn't help but smile at the expats in front of me, who seemed determined to demonstrate their superiority to the *tourists* through well-practised speed and efficiency, and familiarity with the Cypriot cashier.

Once I was all packed up and paid up, I wheeled my trolley outside and into a wall of unbearable heat. I glanced up at the supermarket's digital clock that alternated between time and temperature: 36 degrees. Away from the villa's welcome breeze, it wasn't for the faint-hearted – even for a sun lover like me.

I quickly unloaded the shopping into my Z-plate hire car; a blue Renault Clio – which I preferred to think of as Cleo, just to keep the infantile theme going. With sweat already trickling down my spine, I climbed into the driver's seat and found the steering wheel baking hot to the touch. As I switched on the engine and whacked up the air conditioning, my phone rang again. I peered into my handbag and saw Eddie's name shouting at me.

As I wiped moisture from my forehead, I said, 'Sorry mate, but I'm too hot to get bollocked at the moment,' and let the phone ring out. And as I waited for the air con to do its stuff, I once more listened for the ping of a voicemail that never arrived.

'Oh dear,' I murmured. 'Someone sounds snappy.'

I tested the steering wheel. It was just about good enough to go. And five minutes later, I was parked up in the villa's car port and quickly ferrying the shopping into my own air conditioning.

With everything put away, I stood at the kitchen sink, washed my hands and let the cold water run over my wrists as I looked out at the pomegranate trees I regularly plundered. Beyond was the semi dirt road I'd just driven on and a view of tree-bobbled hills.

After drying my hands, I took a bottle of water from the fridge and as I stood, glugging away, I cast a look at my surroundings, still unable to believe this was my home for now. The open plan living area had a smart black and chrome kitchen with all mod cons. A few steps lead down to the lounge with its sliding doors to the veranda and its table and chairs. There were a couple of smart, black leather couches that made the backs of my legs sweat and slide with squeaky noises if the air con wasn't on. A large, flat screen telly. A chrome and black coffee table. Shelving with books and tasteful, local pottery. And a curved, black leather-edged bar, complete with high bar stools, but sadly, no booze.

Back up the steps, and to the right, the heavy, wooden front door, which served no real purpose when people like Pool Man wandered in by the low, latched gate that not only led poolside, but to my favoured entrance via the kitchen.

Opposite the front door, a corridor leading to a twin guest room with an ensuite bathroom.

And just past the front door, a downstairs toilet ahead of the granite staircase that led upstairs. Off the first-floor landing, a luxury shower room that Cleopatra herself wouldn't have sniffed at. The only other room on that floor was the master bedroom. And man, oh man, I felt like a Queen every time I walked in there – it was massive and caused me to wonder if the villa originally had three bedrooms – like all the others I'd seen when doing my research. I had no idea what size the bed was, but it was a beast of a thing. There were enough fitted wardrobes to house a small family. A stylish dressing table and stool. Two expensive-looking easy chairs. A small, low table. Attractive paintings of local scenery. Patterned blinds and curtains. A mini bar fridge with a freezer compartment (which I stocked pretty pronto), glasses and an ice bucket.

And if all that wasn't enough, there was the glorious balcony – my favourite spot upstairs. Accessed by sliding doors, its canopy came from a large bougainvillea tree which provided shade for roughly half its area. The view from here was basically a higher version of that from the veranda or poolside, but at the end of the balcony, if I looked left and inland, I was greeted by the sight of villas and villages dotted about the hills – their lights adding pretty twinkles at night.

I quite liked the thought of returning the favour and being twinkles in their distance.

And on the nights I didn't fancy a poolside or hot tub nightcap with Radio Aphrodite playing its cheese, I'd enjoy some 'quiet time' relaxing on the balcony and gazing at the twinkles of Coral Bay or the hills. And when a sudden breeze would cause bougainvillea petals to fall and flutter like confetti, the air would fill with the scent of the heavy jasmine bush below.

And for a while, my soul would heal.

Refreshed from drinking the water, I nipped upstairs, threw off my clothes and tied my wrap around me. Returning to the kitchen, I lifted my handbag from the counter and padded outside to sit at the veranda table. After a sigh of appreciation at the scenery, I fished about in my bag and pulled out my phone, the have-a-go pen and postcard I'd bought for Elena. I looked at the front; a group of four old men with appropriately sun-ruined postcard faces, sitting outside a traditional coffee shop and playing backgammon – or *tavli* – to be locally correct. I smiled at the image before turning the card over. With my pen poised for action, I wondered what news to tell her.

Since being in Cyprus, we'd kept in touch via Zoom, but I enjoyed sending her postcards. Maybe it made me feel like I was doing some actual writing. For a change. That aside, I liked to imagine Elena's smile when delivered my latest offering amongst the pile of usual crap. She'd become a good friend, and I owed her *big time* for all the support she'd given me. As it was, she was popping into the flat every once in a while to check on things.

Hopefully, she'd enjoy the surprise I had in store on my return; a luxury weekend spa break for two. Whether Elena wanted me as her guest or not, didn't matter – I just hoped it would go some distance to show my gratitude and thanks for all she had done.

My mind skimmed over all the London friends I'd become so distant from; some wonderful people (one traitor aside), who I'd also be writing postcards to if our relationships hadn't fizzled out during 'the Clarke era'. If *I* hadn't let them fizzle out. Had fought harder. And hadn't been carrying a lead cloak of embarrassment and shame on my shoulders.

The cloak that now hung more heavily with guilt.

As I heard distant cheers and horn-honking from passing quad bikes, my memory flickered through images of loud, boozy nights in London with my advertising chums. Sparky, bright people with a passion and energy for life and creativity. We worked hard, played hard and sometimes, argued hard. But for all the right reasons. Then we'd go to a wine bar or pub and put it behind us.

I'd loved my job. And was bloody good at it.

I loved the vibe of Soho and Camden and Covent Garden and the hidden gems any back street might throw up. I loved the smart places, the grungy places, the surprising places.

And I missed the camaraderie of all those lovely, talented people and the life I once had.

The life I once had...

I reached in my bag for my cigarettes. The bastard things I'd so nearly given up, courtesy of my lengthy hospital stay. The same bastard things I'd so quickly reached for when the trial started. And I became a person of interest.

I lit up and exhaled.

It had been impossible not to wonder how things might have turned out if I hadn't fled to Exeter following the collapse of my marriage. Maybe I'd be at the same agency? Maybe promotion to Associate Director? Or beyond? Or maybe a different agency with different opportunities?

But whichever way you dressed it up, if I'd stayed in London, Spencer would still be alive.

I shifted to a more upright position in my chair and gulped back an all-too-familiar sob. With trembling fingers, I pressed the cigarette to my lips and squeezed my eyes shut.

My phone began to ring. I opened my eyes, glanced down, and after a half-laugh, blew a stream of smoke over Eddie's name.

'I'm just about in the right mood for you,' I said, as I reached for my phone.

'You've got this, girl.'

It was time to hear what Jaws had to say.

After Eddie's call, I hugged up my knees and stared out to sea. As faint rumbles of traffic passed below, I replayed our conversation; none of which overly came as a surprise. Eddie kicked off with a well-deserved moan about my lack of progress – then counterbalanced by asking if there was anything he could do to assist. I'd wanted to say, 'make it so that night never happened,' – but recognised his attempt to help me. And himself. Instead, I told him I'd keep on trying – that was all I could do. I'd try my best.

I waited for some push back. But he left it at that.

We then got onto the real reason for his phone calls: my 'story'.

Another national newspaper. This time, showing interest in a serialisation.

Maybe... if was struggling with the sequel... might I want to consider starting work on that instead?

There'd be BIG BUCKS on offer.

As I said; no surprises.

I answered Eddie in a low, measured voice and in the hope he'd finally understand.

I wouldn't do it.

Not for any amount of money.

I had to protect my sanity. Spencer's memory. And all the other people involved in my life – both before, and after, that night.

And I *certainly* didn't want to spend a moment more thinking about that murdering bastard. Let alone, spend time writing about him.

I was already torturing myself on a daily basis.

And besides any of that, there had already been enough about me in the press.

Eddie's response suggested my reaction had been expected.

'Well,' he began, 'if you don't write your story, someone else will.'

It was as simple as that.

Our phone call ended soon after. Eddie told me to 'digest' what he'd said and 'have a think about it'. Before I could further protest, he jumped in and told me to, "stop getting pissed and fucking about on Twitter, X – or whatever the fuck it's called these days". And that his staff were busy enough without having to clean up 'my bollocks' at all hours of the day.

Without pause, he breezily mentioned it was looking 'bolted on' that Just Susie would hit the bookshops late October or early November – which would 'fit in nicely' with my return to England.

As I tried to digest that bit of information, he briskly told me, 'Get to work, Amber', before signing off with, 'I'll be in touch.'

And that was that.

I must have been lost in thought, as distant whoops from passing quad bikes shook me back to the present. They were probably en route to the rocky coves and shingle beaches of nearby Akamas, where their mode of transport was best suited to the off-road rugged terrain. I was yet to go but hoped to visit before leaving the island. The turtles alone would be worth the journey.

I picked up Elena's postcard and idly flipped it backwards and forwards as I thought about someone writing my biography. Or 'story'. I certainly wouldn't be writing it myself – whatever pressure was put on me. And I had no desire for anyone else to write it either. But who knew how many other 'friends' were out there, willing to spill their – and my – guts for money?

I wondered if things would be better or worse if I had an agent. Eddie's company had been one of the very few publishers accepting direct submissions without an agent. Which left me with no idea if the deal we struck was in line with my industry peers. At the time I'd signed with Eddie, I was so cock-a-hoop at having his interest – *someone's* interest – it never crossed my mind, and quite honestly, I didn't care. I was full of excitement and felt gratitude at having something else to fill my focus. And rightly or wrongly, money hadn't been the overriding factor; I just *needed* something else. The distraction. To feel valued. Both, I suspect.

Would an agent protect me more? Or just throw me to the tabloid lions for a handsome price? I honestly had no idea how it all worked. And at the time – and with the trial looming, my head hadn't been in the right place to question anything.

I pushed away the sudden and unwelcome thought of my October return and placed the postcard on the table. I picked up my pen and sat, poised, wondering what to write, and if it would serve as some form of warm-up to getting some Susie work done. I still felt disturbed by Eddie's call, but there was nothing I could do, except stand my ground. And if I cracked on with the sequel, maybe Eddie would settle for that.

Problem was... it seemed increasingly clear our Susie didn't love me anymore.

Odd, really. I managed to do all that editing after Spencer's death, but that bastard trial just finished me off.

I dipped my head and began.

Hi Elena!

I hope you'll cherish this picture of my latest admirers...

6.

The Game's Up!

Susie has taken to serial shoplifting. It started small and by accident, when she absently shovelled a tube of Fruit Pastilles into her jacket pocket when wandering the aisles of her local supermarket. Unscanned and unpaid for, the Pastilles accompanied Susie to the car park until a burly Security Officer caught up with her.

When challenged about secreting stolen goods about her person, robust and indignant denials were forthcoming. Along with one hearty cry of, 'How VERY dare you!'

As the Officer stepped forward to search her, Susie squeaked and squealed and swatted away at him, but to no avail – he was upon her! During the unsightly tussle that ensued, their bodies pressed together as the Officer determinedly rummaged about in Susie's attire.

With her heaving bosoms squished into his chest, Susie writhed and wriggled and fought to resist, oblivious to the buttons that had pinged off her blouse. But when the friction of the loose fabric against the Officer's body made her nipples stand to red alert, Susie became aware of a near-forgotten tingle in her Thursday knickers.

'Well, helloooo... ' she thought.

And, 'Hello,' said the Officer, as he triumphantly held the Fruit Pastilles aloft in a bunched fist. As he sought to disengage from Susie, she was having none of it, and sought to remain very much engaged. The Officer grimaced and squirmed and told Susie to, 'Gerroff!' before adding a stern, 'That's enough!' Such was the scene they set, any casual onlooker may have been forgiven for thinking Susie was attempting to mount and dry-hump the Security Officer's leg.

In the end, the Officer's jumbo hands won the battle as they prised and then, pushed Susie away from him. Anxious to get shot of her, Susie got away with a stern warning.

As Susie stood quivering, breathy and with her bra on show, she watched the Officer stride towards the safety of the supermarket, (such a firm *grip on those Pastilles...) and like a thunderbolt, she saw a glimpse of her future...*

Before today's unexpected deliciousness... it had been so long since feeling a man's hands on her...

Almost a year, in fact, since Doctor Wellard gave her one up the Khyber and a final fumble before going their separate ways...

And she was *a woman with needs...*

Who maintained a meticulous *waxing regime... should an agreeable liaison present itself unexpectedly or at short notice...*

But truth be told, her heart was still broken... she pined for Wellard... and would feel uneasy if going the whole hog with someone new...

But still... those pesky needs...

If only her Oireish Shagmeister hadn't ignited such a fire in her hungry loins...

Susie gathered her blouse around her and lifted her chin defiantly: she had seen the future and was now a woman with a plan...

And so it began...

Leaving Trewithiel behind (and Brutus to lick his stump in peace), our Susie has taken to travelling to superstores and shopping malls, where she gets a bit light-fingered.

Quickly becoming a mistress of her art, she bundles items into her pockets, skirt waistband, up her blouse and down her bra cups. Out she'd dash – from whichever store – with the pre-approved Security Officer in hot pursuit. The inevitable struggle would ensue. And a rehearsed, staged tumble, would gift our Susie the heady delights of wrapping her legs around the Officer when pinned to the ground.

Look at our Susie go! See how she squirms and wriggles and bucks beneath his pressing body! Hang on... surely, *that blouse didn't unloosen itself?*

And what's this? Susie coming over a bit breathless and howsyerfather as the Officer plunges his hand deep into her clothing to rummage for the stolen goods?

I should jolly well say so.

Alas, Susie's plan couldn't go on forever. And eye-flut-

tering apologies and blaming it on her hormones could only get her off the hook so often... as after a very satisfactory session with not one, but two solidly-built officers, Susie finally got her collar felt.

She was nicked.

And would soon be starching her favourite white blouse for her impending trial.

The charges? Having it on her toes with 3 pairs of American Tan pop socks and a meat tenderiser.

Trial.

Trial...

...

Nope. Not doing it.

I gazed towards the sea for a few moments, then deleted it all.

7.

It's Showtime!

It's still jumbled and hazy in my mind. All of it. The whole 6 days. The jury were out for just over an hour – no thanks to Clarke pleading guilty to manslaughter on the ground of diminished responsibility. But all thanks to one Andrew Harper. Or No. 70, as I'd previously referred to him. The man who bravely battled to save my life that night.

The police had taken my laptop from the caravan and retrieved my phone from beneath the fridge freezer. And while I was being treated in hospital, the messages and threats from Clarke were discovered. It was only when the phone was finally returned, that I realised the blue flashing light I'd fixated on before blacking out, had been a funny (and decidedly smutty) text from Luke.

Clarke's defence team painted me as a semi-alcoholic whore, who had 'rubbed his face' into our break-up by sunbathing naked and going off with various men. Apparently, I'd driven him to it. The jealously and hurt he felt, made his mental state spiral off the scale, and rendered him incapable of rational thought.

M'lud.

Stevie took to the witness stand during proceedings. I can't remember the exact line of questioning, but it was aggressive and designed to achieve confirmation he'd been one of my 'many conquests'. Clarke's statement had referenced seeing Stevie and myself performing sex acts in the front of his van. And was littered with graphic detail.

Stevie used every ounce of his charisma and convincingly lied through his teeth; he'd given me a lift back to the caravan when I'd hurt my ankle. That was all.

Our Double O pact lived on.

As did Stevie and Freya's relationship, as she watched on from the public gallery.

There had been photos of the smashed-up flat.

Accounts of my general behaviour in Flabby's.

And accounts from people who had seen me and Spencer squiffy together on that final night.

Others came and went. Some I knew or recognised. Some I didn't.

Even a couple of the guys from Brokeback Bay got their 5-minutes of fame on the stand: Penguin Man and Mister Tall and Skinny. They both looked unfamiliar with their clothes on and were in and out in a flash. Each managed to throw me a brief, kind smile. I kept myself to myself, they both said. Polite hellos, exchanges about the weather and at their invite, I once joined their group for a beach party. Food. Drinks. Music. A bit of swimming.

Nothing to see here. Move along, please.

Christ. I'd assumed Clarke had only seen me coming off or going towards the beach – not following me onto it. Or maybe... there had been a way to spy on me from the top of the cliffs?

At times, it felt hard to work out who was on trial. And rather than feel uncomfortable about Stevie and the Brokeback guys being economical with the truth, I felt pleased. And relieved.

Clarke had to pay. There was nothing to excuse his actions. It was as simple as that.

And no matter what was denied or omitted, the press still had their field day and the public made up their own minds. And they chose to prefer titillation. Fuelled by outlandish stories from nudey beach, and from some people I had never seen there.

Elena did me proud. She spoke calmly and clearly; detailing how she'd listened to my concerns and fears about Clarke. And later on, Charlie, the (then) assistant manager of The Grub Shack, vouched for having to step in when Clarke made his impromptu and increasingly regular disappearances from the café. He also spoke of Clarke's sudden mood swings and occasional, volatile behaviour.

My own time in the stand remains the most

indistinct. I was the first witness to be called upon. The star turn.

With Clarke only metres away and looking as cool as a cucumber, I became flustered, confused in places and, at times, visibly agitated and annoyed at the personal and intrusive line of questioning – despite being warned what to expect.

Throughout it all, I think I looked at Clarke only 3 or 4 times. The last, when asked to describe our relationship; to go back to our early days. As I spoke, I stupidly glanced his way. And for the briefest of moments, his face creased into a small smile and his eyes glittered with affection as he looked at me. I froze for a few moments, lost track of what I'd been saying, looked away, then stuttered as I struggled to pick up my train of thought.

I didn't look at him again.

Until it was over.

I do recall speaking with enthusiasm and warmth about meeting Spencer that last time, and the fun we had together on our night out in Brightlea. But the mist descended when asked to describe the events that happened later, in the caravan. To assist the jury, there was a floor plan to refer to. And photographs I couldn't look at.

Sensing Clarke's eyes boring into me, I struggled and stumbled, until I finally broke down in tears and sobbed like a child. I was offered water, tissues and a little time. I gratefully accepted them all. Then made myself carry on.

I owed Spencer.

And couldn't let that bastard get away with his outrageous plea.

Andrew (aka No. 70) was magnificent; composed, articulate and unflinching as he gave his account of events. As a result of his courageous efforts, I discovered he'd been rewarded with a fractured forearm, broken ribs, heavy bruising and deep gashes to his body and arms. I can't remember what job he said he did, but it was something in the corporate world. There was no mention of what he was doing in a tatty caravan park. Or his mistress.

It seemed the courtroom was full of secrets.

I sought out Andrew when it was all over and thanked him as I squeezed his hand tightly and held back tears of gratitude. His evidence – along with Clarke's voicemails and messages, had been key. Andrew was careful to stress to the court that he'd seen Clarke striding, then jogging, towards my caravan, clasping an iron bar at his side, which was raised and brought down in a striking action when reaching the top step.

Manslaughter, Clarke?

Andrew hugged me and told me to take care of myself. He shrugged away my attempts to apologise for what I'd put him through – his injuries – *everything.* And when I thanked him once more, I glanced over his shoulder and recognised his attractive mistress, waiting patiently against the corridor wall. No. 70 followed my gaze.

'Things will get better. And work out for you,' he said. 'They have for me.'

As I watched him walk away, his arm wrapped around the woman's shoulder, I knew I owed him my life. Whatever had gone on in his personal life was none of my business; I was just glad he was happy.

With tears welling in my eyes, I croaked, 'Be lucky!' after them. For a moment, I thought they hadn't heard, but the woman twisted and threw me a dazzling smile. Then Andrew raised an arm, gave a small wave, then a thumbs up.

As they disappeared amongst the sea of milling people, I heard my name – spoken as though a question. I didn't need to turn around to know who the soft, Irish accent belonged to.

Luke.

I'd seen him earlier, of course, when he took the stand. How strange it had felt, seeing him for the first time since our afternoon of pleasure on the beach. He'd looked so different in his sharp suit. The summer tan long faded. His searching eyes located me in the public gallery, and he when gave a warm smile of reassurance, I had to look away.

Later on, a large photo of a smiling Spencer was displayed, and much was made of Clarke's case of mistaken identity as the physical similarities between Spencer and Luke were put forward. Similar height, build and salt and pepper hair. And only a five-year age difference between them.

I couldn't bear to watch, having already spent

countless hours thinking about how – from a distance, one could be mistaken for the other. Unsettled by Luke's presence and my head a whirl of sadness, confusion and exhaustion, I only half-listened to the drone of proceedings. But when Luke was questioned about the nature of our relationship, my ears pricked up.

'Was it purely sexual?' he was asked.

The prosecution barrister objected. But the defence put forward they were only trying to form a picture of my behaviour. The behaviour which sent Clarke mad with jealousy. And to kill.

I kept my head down and waited. Unsure what I wanted to hear. If anything at all.

Luke cleared his throat before speaking.

'No. Not at all. The physical aspect was just one component. We shared common interests, talked a lot and enjoyed each other's company. In fact, I believe our relationship had a strong enough foundation to become serious.' After a pause, he added, 'Very serious.'

As another wave of confusion pulsed through me, my head remained down.

Luke had already had some of the 'juicier' information extracted from him. About us. I'd managed to block out most of it, but from what I heard – despite being dressed up in eloquent wording – it hadn't painted a picture of wholesomeness. And now, with a romantic aspect thrown in the pot, it was no small wonder Eddie and the other sharks were circling for my side of the story.

As he stood beside me, I looked into Luke's face as he waited, unsure, for some form of response. Despite the paler skin, he looked as handsome as ever and his expression was one of concern.

I had no idea what to say, so numbly shook my head at him.

He reached out and lightly touched the sleeve of my trouser suit.

'Amber?' he quietly repeated.

As I squeezed my eyes shut and continued to shake my head, a lone tear trickled down my face.

'I can't, Luke... I just... *can't...* '

I wiped away the tear and raised my face.

Luke smiled at the progress. He cast his eyes over my dark hair but took care they didn't rest on my scar. 'I've missed you, Amber,' he said. 'And I'm so terribly, terribly sorry about what happened. I just hope today brings you some kind of... if there's *anything* I can do to... '

I interrupted him before he could continue.

'There isn't,' I said as firmly as my voice would allow. Unable to look into those grey-blue eyes, I turned my head to one side as I spoke.

'I got all your voicemails and messages when I finally got my phone back from the Police,' I began. I bit on my lip and shook my head, as I tried to push away the memory of laying in hospital when a female Police Officer breezed in and cheerily handed over my mobile in a clear plastic bag. 'All done!' she announced, as if just finishing a waxing session on my legs. My jaw was so awful at the time, I couldn't even speak. The phone remained on my bedside table for days before I felt brave enough to charge it and see what was waiting for me. The state I was in, I was half-expecting something from Clarke to be lurking there.

'Anyway... I know you got in touch. Quite often. And... thank you. I know you care... '

'I do care, Amber. I care about you a *lot*.'

I threw Luke a tight-lipped glance to silence him.

'But... I *can't*. *We* can't. There's nothing for us anymore. So... let's just leave it. We have to. It'd just be... *wrong*... '

He began to protest. He wanted to help me through everything. Be there for me. But I waved him away. And walked away with tears falling freely. I found Elena, donned my hat and sunglasses then, arm-in-arm, we went outside to push our way through the sea of microphones and cameras.

I've tried to keep Luke in a compartment I avoid exploring too often – a bit similar to Spencer's, I suppose. Both painful, but for very differing reasons.

But occasionally, Luke's words at the trial would unexpectedly pop into my head. He was right, of course; there'd been every sign our relationship would develop further and strengthen. And I knew myself enough to know he was the type of person I could fall in love with. After all, Luke was a really great guy.

But scratch away at the surface of my grieving for Spencer, and there was always the fact that Clarke got the wrong man. God knows, I didn't want Luke killed instead – I didn't want anyone to have been murdered. *Especially* because of me. But the confusion, self-disgust and overwhelming sadness and guilt I felt as I tried to examine and process my feelings, got me nowhere. Only halfway around the twist.

But one thing was clear – I had to deny myself Luke.

I didn't deserve him.

And it would be a betrayal to Spencer.

Besides, Luke would be better off without me; I was damaged goods. And despite the mixed publicity the trial provided him, I hoped it would help sell some of his paintings and that he'd find someone new.

Luke deserved some happiness. Just with someone else.

Yet, when he spoke to me – and just for a moment – I'd wanted to hug him. Or scream at him. Or both.

I'm so totally fucked up.

Clarke didn't take the stand. He wouldn't do it and didn't have to. Instead, he spinelessly left it to his defence team to pull me apart. How predictably typical of him. Anyway... it was claimed I'd shown such a level of 'wanton behaviour' that his spiralling feelings of belittlement and jealously finally snapped, making him irrational and out of control. It was even suggested that when I stayed at the Exeter hotel – after Clarke had struck me and prior to my leaving him – it had been to 'pick up men' just to 'rub him up the wrong way'.

It was extraordinary. And I did well to keep my head down and my mouth shut.

But between most of my alleged conduct being put down as hearsay or inconsequential, the details and graphic photos of my injuries – which were more appalling than remembered and caused gasps around the court room – meant all the evidence was stacked against Clarke. And he was duly found guilty of murder, attempted murder and GBH.

Clarke stood to receive the Jury's verdict.

And that's when I gave him my full attention.

Wearing a dark grey suit I recognised, Clarke was noticeably thinner with dark shadows rimmed beneath his eyes. But his stance was straight and confident, and as the foreperson of the jury (a portly lady with the air of a headmistress) was asked if the jury had reached their verdicts, Clarke defiantly tilted his chin upwards and fixated on the ceiling.

As the word, 'Guilty' rang out the first time, and as I trembled with emotion, I saw Clarke's jaw clench and a tiny jolt run through his body before composing himself once more. When said for the third and final time, he pressed his lips together, nodded his head as if in acknowledgement, then turned his eyes towards me.

The slow smile that spread across his face chilled me to the bone.

With a determination that was resolute, I refused to give Clarke the satisfaction of looking away. Our exchange was only broken when two Custody Officers began to lead him from the courtroom. About to disappear from view, he twisted his body and with his face contorted with rage, screamed at me, 'JUST REMEMBER THAT POOL OF PISS YOU WERE IN – YOU FILTHY FUCKING WHORE!'

Before he could bellow anything else, Clarke was swiftly ushered away and out of sight.

As I felt the blood drain from my face, I became aware of heads turning my way and someone encouragingly telling me to ignore him; that he'd be rotting in hell for a very long time. My shoulders were squeezed. My hand shaken. Fucked up congratulations were offered.

For what?

No one had won.

Spencer was dead.

And I was left to exist in my own kind of hell.

Clarke was sentenced two weeks later. I didn't attend for a great number of reasons. But Missus Mouth Almighty had been more or less right; life imprisonment with a minimum of 25 years. It was impossible to describe my feelings when the phone call came through. I just remember sitting in the flat, knees hugged up, and bizarrely thinking about my childhood and parents. Daisy chains, beaches, art, drugs and madness.

I suspected – or possibly, hoped – they were none the wiser about Spencer's murder and what had happened to me. With Mum's refusal to watch, listen or read any news, it afforded her the luxury of living in her hippy bubble, ignorant to the evils of the big, bad world.

It almost felt appealing.

Maybe I should have gone to see her – Dad pointless, as he was off with the fairies – but I simply didn't have the energy, capacity or, to be honest, the inclination to get embroiled in another painful scene. Besides, they'd never met Spencer – our courtship, wedding and divorce – were all played out during my exile for succumbing to the corporate world. And whilst Mum would doubtless have approved of his creativity, it wouldn't have stopped her spitting bile about him earning big bucks for the advertising fat cats.

What a mess. All of it.

I checked my phone; it was time to be getting my arse into gear and making some dinner. But despite my earlier shopping trip, preparing and cooking some food seemed beyond my reach. I guessed, revisiting the trial had dampened my mood for getting creative in the kitchen.

I lit a cigarette and gazed across the horizon to the beginnings of a streaky sunset.

Yeah, bollocks to cooking, I decided. I'd do the 15-minute stroll into Ketra. Get fed. Then get watered in one of their bars. Probably The Red Lion. I liked it there. And liked getting watered there. In fact, getting half-cut each night was the only thing keeping me together.

As I flicked some ash, a memory of Luke invaded my mind: the first time we met on nudey beach, when he cheekily came over to borrow my lighter and introduce himself. All smiles and Irish charm.

Despite myself, I couldn't help but smile.

I would have loved to have seen his Ireland with him.

Such a great, great guy.

So interesting.

Such a fantastic lover...

And now, probably someone else's...

With a sigh, I stubbed out the half-smoked cigarette, put Luke back in his compartment and firmly closed the lid.

'It's all for the best,' I muttered as I looked at the pink-tinged sky.

8.

House of Lunge

'House of Lunge' was my favourite eatery in Ketra. Tucked away in a cobbled side street, it was basic and cheap, but served the most delicious, traditional food. I found out about it when I met the owner, Lunge (as I'd christened him) in The Red Lion. Mid-to-late fifties, thick black hair, thicker eyebrows and the standard sun-damaged face I'd grown accustomed to seeing. He'd just finished work for the night and was enjoying a few whiskies at the bar.

It hadn't taken long to give him his nickname – he was a randy old bugger and took any opportunity to squeeze an arm around a woman's waist, before casually moving his pressed hand up in increments until sitting beneath a breast. Then, in a series of small, jerking tugs, he'd pull you closer. Causing boobs to bounce. And his hand to surreptitiously edge further upwards to feel the full weight of the jiggle.

He tried some of that malarkey with me. Once. And before I knew what the score was. It happened when sitting at the bar one night and asking for recommendations for places to eat. A smug expat, perched a couple of bar stools along and wearing a gaudy short-sleeved shirt, made the introduction. Lunge, who had been quietly nursing a large whisky nearby, was called over and introduced himself as Savva. Expat told Savva to tell me about his restaurant, which led to expressive, pointy directions and, 'good food' proudly mentioned a number of times. Then he plonked himself down beside me and we embarked on the painful journey of trying to converse in pidgin English.

Yes... here on holiday. A L-O-N-G holiday. B-I-G holiday. (Said with my own elaborate hand gestures.)

Holiday, yes?

Yes. Holiday.

You come *avrio*? Tomorrow? Good food.

Yes. Tomorrow I come restaurant. *Av... eo.*

Avrio. Tomorrow. Yes?

Yes.

And so it went on.

He seemed like a harmless chap. And was evidently tired after a long day. He worked his way through a couple of hefty whiskies and nattered away at me in a mixture of our languages. I picked out the scraps of English and tried to throw in some of the few Cypriot words I'd learned. And with squinty-eyed, drunken grins, I was toasted with a slurred, '*Yiamas!*' practically every time he took a mouthful.

So, there we sat. Not entirely understanding one another. But giving it a go. And getting pissed along the way.

Marvellous.

Before too long, Lunge's smiles developed a droopy crookedness, and heralded the point at which all further attempts at English were abandoned. Instead, he happily jabbered away at me in Greek and threw in the occasional hand gesture. I didn't mind any of it.

And when it suddenly became clear he'd done his drinking for the night, he stood, threw some Euros on the bar, bade the barman, '*Kalinihta*,' turned to face me and prodded his fingers into his chest.

'My restaurant. You come tomorrow? *Avrio?*'

As he beamed at me – all unsteady and squiffy – I marvelled at how someone from a developed country could possess such tobacco-stained teeth.

'Yes, yes. *Avrio*. Your restaurant.' I said, pointing at him. For good measure, I threw in some idiotic eating actions and a thumbs up.

As he took a step towards me, I naively assumed I'd be receiving the usual continental peck on each cheek.

But he titted me up instead. And in the process, half-squeezed the air from my body.

I extracted myself from his grasp and pushed

him away. 'Whoah! Get the fuck off me!' I cried.

Lunge shrugged. Gave me a gummy grin. Good-naturedly flapped a hand my way. Mumbled, 'Sorry. *Avrio*.' Shrugged again. Flapped again. Then merrily bimbled away.

And I was left with the expat sidling up to me and almost tripping over his tongue in his eagerness to give me the lay of land. Within minutes he'd told me how long he'd lived in Cyprus, how he knew *everyone* there was to know, and that Savva/Lunge was a 'really good guy'. Despite his wandering hands.

If I'd the energy to engage with Mister Expat, some plot-explaining would have been thrust his way. Instead, I wearily let him prattle on about eateries he'd 'stumbled upon' and how he was '*close* friends' with various owners – even listing their names as though I cared, would remember or be impressed.

I peered gloomily into my glass and suddenly mourned the absence of Lunge.

Yet, despite TitGate (and warily giving the benefit of the doubt) I was as good as my pissy pants word and visited House of Lunge the very next night. Only to fall in love with the place immediately. It was the epitome of rustic; old wooden furniture with dining tables covered with the obligatory blue and white checked cloths; twinkly Greek music was playing, and the stone walls were covered with dog-eared maps, decorative plates and faded photos of grim-looking village folk of yesteryear. In the corner above the small, crooked bar, perched an old TV. It was showing a Greek soap opera; its sound just about audible. But when screeching violins struck up, eyes dramatically flashed between characters, truths were seemingly revealed, challenges made, and a female in heavy make-up and impressive shoulder pads, neatly flopped to the floor.

Splendid.

On one of the eight tables, a group of old Cypriot men divided their attention between loudly commentating on the soap and loudly commentating on the two games of *tavli* taking place. The boards were the lovely, old traditional ones, and when the counters were slammed down for a thwarting move, I was reminded of an East London pub I'd visited many years ago, where old West Indian guys enjoyed a lot of slamming during their animated games of dominos.

When Lunge appeared, he looked fresher and sober. And promptly greeted me by calling me Sally.

'Ah! Sally – you come!'

He showed me to a table and handed me a laminated menu – thankfully in both English and Greek. Not overly hungry, I cobbled together some starters for my meal. Lunge memorised my order of halloumi, lounza, olives and salad. And just a bottle of water, please.

The water arrived within moments and as I gratefully drank, I took a snoop at what some of the other diners were having. All of it looked delicious, generously sized and mainly consisting of grilled fish or meat.

After a while, a shuffling woman – aproned, headscarfed and fiercely moustached – who I assumed to be Mrs Lunge, brought the dishes to my table. The salad alone was worth the visit. Heavy on coriander, a touch of basil, and with a perfect oil and vinegar dressing. After briefly disappearing, Mrs Lunge returned with a basket of warmed pitta. I smiled warmly and thanked her, but she was unreceptive to both. No matter – I'd tried. Left alone, I happily munched my way through pittas filled with halloumi and salad between picking on olives or pieces of lounza. And despite the battle between the Greek music, soap opera violins and slamming *tavli* excitement, I was feeling just about as good as it gets without alcohol. All things considered. And despite the clonky overhead fans needing a kick up the arse.

With my meal finished, I declined dessert by patting my satisfied stomach, but Lunge wouldn't let me go until I was given a generous brandy on the house; no interpreter required and refusal seemingly futile. With the restaurant quietening down, he'd already had a few whiskies by then – having grabbed free moments to join the postcard faces for a quick slurp and add his commentary to the relentless *tavli* duels. I took my drink outside to one of the recently vacated tables and immediately felt grateful for the hit of warm breeze. As I smoked a cigarette and sipped brandy, I gazed up and admired the stars that appeared to communicate with one another as they took turns to pulse bright twinkles. Against the jet-black sky, they were bigger, brighter and more beautiful than any I'd seen back home. Simply mesmerising.

I was shaken from my star-gazing session as Lunge suddenly rumbled into action as he escorted a couple of middle-aged, German-sounding women out of the restaurant. It was all boozy, goodnight cries of, '*kalinihta!*' A bit of a gurn from Lunge. Then – boof! He lunged and efficiently titted-up the closest woman.

Who… *remarkably*… seemed to welcome it.

In fact, as he squeezed her closer – his hand nudging the base of her right breast, and twittering something about '*kleftico*' and 'tomorrow' with a bleary-eyed grin, I watched on in wide-eyed-soap-opera amazement (cue the screeching violins), as she cupped a hand over his and shifted it higher and deeper into her flesh. Lunge whispered something in her ear, causing her to throw her head back in a throaty laughter. He edged his hand a tad higher – Dear Lord, was that nipple territory? A final squeeze. The reluctant release. Pecks on the cheek for the less attractive friend. More choruses of '*kalinihta!*' Royal waves all round. The women toddled off. And Lunge's work was done.

A quick adjustment of his crotch. A replenish of his whisky. Then back to his cronies to boisterously add to their running commentary. He seemed well chuffed with himself.

Left to finish my brandy in peace, I sipped away

and struggled to understand why a decent-looking woman would let someone like Lunge cop a feel. But I already knew the answer; the feeling of escapism; a sense of freedom, and the lack of inhibition that came with holiday drinking and hot weather. Enough to make a lot of people feel randy. Myself included. And I knew for a fact – were I still in England (given everything that had gone on) – sex would probably be the last thing on my mind.

I shrugged away the sudden memory of the two happy chappies I'd picked up. I'd done what had suited me at the time; I was a free agent, after all and supposed I might not be averse to some more no-strings-attached dalliances whilst in Cyprus.

What with us sexy pirates being a bit on the frisky side.

I'd see.

Besides, any distraction to take my mind off other matters would be most welcome. *Plus...* having sex with a tourist came with the added bonus of them going home before too long.

I had to smile and shake my head at that; I sounded as bad as the smug expat. I *was* a tourist! Albeit a longer staying one. Jeez. Get over yourself, Amber – or you'll start dishing out guided tours in a minute... silly cow.

When it came to paying my bill, I kept Lunge at arm's length and swiftly exited stage left. Heat or not, I'd really prefer to secure the services of someone who knew what the end of a toothbrush looked like.

What it was for. And moreover, used it.

He laughed and held his arms up in mock surrender when his advance resulted in me hastily taking a few steps back. Stretching forward, I shook his hand instead.

'Good food?' he asked.

'The best!' I replied.

'You come again?'

'Yes!'

As I slowly extracted my hand, Lunge beamed me a broad smile. '*Kalinihta*, Sally!'

'*Kalinihta*, Lunge!'

He didn't have a clue.

Ooh... those teeth...

*

After a lengthy shower, I dressed, and with the aid of my phone torch, took a slow walk along the semi dirt road until reaching the streetlights of Ketra. I was still struggling to adapt to how early the sun set in Cyprus and surprised myself by occasionally missing the long, light summer nights back home.

Which was probably the extent of what I missed.

When I arrived at House of Lunge, my shower seemed like a distant memory. Despite Ketra being in the hills – and therefore, cooler than Coral Bay, I felt a large patch of sweat on my back and my forehead sopping.

Gratefully snapping up one of the outside tables,

I quickly set about dabbing my face and neck with thin paper napkins tugged from the table's plastic dispenser. With another handful, I reached beneath my vest and swiped at my back and chest, before crumpling them into tight balls for later disposal. Feeling a little more comfortable, I sat back in my chair and took a few deep breaths. Jeez. That *had* been a challenging walk in the heat. And despite being reasonably fit.

As I fanned my face with a hand, I saw Lunge coming over to greet me.

He did the Sally thing. I did the Lunge thing.

I pointed at the meals being enjoyed on the next table.

'Special,' he announced.

'Special,' I confirmed with a nod.

'Drink?'

'Vodka. Diet coke. Please,' I said.

'Coca-Cola Light,' Lunge corrected.

'Yes. Coco-Cola Light. Thank you. *Efharisto*.'

Lunge flashed his horror gnashers and walked away with the redundant menu.

Relieved to be sitting down, cooling down and feeling a tad 'expat smug' about our *ultra* fluent exchange, I decided to fish out my phone: I was just about in the right mood for a snoop at X.

Let's give it a go...

As I bent my head over my phone, I became aware of loud English voices and looked up to see a podgy middle-aged couple further along the cobbles. They'd obviously come from the village square and as their nearing voices became more distinct, it unfolded they were bitterly complaining about the heat and bickering about where to eat. With the husband protesting about all the 'foreign muck' on offer.

Despite the distance, I could clearly see he was getting agitated, as he repeatedly mopped sweat from his bald head between snarling at his wife. I saw her point towards House of Lunge (or 'Manolis Restaurant' to everyone else) as a suggestion. His anger and exasperation boomed across the cobbles.

'I'm telling you, Paula – I want a fucking curry for my tea! Not any of this shit – and that's all there is to it!'

All heads turned their way, but oblivious to spectators, they continued to row. As the wife complained of 'this fucking heat' and them 'traipsing around like a pair of pricks', a taxi slowly rumbled across the cobbles and pulled up outside. A party of four alighted and passed me to enter the restaurant.

The air filled with the sound of a piercing whistle.

'Hold up!' the husband bellowed. 'Oi! Taxi! Manuel – wait for us!'

With his face showing signs of exertion, the husband picked up pace, leaving Paula to unhappily trail in his wake. Unable or unwilling to speed up.

Reaching the taxi, he turned and shouted, 'Hurry up, you lazy cow!' Before banging its roof and dipping his head through the window.

'Coral Bay!' he barked at the driver.

I exchanged disapproving, tut-tut head shakes with fellow dinners. Eyes were soap opera rolled. Whispers. Nudges. Huffs. Puffs. And a bit of 'dear-oh-dear' as loaded forks hovered midway between plates and gaping mouths.

As Paula finally lumbered past, she at least had the decency to throw us an embarrassed glance before telling her husband to 'shove up' and heaving herself in.

We watched the taxi pull away. Their arguing heads visible through the back window.

It seemed he'd be getting his curry after all.

And with any luck, The Taste of Bengal would be notching up another victim.

Order restored, Lunge made a timely arrival with my drink; a gargantuan serving of vodka over chunky ice cubes. As he opened the can of mixer and set it beside my glass, I wasn't entirely sure any of it would fit in.

'*Endaxi*, Sally?'

Okay? he'd asked.

I laughed and pointed at the jumbo vodka.

'*Poly endaxi!*' I replied. Everything was 'very okay'.

And wasn't I a fucking whizz at Greek?

Or roughly twenty words of it.

Happy with my response – or more likely, my effort to use two of my twenty words, Lunge trotted off. I plucked out some of the ice cubes and threw them into the kerb. Space made, I poured in some mixer, swirled the glass, took a mouthful and winced.

Fucking Nora! That had the kick of a mule!

But I'd be brave. I'd struggle on...

Abandoning all thoughts of X, I sipped my drink and admired the small street that was home to House of Lunge. Old stone houses with pastel-coloured wooden shutters. Ornately carved front doors that led directly onto the cobbles. Brightly painted flowerpots filled with geraniums and lavender. Yawning or snoozing cats curled up beside them. And a real feeling of time standing still.

Mrs Lunge – who clearly knew less English than her husband, brought out my meal and silently placed it before me; a mix of grilled chicken and *sheftalia* – a form of pork and lamb sausage. They were packed into a large open pitta with cabbage, chopped onions and heavily sprinkled with fresh parsley. Aside from chips, it came with a chunk of cucumber, tomato slices and half a lemon to squeeze over the meat. It looked delicious. And Mrs Lunge looked tired.

'*Efharisto*,' I said, eager to show off my latest Cypriot word.

She gave me a ghost of a smile and walked away.

The meal was the perfect base for the drinking I had in mind and as tasty as it looked. And with silent vows to do extra lengths, I even polished off all the chips. They were simply irresistible, and due to the quality of Cypriot potatoes, far better than any back home.

The obligatory brandy was forthcoming from

Lunge, and as it collided with the vodka I'd finally ploughed through, it didn't seem the best match made in heaven. I paid my bill, got called Sally again, called him Lunge again, repelled his half-hearted Lunge, said *kalinihta* and on slightly unsteady legs, wobbled over the cobbles towards the village square and The Red Lion.

A few minutes later, I was safely at the pretty, outside circular bar and feeling a bit boozy-triumphant when securing one of the bar stools with arm rests. As I waited to be served, I admired the backdrop of the impressive Byzantine church across the square. At night it was illuminated by coloured spotlights – which tied in perfectly with The Red Lion's strings of bulbs and fairy lights that draped around the bar and perimeter. And in the centre of the paved beer garden, an ancient olive tree took pride of place with green spotlights trained on it. The whole place was just *so cute*, and with its vibe more relaxed than the bustle of Coral Bay, I was glad to have options to suit my mood.

I was shaken out of my thoughts by Johnny standing in front of me.

'The usual?'

I had to beam; the words were like nectar to any drinker's ears. And I still found it incredible – but highly welcome – how most bar tenders remembered my drink out here. Particularly as a reasonably new and somewhat sporadic visitor. The same admiration went to all the waiters who shunned a notepad and memorised orders. Not something I'd be able to do; I could barely remember what I had for breakfast most days...

As I said, 'Yes, please,' I noticed Johnny's eyes momentarily flicker over my scar. I didn't mind; it could be pretty hard to ignore sometimes. Besides, it was only the gawpers that got on my nerves or made me feel uncomfortable.

Johnny patted the bar twice and as he went to make my drink, I wondered what it was with all the bar-patting malarkey out here. Dunno. I extracted my cigarettes, lighter and phone from my bag and, as I lit up, looked around to see who else was out tonight. Well, not the smug expat for starters. Maybe he had some poor sod pinned to a wall somewhere and was boring the arse off them about 'fabulous little eateries he'd stumbled across' or 'amusing anecdotes he'd shared with the President over a cuppa'.

Instead, there was a 50/50 mix of Cypriot men (the women only an occasional sight, I'd noticed) and expats or tourists. So very different from the tourist-dominated bars of Coral Bay where only small pockets of Cypriots could be seen. If at all.

Johnny was back with my drink and a small bowl of pistachios.

'So, how's things with Amber?' he asked with a smile.

There were no communication problems to be had here; Johnny was a 'Charlie' (as I'd learned) – meaning an English-Cypriot – and born in North

London: my twenty words could stand down for a while. *Yet...* he sometimes spoke as though his first language was Greek – which made me wonder if it was an unconscious habit he'd picked up from talking in simple English to various tourists over the years.

'I'm good, thanks. Just trying to recover from one of... Savva's colossal brandies on the house.'

With a laugh, Johnny brushed a hand through his thick, black hair. And for a moment, I was once more reminded of Stevie and his claims of Italian descent. Johnny could almost pass for his older brother and looked to be roughly my age.

'What can I say? Us Cypriots are very generous people!'

I reached for my drink. 'Well, he's certainly very generous with his hands.'

Johnny laughed once more. 'Ah! It's in our blood! We see a beautiful woman... what can you do?'

I raised a disapproving eyebrow over my glass.

'Well, I'm not sure the Me Too movement would quite see it like that. Maybe I should have given him the nickname of 'Weinstein' instead.'

Johnny leaned his tanned arms on the bar. 'Instead? You've given Savva a nickname? Now I am intrigued.'

'I called him Lunge,' I said, with a wide-eyed innocent smile. 'And better than that, I call his restaurant House of Lunge.'

'Lunge?' Johnny blurted out a hoot of laughter. 'That's brilliant! Does he know?'

'Well,' I began, as I coyly swirled a finger amongst the ice cubes, 'we do seem to have a house special arrangement in place. For some unearthly reason he calls me Sally. And I call him Lunge. He's none the wiser and seems rather attached to it.'

'Don't worry, Amber – I'll keep your secret. But... Lunge... it's perfect.'

I put my drink down. 'It's not really, though. Is it?' I had no desire to get heavy or bring the mood down, but Johnny's earlier comment had grated.

Recognising my change in tone, Johnny edged further across the bar and spoke to me quietly.

'How long have you been in Cyprus, Amber?'

'Seven weeks? Something like that.'

'So, maybe enough time to see a few things. I've been here five years, had two pubs in Ayia Napa, one in Coral Bay and now this one here. Now... I'm not saying things are right in Cyprus – but what you have to understand is that *this*... ' he paused to gesture around him with his hand, '... is not real life – *particularly* in the tourist resorts. And a *lot* of tourists go on holiday for a good time. You know what I mean? Open your eyes and you'll see for yourself. I've seen honeymoon couples cheating on each other. Long-time married couples – the same. Women throwing themselves at men – it's not always the other way round. One time, I was working at a bar and a middle-aged couple were drinking with the waiters from the restaurant they'd eaten in that night... they got the husband so drunk he could barely stand. He was put in a taxi back to his hotel and the wife was happy to go off with two of the waiters. She was even groping one of them behind her husband's back. All this madness goes on, Amber. As I said, this isn't real life. People don't behave like they would back home. And as for Savva – or Lunge, as you call him – you and I can say the way he behaves isn't right... but believe me, there are some women out there who don't mind. In fact, they welcome it.'

It was quite a speech. And left too much to debate with the vodka and brandy rattling around inside me. But I very much had the gist and recalled the German woman who'd seemed happy enough with Lunge's attention.

'Doesn't his wife mind?'

Johnny did the Cypriot shrug. 'Either she doesn't know or doesn't care. Or maybe she's just happy he's not pestering her for sex. Like I said, I'm not saying any of it's *right*, I'm just saying how it is.'

'So... do any of these women go *off* with him?' I asked. 'I mean, I don't want to sound harsh... but... *those teeth...* '

As soon as the words left my lips, I realised the hypocrisy; me sitting there with scars on my face and a selection of teeth that weren't my own. But Johnny just laughed.

'You'll be surprised, Amber,' he said, simply.

'Blimey... ' I muttered in wide-eyed realisation.

Johnny checked over his shoulder. Some of the

Cypriot guys were beginning to tease him about the lack of service. One of them – who looked a real character, held an empty glass above his protruding tongue as he tried to shake out a final droplet to good-natured jeers and laughter.

'*Yiannis!*' they repeatedly cried.

Keen to learn another word, I asked, 'Yan-iss. Does that mean 'service'?'

Johnny straightened and laughed. 'No! *Yiannis* is my name in Greek. It translates to Johnny.'

'Ooh! Who *knew?*' I said with an unexpected touch of campness.

'Catch you later,' he said. Then he did the bar-tap thing, walked over to the Cypriots with his arms thrown in the air, and began jabbering away at them in Greek.

I threw a small salute to Johnny's back and was left to my drink and thoughts.

When did I start getting so prudish about a bloke chancing his luck? After all, I was hardly a nun, myself.

But... what about the women who didn't want to be lunged at? Were they fair game out here, in the false reality of a fortnight in the sun? But then again... it did seem like Lunge was getting his tobacco-stained leg over...

The drinks had made my head a bit woozy. Now was not the time for such *complicated* deliberation. As I pushed away all thoughts of Mediterranean gropers, my earlier phone call with Eddie tried to muscle its way in.

'And you can fuck right off,' I quietly murmured.

I drained the rest of my drink and as I slid the glass forward for Johnny to replenish, regretted downing it so quickly.

Yipes...

I looked around. What I needed was a bit of light relief. Someone to play with. Casting my eyes around, I was only met with couples and a group of four engrossed in each other's company, the Cypriot guys and one sorry-looking cat having a kip. Just *where was* the smug expat when you needed him for a piss-taking session? Lunge, even?

Pfft.

I lit a cigarette and picked up my phone.

And to my utter delight... there... on X... I was immediately greeted by the magnificence of a tweety post from @ballbagderek.

'I am now identifying as a wide-toothed comb'

As I snorted with laughter, I noticed the fresh drink beside me. Taking a sip, I wondered how naughty it would be to respond. Or message.

Tilting my head to the stars for the answer, I tried to weigh up the pros and cons. But it all seemed so terribly confusing for my pissy pants brain. As my head began to feel a little fuzzy, I straightened up, gave it a little shake and looked again at the post.

It would be a *terrible* idea. Wouldn't it?

Yeah. Deffo. He could be *anyone.*

But his profile picture was a bulldog wearing glasses. His bio said, 'Pissing my way through life one lamppost at a time'. That's funny. *He's* funny.

And I need some fun.

Maybe. But it would still be a *terrible* idea.

And what would Eddie's team have to say?

Hmm...

Fuck 'em. Fuck. Them.

And to demonstrate my defiance, I had a little drinkie to show the world what tough chick I could be.

Then I did the unthinkable. And began tapping away on my phone.

9.

A Funny Old Day

Pool Man spoke to me!!

Which was all rather unsettling, as I thought we had an understanding; he silently does his sweep – and whatever other bumfuckery he gets up to – he either does or doesn't take a peep at me nudey sunbathing (through the bastard sunglasses); I stretch out and, by and large, ignore him. *Or...* I occasionally adopt a mildly, fruity pose if the mood takes me. Or if I'm feeling ignored. Or ugly. It's been a marvellous arrangement. And having got our earlier exchange out the way, one that has worked perfectly well.

He comes. He does. He fucks off.

All very civilised.

The old boy of a gardener is from the same stable. I've only seen him the twice; pottering around in the relative coolness of early evening. A knackered-looking cap. Buttoned-up shirt. Tucked into belted trousers hoisted too high. The two times I've seen him, I was sitting at the outside table, sunbathing finished for the day and glumly staring at my latest Susie attempt. He's yet to acknowledge my existence and with his advanced years, I wonder if his eyesight and/or hearing might be a bit dicky. That said, I do harbour a suspicion he's one of the postcard faces I've seen throwing back whiskies at House of Lunge and getting vocal about backgammon and the violin-themed soap opera. Either way, he's never thrown me a glance, let alone attempted to speak to me. I even fleetingly wondered if he was in league with Pool Man of the non-specific nationality and they'd formed some kind of pact to silently 'do' and 'fuck off'.

So when Pool Man uttered his first words to me for weeks, I initially ignored him. At the time, I'd been merrily soaking up the brutal rays, contemplating a swim once he'd fucked off and listening to a phone-in on Radio Aphrodite, where some self-catering Brits were asking for advice on how to keep ants out of their cornflakes. Willing the presenter to tell them to just shut the fucking packet properly, put it on a high shelf and CLEAN AWAY YOUR SHIT in the kitchen, I'd been eagerly awaiting said advice from Sunshine Sam (for ALL your holiday problems). Which, in turn, meant it didn't compute for a while, that Pool Man had broken his oath of silence and now stood a few metres away, pole in hand and expecting a response.

As I half-mouthed the words, '... and tell them to take their fucking rubbish out once in a while... ' I felt daftly hopeful of an airwaves ding-dong and that Sunshine Sam was going to give them a bit of what for on the hygiene front.

Sadly – and I mean, *very sadly* – I was all ears.

But instead of gripping talk about crumbs, sponges, Dettol and have-a-word-with-yourselves, my ears picked up sounds of something else.

There it was again.

I opened my eyes and squinted into the dazzling light.

And behold...

Pool Man. Pole. Expectant look.

I shielded my eyes with a hand.

'Did you say something?' I asked, sure in my mind that he hadn't, and was just looking at my naked body whilst performing pole activities.

He didn't respond. He just stood there with those grinning wraparound sunglasses. As I was about to close my eyes again and pick up on CornflakeGate and the mention of a 'ruined holiday' and compensayshun, I very definitely heard Pool Man utter words in my direction.

Which was all very unnerving. And not part of the deal, at all.

I bristled myself into a sitting position and unattractively scrunched my face into an old man, 'I can't hear you' expression. All that was missing was a hand cupped to my ear.

'Beach barbeque,' he announced, as though answering a quiz question.

For a second, I thought he'd picked up on something on the radio, but as I momentarily diverted my attention back to Sunshine Sam, the Brits were moaning about 'and *another* thing' – a tub of open and unattended Pringles being invaded by the same army of peckish ants.

I reached for my sunglasses and popped them on.

'What beach barbeque?' I asked, still scrunching.

Pool Man remained silent. Dear fucking Lord, I thought – it was like getting blood from a stone.

I was anxious to get back to Sunshine Sam's slot, as I could hear him battling to reason with the Brits, and mentioning things like 'hot country' and 'staying on top of things with the ants'. But the Brits Abroad were seemingly having none of it. Apparently, they'd 'paid bloody good money' for their holiday, Pringles and bloody cornflakes.

And on lazy, hot, summer days – when you can't string more than five words together on a laptop, such things fill your life. Particularly if it sounded like it might kick off.

But there was nothing doing about beaches or barbeques.

Silence. Those fucking sunglasses.

It could go on forever.

In exasperation, I hunched my shoulders and shook my upturned palms to Pool Man in a 'get on with it' gesture.

'Tomorrow night,' he said.

I nodded. I understood those two words. I just needed *more*. So I shook my palms at him some more.

'Tomorrow night,' he repeated. 'Barbeque. And beach party. By the sea caves.'

Ah ha! Progress!

I lowered my sunglasses over my nose and looked at him. 'Ooh… I *do* love a beach party.'

Pool Man tilted his head to one side. 'You come?'

I fought back a childish urge to reply with, 'I did the last time,' but instead asked, 'Go with you?'

'I take you if you want to go.'

We entered another silence as I considered. My last beach party had been at Brokeback Bay and that'd turned out *most* satisfactory, thanks to Olive Man. And anything involving beaches, hot nights and alcohol *could* lead to… well, *anything*. But was I meant to go as Pool Man's *date?* I mean, he was quite interesting in that craggy, keeping-his-trap-shut kind of way – but as his date? And all that could possibly entail?

I pushed my sunglasses back up. 'Who else is going?'

'Many people,' he replied with a shrug. 'Every month, second Saturday – beach party, barbeque. Sometimes music. Sometimes lots of people. Sometimes not so many. Normally many.'

He was selling it to me and was probably the kind of thing I needed, but I could feel Pool Man's eyes through those sunglasses.

'I go with you?' To get over my meaning, I tapped my chest then pointed towards him.

A slow smile spread across Pool Man's face – the first I'd seen from him. It was broad and amused and had an edge of mischief that brought to mind Jack Nicholson's wicked grin.

'I take you,' he said. 'That's all.'

And suddenly, from not wanting to be saddled with Pool Man at the beach party and him thinking I'd be a shoo-in for sex, I felt an acute sense of rejection. Without thought, I raised a hand and my fingers sought out the scar above my eyebrow. In the unforgiving light, with no make-up and covered in a sheen of sun oil and sweat, I knew my injuries looked at their worst.

Of course he wouldn't want me as his date. Even if I was sitting there naked.

I turned my head and looked at the stunning bougainvillea that decorated the villa's walls.

Okay Amber, get over yourself. He's probably got a wife or girlfriend. Or a boyfriend. Or he's just not into you. And you're not into him – *despite* him seeming a bit more intriguing now you've been blanked. Besides, not everyone's Lunge. All he's done is offered an invite to a party. Which is kind and thoughtful. Don't. Be. A. Twat.

I turned my head and beamed at Pool Man.

'That sounds great. Thank you. Do I need to bring anything?'

Pool Man shrugged. 'Some drink. If you like.'

'Okay. What time?'

'I come for you 8 o'clock. Tomorrow.'

'*Avrio!*' I said, proudly showing off one of my words, but he remained silent and just stared at me through those grinning sunglasses.

Feeling a need to fill the void, I tagged on, 'Okay. Tomorrow at 8. I'll be ready.'

Pool Man threw me a quick Jack Nicholson then returned his attention to dragging his pole through my pool.

Hmm...

As I removed my sunglasses and settled back on my sun lounger, I felt surprisingly pleased I had a party to go but, and more importantly, I was tragically anxious to pick up on AntGate. But Sunshine Sam's slot had finished and Big Mountain's, Baby I Love Your Way was playing. As I listened to the song, all daft thoughts of rejection floated away and were replaced by an overwhelming feeling of holiday mode. Free and relaxed and with a date in my diary. As the song made my mind drift to the party, where I imagined myself dancing to it on the beach, I suddenly wondered if I should take some food as well. I lifted my head to ask Pool Man.

But he had vanished.

Funny old thing.

I did it. I boldly returned to Sonny's and thrust my overdue Euros upon Andreas who, in turn, appeared highly amused and bewildered about the long-winded hullabaloo of an apology I dished out about the delay. He also had the manners to make no mention of Miss Mouth Almighty nor the scene that had unfolded.

When I finally ran out of steam, he leaned across the bar and patted my hand.

'Amber, there's no worries.' He spoke in a soothing tone which made me feel as if he were addressing a toddler whose balloon had just blown away. About to thank him again for being so understanding and not setting his numerous cousins on me, I changed my mind and decided to tell him my BIG NEWS instead.

'Guess what? *I've* been invited to a party tomorrow night!' I threw Andreas a smug nod to let him know, *aren't I* the one, then ruffled a hand through my hair, took a sip of my drink and attempted to adopt the air of an international woman of mystery.

Which was short-lived.

'Yes. Down by the sea caves. Are you going?'

Andreas laughed at my crestfallen expression.

'There's a party... ' he began.

'Every month... ' I interrupted, '... on the second Saturday.'

See? Not totally useless.

Andreas lifted both palms in the air. '*Brávo* Amber!' he exclaimed. And as he walked away to serve someone, I was left feeling like a seal who'd clambered on a bar stool and was waiting to be thrown a fish.

Resisting the urge to clap my flippers together, I picked up my drink instead, took a mouthful and looked around. Tonight was Reggae Nite. Bob Marley was singing about Buffalo Soldiers and the puny DJ was ridiculously swamped by the dreadlock wig he was wearing beneath a woollen Rasta hat. Even from my vantage point, I could see rivulets of sweat running down his face as he struggled to navigate a headphone to his ear through the mass of synthetic fibres.

'Let it go, son... ' I murmured to myself. '... it's too fucking hot. Take it all off. Let. It. Go.'

Jeez. He'd be going up in flames if he wasn't lucky...

There was nothing doing on the dance floor and the tables were only half-full, with some of the tourists fanning themselves with their hands or plucking damp tops from their bodies for an aerate.

The oppressive heat was relentless and despite having adapted to it a little, I decided to follow suit and wiggled the front of my vest about for a few seconds. As I idly wondered about the poor turnout in the bar, I remembered Andreas telling me about the large hotels' changeover days being a bit quieter and supposed that was why. From the way things were going, it might be worth drumming up some business by advertising the imminent collapse of the DJ, whose legs seemed to be buckling more by the minute.

Hmm. It'd been a funny old day. And could

possibly get funnier if DJ Puny managed two twists and a pike before hitting the deck – or decks – with his nut on fire.

The morning had begun with a lengthy swimming session before enjoying an alfresco breakfast as I watched the swallows reclaim the pool with their delightful antics. Then, with a whack of endorphins and feeling of, 'This is the day!' I got my head down with some writing...

... only to rattle out a few words about a pining Susie getting 'Wellard' tattooed on her tit. Instantly regretting it. Instructing the tattoo artist to disguise it... and ending up with something resembling a deformed cabbage on her knocker.

At which point, I waved the white flag and retired to my sun lounger for a bit of Sunshine Sam and my subsequent weird exchange with Pool Man. Which, thinking about it, could have done with some soap opera violins to fill those silences.

After a fruit-based lunch, I went indoors to get some ironing done and made sure to put on the air con. My first laundry session at the villa had seen me struggling in the suffocating heat and dripping sweat onto clean clothes before realising the error of my distracted ways. Anyway, lessons learned etc.

All good.

Or all good until earlier today, when I looked up from the shorts I was pressing and saw a lizard on the kitchen work surface a few feet away. After my initial squeal of shock, I shooed it away with my arms and chased it to the gap in the veranda doors.

All good (Vol II).

However... at the point the lizard had its backside halfway out the door, it had a sudden change of heart, (or simply thought, 'fuck this for a lark') made a U-turn and had the temerity to charge towards me. Which resulted in a swift role reversal of aggressors, as I flapped and screeched my way around the lounge and kitchen in a series of bare-footed hops, as if the floor was made of hot coals.

Not good.

Fearing for my tootsies and life, I pegged it out the kitchen door and fled to the sanctuary of Chez Cleo to flop on her cushions with sighs of relief. But after a period of regrouping – which involved a hastily smoked cigarette, I remembered the dated and unreliable-looking iron was still switched on and feared for my going out shorts. And the villa burning down.

Not good at all.

Action (unfortunately) was required.

When I tentatively re-entered the villa, Mr Lizard was naturally nowhere to be seen and I had no idea if he'd buggered off outside or was lurking with intent somewhere. And possibly armed. I switched off the iron (gladly noting I'd left it upright), picked up two hangers, and after a few deep breaths and murmurs of, 'Motherfucker,' I channelled my inner Lara Croft and thudded about, poking my hangers in this place and that with booming shouts of,

'Gertcha!!!' or 'Gerrout of here, fuck head!'

And when I roughly rustled the heavy drapes that hung by the veranda doors, Mr Lizard casually poked his head out, only to find me doing some form of hysterical war dance on the spot and brandishing a couple of plastic hangers in his direction. 'Gertcha!! Gertcha!!!' And to my deepest joy, Mr Lizard promptly gertched the fuck out of it through the gap in the doors, over the veranda and scampered off somewhere deep into the garden. The little shit.

But all good.

I slid the doors closed and eyed the pile of ironing yet to be done.

Nah. The moment had passed, I was *emotionally drained* and still coming down from the chase.

I *had*, after all, just fought a small war on my own...

And note to Amber: when you put the air con on – make sure all the doors are closed properly. El Twatto. And maybe see if the agents can rustle up a better iron.

Grabbing a bottle of cold water from the fridge, I wandered outside and returned to Chez Cleo. As I glugged down large mouthfuls and cast a cautious eye around for Mr Lizard, I wondered if my tragically pathetic (yet comedic) display had any mileage as Susie material.

Probably not. But it showed how desperate I'd become.

I idly picked up my phone from the cushions and

scrolled through my emails. A brief one from Elena, thanking me for my postcard. The flat was fine. Work was manic. She was seeing someone.

Ooh er Missus! How brilliant! I'll drop her a line later and ruthlessly quiz her about her new man.

Scroll. Various nonsense. Scroll. Scroll. More nonsense. Bollocks. Offers for various bollocks I don't want or need. Scroll. Scroll. Ignore. Ignore for now. Scroll.

Ah. Eddie...

Oh dear. He was asking me who the hell @ballbagderek was.

Seems his team picked up on our messaging session...

Blah, blah... better things to do... blah... if I put half as much energy into my writing... blah... invested heavily... whooping it up and getting pissed every night... blah, blah... if I could kindly extract my messaging finger from my arse... blah, blah, blah... and... ... blah.

Not good.

Not good at all.

But rather than feeling the intended sting on the back of my legs, I found it hysterical and threw my head back for a lengthy bout of rare laughter.

Yeah, it'd been a funny old day.

So, all good.

Better, in fact.

*

I drained the rest of my drink and smiled over at Andreas for a refill, who gave a nod of acknowledgement before turning to the bank of spirits on the back bar. I liked Andreas, he seemed a good guy and had never once mentioned – nor barely glanced at – my scar. He never questioned. And just took whatever information I chose to offer. Meaning, as far as he was concerned, my extended holiday was to get over a recent and messy divorce.

'So, are you going tomorrow night?' I asked, when Andreas brought my drink over.

He considered my question for a moment. 'Maybe.' Then with a shrug and a sigh, 'Maybe not. Depends what I feel like when I finish here. It's a tough time of the year. Yes?'

'Yes – I bet it is,' I replied in all seriousness.

With a tight smile, Andreas patted the bar twice then walked away to chat to his Cypriot chums at the far end. Leaving me to wonder how exhausting it must be to work such long hours in the relentless peak time heat.

He must be as whacked out as Eddie having to tell me off all the time, I thought with amusement.

Eddie... Eddie... which reminded me...

I needed to swerve Ball Bag away from messaging on X.

With a smile, I thought back to our daft exchange that had started at The Red Lion and continued after I'd unsteadily wobbled my way back to villa and settled on my bedroom balcony with an unnecessary nightcap, my bougainvillea canopy, twinkling lights and the sweet smell of jasmine. Our messages had been total nonsense. Lots of little parcels of fun. I'd snorted out loud at some of his offerings. And felt mightily chuffed at some of my dazzling and *hysterical* responses.

At some point, I'd felt the heavy hand of reason rest upon my pissed shoulders, so I apparently signed off with, '*Laters. Bit wankeered*' and happily toddled off to bed.

The next morning, aside from discovering one of my sandals bobbing about in the swimming pool (dunno) I also found Ball Bag's response; '*Have you been on the E's tonight?*'

Funny guy.

And no small wonder Eddie thinks I'm on the lash the whole time...

Thankfully, there was no hideous hangover to contend with as, for some peculiar reason, I just didn't seem to get them in Cyprus. Maybe it was to do with the copious amounts of water I drank. Maybe it was do with the amount of sweating I did. Or maybe a mixture of both. And given the amount I was necking on a regular basis, I was grateful for the reprieve. However it was gifted.

Anyway, if I wanted to continue my jocular bullshit sessions with Ball Bag, it needed to be in laboratory conditions and away from the prying eyes of Eddie and his team of raptors who kept dibbing me in.

As I sipped on my drink, I wondered if I was being stupid. After all – and as Eddie had asked – who the hell was he? He could be a reporter, a stalker, a perv – anyone. But a snoop at his account had revealed nothing of note or concern. And it had been *me* who'd initiated things. He was just a funny bulldog pissing his way through life one lamppost at a time. Totally reasonable. Plus, I didn't want to *overthink* it. He made me smile. Simple as that. And smiling is all good for Amber.

I picked up my phone and tapped away.

'*Dark forces have gathered and we must abort to another planet for all messaging activities forthwith!! Preferred planet?*'

I re-read my words, took a large mouthful of vodka and pinged it off before I could change my mind.

Which left me feeling *very* naughty; Eddie and his raptors could go suck on *that* message.

Putting my phone away, I looked around hopefully for a bit of sport factor to keep me amused. Hmm... not much doing. Maybe it'd be a good idea in the future to abort to the Red Lion on changeover days, where the vibe was perma-chilled and charming, no matter how many people rocked up.

As Jimmy Cliff begun to belt out, 'You Can Get It If You Really Want' two couples took to the dance floor and tamely shuffled about without the energy, inclination or common *decency* to milk an imaginary cow. I glanced beyond their uninspiring efforts and was greeted by the magnificent sight of DJ Puny minus the Rasta hat and his dreadlock wig pushed so far back off his forehead, it looked on the verge of sliding off completely. And maybe dragging him down with it. He looked ridiculous. On the brink of collapse. And so *unbelievably* white. Bordering on translucent, in fact. How could *anyone* be so pale out here?

'For the love of God, lose the fucking wig!' I murmured with a half-laugh.

As nothing else was doing, and Andreas otherwise engaged serving dribs and drabs of customers, making orders for the Eastern European girl who efficiently waited on the tables or chatting to the chain-smoking Cypriots, I looked hopefully towards the street, where it seemed like a group of lads in their mid-twenties had just come from Coral Big Buns next door. I was yet to sample their culinary delights, but judging by their smeared faces as they happily wolfed down burgers, it looked like they did the job.

As a couple of them picked up on the music coming from Sonny's, they stopped in their tracks, with one of them indicating inside with his burger. With shrugs of 'why not' and nods of agreement, they hastily finished their food, wiped their mouths on paper napkins, before scrunching them and the wrappers into balls and sending one of them back to Big Buns to offload their rubbish.

I was yet to see a group of lads in Sonny's – they always seemed to favour the more boisterous bars with their banks of TV screens, up-to-date music, younger clientele and single women. Not us old scrotes getting pissed on our own or pant-swinging on the dance floor. God knows what they were doing, wandering in here.

Ah. Changeover night...

As they bowled in, I noticed there were five of them – all smartly dressed and looking a bit sporty and/or as if they worked out in the gym. Maybe some frantic pre-holiday weight sessions to pump and flatten. Although they were laughing and a couple raised their arms in the air and, 'Oi! Oi'd!' to the song, they looked like no bother at all. Just lads on holiday, trying to find a decent drinking hole and have a good time.

But evidently, DJ Puny was unaccustomed to a testosterone invasion (his translucency had made me wonder if he was fresh meat to the island – or maybe being kept captive under someone's bed between DJing sessions) and perhaps imagining an element of threat, he pulled himself up to his full diminutive height and adjusted his wig so it sat squarely on his head once again.

Surely, this wouldn't end well...

As I smiled and reached for my drink, I noticed one of the lads looking my way. He was the most muscular of the group, attractive and with blond, tousled hair like a surfer boy. His friends had decided on a table and were busily rearranging the seats so they all faced the dance floor, but he remained rooted to the spot, seemingly transfixed on me.

My immediate reaction had been to give him a small smile, but in the instant it'd formed, I noticed a narrowing of Surfer Boy's eyes and a shift in his focus.

He'd homed in on my scar. He recognised me.

I quickly spun on my bar stool to face the bar and dived into my bag for the prop of my phone. As I bent over the screen, I could see the rapid rise and fall of my chest and prayed that my increased heart rate would go unnoticed by Surfer Boy.

If I just kept my head down and pissed about online... oh, God... please don't let me have another scene in here...

With a heavy sigh, I further thought, for fuck's sake! Is *this* how it's going to be for the rest of my life?

Without realising, the fingers on my free hand had sought out the scar on my forehead. I snapped the hand down and tried to focus on my phone, but my attention was attuned on trying to sense if Surfer Boy was homing in on me. As I felt my anxiety heighten, I heard the most welcome voice of Andreas.

'You look confused, Amber. Too many nice men on Tinder?'

As I looked up at his wide grin, I blurted out a laugh that included a mixture of relief and nervousness.

'Very funny,' I said.

'Drink?'

'No, I'm fine, thanks. Look... could you do me a favour? Those five guys at the table... are they all sitting down?'

Andreas moved his look of amusement from my face to over my shoulder.

'Five guys,' he said with a shrug. 'Sitting down.'

'Sure?'

'Yes, I'm sure. Your dates from Tinder? Which one you like best?'

As I struggled to think of a witty retort, I felt the tension in my body drop a few notches.

'I don't know,' I replied. 'All of them, probably.'

'Well, here comes Martha with their order – I'll make sure she tells them.'

'Don't you dare!' I cried as I playfully took a swipe at Andreas.

He tapped the bar twice then pointed a finger at me, 'Ha! Ha! Gotcha!'

I felt relieved to see Martha at the bar seconds later – particularly as I could faintly pick up on her asking Andreas for five pints of Keo.

If she was here, then Surfer Boy should be at the table with his mates.

Maybe I'd got it all wrong. Perhaps he'd just been checking out what lagers were on draft. Or something like that. After all, the whole planet didn't revolve around me and my pathetic paranoia.

As I felt the first pulse of a headache descend,

I decided to have an early night for once and leave after I'd finished my drink. Besides, there was the beach party tomorrow night and my stamina wasn't *quite* what it used to be...

Still uncomfortable with the thought of turning around, I gave my phone my full attention. Nothing yet from Ball Bag but... hello... a tweety post from a couple of hours ago; '*Is it just me who tries to count their teeth when drunk?*'

Ha! Where *does* this guy get this stuff from? He's *seriously* off-the-wall!

As I smirked at his ridiculousness, I thought once more of our evening of nonsense. It was like a little sparring match – each trying to outwit the other. Naturally, Ball Bag had won, hands down – but I'm guessing he didn't have several large vodkas and a Lunge-sized brandy swirling around his stomach at the time.

Mind you, he'd have outwitted me even if I was sober.

My gain.

It had been delightful to engage with someone back home without any mention or questions about what'd happened. Or Susie. And for my part, I didn't particularly want to know anything about Ball Bag – I wouldn't ask, and it seemed unlikely he'd start quizzing. Maybe he already knew everything he needed or wanted to know about me.

Back home...

With a blood draining jolt, I wondered if Ball Bag

could be here, in Cyprus, and not back in England. Where I'd always assumed he was. Perhaps he was watching me. I quickly re-examined his feed on X... ... lots of his wonderful nonsense... including a post I'd previously missed; '*I am yet to meet a cucumber I trust*'... more nonsense... a random photo of an Afghan hound dressed as a mermaid and sitting in a rock pool somewhere on an English-looking coastline, with Ball Bag's caption of; '*Have you ever seen a mermaid say 'Sausages'? I have.*' More nonsense... then another photo from a few months ago... taken at the Chelsea Flower Show and depicting a disinterested-looking guide dog cocking his leg and tinkling over a medal-bearing male judge on the brink of presenting to a gummy woman in dungarees.

'*Doing it in style*' was Ball Bag's caption.

Hm... they could be stock shots lifted online, but something about them made me think they'd been snapped on a phone. Perhaps I was wrong... *but*... I did feel encouraged by Ball Bag's interest in the famous London flower show. Plus... that coastline didn't look like Cyprus *and* I'd barely seen a dog since I'd been here. An Afghan hound? In Cyprus? In a mermaid outfit? *And* saying 'sausages'? Nah. I don't think so.

I scrolled a little further and came across a photo of various members of the England football team looking crestfallen and somewhat confused after their latest defeat. '*Ball Bags, indeed...*'

I'd seen all I needed to see.

And I was beginning to drive myself nuts. Again.

And as much as I could be, I felt satisfied; the posts were all very civilised. Granted, they were totally nuts – amusing nuts – but civilised nevertheless, and there was nothing to cause me, nor Eddie's team of raptors, any concern.

Just remember that, Amber. And stop freaking yourself out. For once.

As I drained the last of my drink, my headache began to crank through the gears. It was time to get back to the villa. I called out to Andreas, and when he looked over, I mustered a smile and patted the bar twice before waving him goodnight.

I climbed down from the bar stool and as I made my way towards the street glanced towards DJ Puny. The wig was nowhere to be seen. The oversized baseball cap was back. His eyes tracked me with something akin to a glare.

Where was the wig? Had I imagined it?

Why the dirty looks? Could he somehow read my piss-taking thoughts?

As I continued walking, I neared the table with Surfer Boy and his mates. They were each huddled forward, nudging and whispering to one another. All eyes were on me. As one of them lifted their phone from the table, I panicked, fearing my photo would be taken.

Instinctively, my fingers flew up to cover my scar as I looked away and picked up speed. And when I reached the street, I kept walking past the bars and restaurants and shops until I felt a little calmer. A little safer.

This was no way to live.

Paranoia. Too much drinking. Too much heartbreak.

And when I hailed a taxi and rode back to villa, it was in silence and with my head bowed.

10.

Dreams and Danglies

The early night did wonders for me; I woke up refreshed and headache-free – despite a peculiar and trippy dream that bordered on being a nightmare. It involved me swimming with pinchy lobsters, scissor-wielding mermaids, grinning raptors and someone who I knew was Lunge – despite it looking nothing like him – with mammoth, decaying teeth that were bared and too big for his distorted head. They were swirling around me trying to nibble, bite, slash or worse.

As I silently screamed, 'Nooooo!!' into the murky water and thrashed my legs in a futile attempt to escape (which probably accounted for the tangled sheets when I woke up), water began to fill my lungs as my body sank deeper and my predators continued taking turns to sweep by in attack. As I began to descend into nothingness, I felt a solid bulk beneath me. I wrapped my arms and legs around its form and felt it powerfully swim away and climb through the depths of the water.

Within moments we broke into dazzling sunlight.

As I gasped in air and wiped water from my eyes, there was nothing but blue skies and sea.

And the shark I was clinging onto.

As it skimmed through the water at speed, I squinted into the distance and saw the deserted, palm-tree-lined coastline we were heading towards. Within seconds, we arrived. And as the shark screeched to halt – after sharply skidding its body parallel to the beach – I was thrown off to land on my arse in the shallow water and found myself face-to-face with Eddie the beady-eyed shark.

'I saved you. Now get to work,' he said.

Then with a flip of his tail – which caused a deluge of water to knock me onto my back, Eddie buggered off into the sunset. Wiggling his fin and whistling to Mack the Knife.

That's when I woke up.

And as an indictment to my state of mind, I just stared up at the spinning ceiling fan, scratched my head, then promptly fell into the most delicious and deep sleep. And slept the longest since being here.

Weird shit. Indeed.

I went for a long swim after breakfast and occasionally found my head dipping beneath the waterline with a smile to check Lunge wasn't lurking anywhere with his jumbo gnashers. Or wandering hands...

As I pounded out the lengths, I also had a word with myself about my paranoia. Surfer Boy was probably just staring at my scar (and *doubtless* telling his mates what a sexy pirate I was...). And DJ Puny was only scowling because he felt bereft (or less of a man...) at having to ditch the wig. So get a grip, Amber.

Exercise done, endorphins pumping and feeling invigorated, I sat at the veranda table and did what I should have done a while ago; I opened my laptop and wrote an apology email to Eddie. After all, it was *me* who had submitted my work to *him*. He *was* in the business of making money. And all he was guilty of, was investing in our success, and although I didn't like it – sniffing me out for 'my story'. And merely advising me to get in there first. I wouldn't do it. But he was hardly holding a gun to my head either.

Then there were Susie's readers, some of whom wanted a sequel. And there was nothing terrible about that. It was fantastic, in fact. These were the fans who'd soon be providing me with my first royalties which, according to Eddie, should be 'pretty tasty'. And in return, what had been the result of my *extensive* efforts before going out last night?

'Jeremy advances knob first towards Cornwall, determined to win back Susie's affections...'

Yup. That had been the total sum of it.

Pathetic.

When I'd finished the email, I sat back and re-read it with a feeling of satisfaction; it was undoubtedly the best thing I'd written since being in Cyprus. I'd apologised for my abject failure at progressing with the sequel and explained that I was honestly trying my best; I *wanted* to get it done. I explained that I was still feeling 'meh' but having some days better than others. I'd push on. And despite Cyprus undoubtedly helping in my healing process, I did wonder if I'd be able to get my head down *properly* when back in England in several weeks' time and not feeling in perma holiday mode.

Which led to my pissed tweets and messages to Ball Bag...

Sincerest apologies to the team – but as they would have seen, 'all-things-Ball-Bag' have now ceased. Along with any drunken tweety posts.

I rounded it off by saying; if the convention went ahead, I hoped it wouldn't require my presence as I'd probably find it a bit much (and just wanted to get that 'out there'). But I would happily attend Susie's launch (which I understood would mainly be a trade event?) and we could look at some bookstore signing sessions, *if* there was some form of strategy for dealing with undesirables, *and* I wouldn't feel like an exhibit in a Victorian Freak Show. I hoped he understood.

I wasn't entirely sure how much of that last bit was true, but my intent was to try and rebuild a 'normal' life when I got back. I couldn't hide away forever – as appealing as the thought was. Besides, I was hopeful I'd soon become yesterday's chip paper on the trial front, and I *did* want to build some form of writing career. And preferably, away from Susie – who had *really* begun to get on my tits.

I signed off by thanking Eddie for his support and understanding. Then I tagged on as a PS that I'd be watching my drinking and limiting myself to 'just the one' litre of Ouzo a day...

I pinged off the email and felt good about it.

Maybe he was saving me, after all.

As I thought about seriously knuckling down to write on my return and getting into a proper routine, I wondered for the first time, if I should move from the flat. Surely, it wouldn't do me any good to stay there.

Yeah. Fresh start. Fresh digs.

Sounded a plan.

I lit a cigarette, smiled at my beautiful surroundings and acknowledged how unusually chipper I felt. One good night's sleep – albeit with a trippy dream – a whack of a swim, a half-baked plan and suddenly the world didn't seem *quite* so bad. As I brushed some bougainvillea petals from the table and aborted the plucky stab at putting one in my cropped hair, I suddenly remembered...

... Ball Bag!

I'd found him lurking in my DMs once I'd rattled myself from my heavy sleep. His message had been short and sweet: '*Planet email*'

Then his email address of *ballbags4U@hotmail.com*

I was initially a little surprised he hadn't chosen

text or WhatsApp, but after a micro head scratch, decided it was better we weren't dishing out phone numbers. An email address would be perfect. And safer. Just in case.

With a blurt of a laugh, I entered Ball Bag into my contacts and pinged off an email.

'Testing. Testing. Is this Planet Ball Bag?'

I switched off my phone and placed it face down on the table. It was time to sunbathe and top up my tan for the party. I'd already decided to limit my Ball Bag time and just dip in and out whenever I felt like a bit of humour, so wasn't going to give up precious time in the rays waiting to see if he responded straight away. Keep him at phone's length, Amber, and just use him for his wit. When it suits. And in little bite-sized chunks.

I stubbed out my cigarette, stood and stretched, then gazed out towards the stunning azure sea. As I hugged my arms around my waist, I smiled; I was actually feeling pretty positive about things. For once. And for the first time. Since.

And hopefully Eddie and the raptors would calm down after my email and see that we were all on the same side. I just needed a bit more time. A bit more patience. But I had a feeling it'd all pan out okay.

I padded down to the Chez Cleo and picked up my sun oil. As I began slathering it on, I abruptly stopped and laughed out loud.

'Eddie and the raptors!' I said to no one. 'Sounds like a brilliant name for a rock band!'

I was well chuffed with myself and smirked all the while I finished off applying the oil.

Today was going to be a *good* day, I decided. And if I was lucky, I'd be catching another phone-in with Sunshine Sam.

Those pesky ants can be right bastards.

Before starting to prepare for the party, I toyed with the idea getting a bit frisky with myself on the bed. The heat, my oiled nakedness, the smell of jasmine that invaded my bedroom... plus the anticipation of going to a beach party and how that might unfold...

But there was a problem.

Whenever I settled down to enjoy a lengthy masturbatory session – whether on a lounger, my bed, in Chez Cleo or the shower – when I was sober, I just couldn't see it through. I mean, I'd start off fine, and at times, rue my decision to leave my toys back in Exeter (them being the last thing on mind when I left), but as I'd gather momentum and arch my back and pinch a nipple with my free hand or plunge fingers inside, inevitably, Luke's face – or the memory of our afternoon on nudey beach, would zoom into view.

So I'd abruptly (and reluctantly) stop and wrestle him back into his box.

Being drunk helped. Fantasies about randoms being filthy with me. Me with them. And mostly that would work. Unless I was *really* plastered.

Which was... oh... is that the time?

I looked at the bed with regret and closed the sliding doors to the balcony; it was time to switch on the air con or my make-up would be dripping to the floor the instant I applied it.

After a refreshing shower, I inspected my washed hair in the bathroom mirror with a sigh. I had been hoping to avoid another visit to Coral Cutz or moreover, their nosey stylist, Julie. But whether it was the hot weather or not, my hair had sprouted like mad since its last trim and my dark roots were already making a dart for freedom.

Maybe I could hang on until my return to England, when Elena would be able to sort me out.

Granted, Julie hadn't done a bad job on my past two visits, but her relentless hairdresser questions – that seemed to probe deeper than the norm – married with her unabashed gawping at my scar as she spoke to me in the mirror with her head tilted to one side, hadn't made it the most relaxing customer experience. Then there'd been the episode when her scissors had caught the edge of my scar and I'd had to endure the near-hysterical cries of, 'Oh my God!!! I haven't hurt you, have I?'

All that aside – and based on her passable results, I did return – as I reckoned there'd only be a similar scar-gawping session under the unforgiving lights of any other salon.

Yeah. Maybe I'd hang on for Elena.

I wandered into the bedroom and immediately felt the effects of the cool air circulating around. As

I dithered over my choice of clothes, I thought back to my earlier call with her – just after I'd finished my Sunshine Sam session and had taken a much-needed break from the heat. Sam had put me in the highest of spirits when a disgruntled caller had questioned the calibre of meat in The Taste of Bengal (no less!) and voiced the concern he'd been given 'an old goat with the pox' to eat, rather than the lamb jalfrezi he'd eagerly ordered.

Either way, he wasn't straying far from his hotel toilet – where, at one point, it sounded like he was calling from...

Quality.

As it was unscheduled, I'd been extremely lucky to catch Elena between clients, with her incoming running a little late. When her face came up on the screen, I couldn't fail but notice how glowing she looked. After she'd reached the small staff area at the back of the salon, I'd been quick to ask her about the new man in her life and tell her he was clearly having a positive effect on her.

We managed to chat for about ten minutes before her client arrived. And it turned out, that Adam – the man who was putting such a smile on her face, was the owner of the burger bar a few doors along – which had replaced The Grub Shack. It was truly great to see her so happy. She told me about their gradual flirting when she occasionally picked up some lunch. Her finding the courage to ask him out. Then discovering a real connection with him over their subsequent dates. Still early days, but there'd already been loose talk about moving in together if things were still strong after the six-month (or so) mark.

Which reminded me...

I told Elena I was kicking around the idea of moving from the flat. No sooner than the words were out of my mouth she cried, 'Yes! Yes! And yes! Do it!' She asked if I'd stay in Exeter. I told her, I hadn't thought that far. Perhaps. Maybe. I didn't know yet. But after brief discussion we were both agreed that a fresh start, away from the flat, would be bang on.

I then gave a condensed run down on what I'd been up to since we last spoke. And proudly let Elena know I had a party to go to. Go me!

'Well, knowing you, I'm sure you'll have a brilliant time!'

Just before we signed off, I told her she'd be tackling my hair before too long and mentioned Julie's scar-gawping and scissor-wielding antics.

'And you think you'll be getting anything different from me?' Elena asked with a laugh.

'I live in hope,' I told her.

'So, when are you back, exactly?'

To be truthful, I wasn't entirely sure how many weeks and days were left. I knew the date when my 90 days were up, but had gladly lost all track of time in Cyprus. That aside, a big chunk of me didn't want to leave. Or think too much about my return. And the possibility of any subsequent setbacks or pitfalls.

'Next month, sometime. A few weeks. I think. It's *very* hard to tell.'

Elena's tinkling laugh travelled across the miles. 'What *are* you like? Okay, I'll see you *sometime* next month. Have fun tonight. Catch up soon.'

'Thanks. Will do. Glad you're loved up, you filthy minx. Bye-eeee!'

And that had been that.

As I stood in front of my opened wardrobe, I wondered how on earth I'd be able to decide where to move – given I had no real ties to anywhere and couldn't even select some clothes for a night out. But the fact was, I was very much warming to the idea of getting away from the flat. Maybe somewhere with a bit of a view, where I could set up a writing desk and get some inspiration.

Dither, dither. What to wear...

I wondered if anyone would be going into the sea later and supposed, given how hot the nights were, it wouldn't be outside the realms of possibility. My (as yet) unused bikini would be a good starting point.

Yay! A decision! Cue the street parade!

Having extracted my green and black bikini, I had a moment of *total* genius and reached for a stretchy, above-the-knee lime green skirt (to easily peel off for any sea ventures) and a long, black halter neck top (ditto) which would also cover the lumps of the ties on my bikini bottoms. Sorted.

See? I'm not a total tit. Give me a bit of encouragement and boof! I'm up and running!

I laid the items on the bed, closed the wardrobe and went over to the dressing table. A quick inspection of my phone told me I had half an hour before Pool Man would be rocking up.

Good, good, good.

And... ooh hello... and email from Ball Bag.

'I receive you Planet Amber. This is Planet Ball Bag requesting permission to dock for late night talking of bollocks.'

I blurted out a snort of laughter, but felt no need to respond. Odd, really, but now I had the direct contact sorted, it somehow felt less 'naughty' to message. And to risk the wrath of Eddie and his sharp-toothed mob. Besides, I'd already decided; to just dip in and out, as and when suited. All that to one side, I really didn't want to get too friendly with someone who hid behind a pissing dog.

That would *never* do.

On the subject of Eddie, I noted there was nothing from him – but as it was the weekend, guessed he'd respond when back behind his imposing work desk and ruling the world with an iron fin. Or perhaps when he'd finished picking fish bones from his teeth. Or maybe my email didn't warrant a reply. We'll see.

Not much else on the emails front.

Let's risk a quick delve into X while I'm here...

Christ... apparently, I was hoping to share 'exciting news' before too long. Guessing that's meant to be a vague date for the sequel. Or that pesky convention. And... oh fuck... what's this?

"I'd rather put pins in my eyes than read anything from that grotesque slut of a murdering bitch."

56 likes.

And counting...

I blinked at the screen and re-read it twice. Then I calmly switched off my phone and placed it on the dressing table. I looked at my reflection in the mirror; my face had a flush that was nothing to do with the sun and I could see my chest rise and fall in line with my snatched breaths.

But as I watched on, my breathing settled back to normal. Almost as fast as it had begun. The pink in my cheeks began to fade. And I felt oddly detached for some reason.

Or maybe it was as simple as he or she (NeBan785 with a plain blue avatar) had caught me on a good day. Although clearly not a day the raptors were monitoring my account. But what could they do? Block someone, only for them to return under a different account? Report it? X was like an ancient, foreign language to me. Unfathomable. I put a hand to my cheek. No, I was alright. 'This' was nothing I hadn't seen before, and I would doubtless be seeing similar again.

'You're having a *good* day,' I calmly told my reflection. 'These people are knobs and trolls. They are knobby trolls. They spend their time in darkened rooms, crouched over a keyboard in their festering underpants, angry at the world and with nothing better to do. Whereas... *I*... have a party to go to. So go fucking swivel!'

I laughed at my reflection with relief; I felt surprisingly okay. Then watched as my forehead creased into a frown, making my scar slightly bobble beneath the overhead lighting. Was I getting better? Stronger?

It felt like it.

For sure, I'd had a nasty shock when I read the message. But then quickly recovered. That had to be a good thing. Right?

Bloody right.

I picked up my phone rattled it in front of my face.

'Bore-ing!' I sang to it. 'Bore-ing!!'

I laughed at my ridiculousness but failed to give a single flying fuck.

Right. It was time to get a wiggle on. Pool Man and his chariot would be pulling up before too long. And the trolls could go fuck themselves. And their festering underpants.

Because *I* had places to be!

I sat down on the dressing table stool and took extra care with my make-up, applying the smokey eyes look I normally reserved for special occasions. Then a couple of coats of waterproof mascara. Light brushes of bronzer on my cheeks. Some swipes of tinted lip gloss. And BIG squirts of Duty Free perfume.

I assessed the results and felt pleased with what I saw. Scars aside. And despite the best efforts of the expensive foundation used on both my forehead and beneath my chin.

Sigh.

There was nothing else I could do. Except live with them.

After quickly applying some texture to my hair with a dab of wax, I opened the small cardboard box that contained the handful of jewellery I'd distractedly scooped up for my trip. I was after some earrings but wanted something secure, in case I went in the sea. I plucked out a few options, dismissed them and settled on a simple pair of silver, hand-hammered hoops.

Earrings in place, I gave myself a final once over.

The earrings were perfect. I had no idea why I hadn't worn them for so long.

Yes, I did...

They had been a gift from Spencer. From one of our early dates; a day trip to Whitstable. Ice cream, seagulls, a walk along the beach and a wander around the shops. We came across a small, independent jewellers and wandered in. Spencer had wanted to buy me some expensive and elaborate earrings and was quite taken with some dangly, sparkly ones with gemstones hanging from their tips. As he enthusiastically held them up to my ears, I caught sight of the price tag and pretended they weren't quite 'me'. Instead, I asked to look at the hoops – which had earlier caught my eye.

'I prefer these,' I'd said. 'See how the little indents catch the light. Understated but pretty.'

'You're sure?'

'Only if you're sure you want to buy them for me.'

'I'm very sure I do.'

'Then these little beauties are the winners. Thank you, they're lovely.'

'Sure I can't tempt you with my danglies?'

'Only when we're back at your flat.'

'You're a keeper,' he'd said with a broad grin.

As I fought back the all-too-familiar threat of tears, I stared at my reflection as I slowly and defiantly negotiated each earring through the pierced holes and snapped shut the catches at the back.

'You're having a *good* day,' I told myself once more.

I flicked a finger at one of the earrings and watched the light dance off it as it swung about. Then I stood up, went across to my bikini and clothes and got dressed. After I'd slipped on some flat sandals, I walked back to the mirror for a final appraisal.

'Come on Spencer – we're having a night out.' I held my own gaze for several moments, then broke into a wide smile.

11.

Did Amber Have a Good Time?

Pool Man didn't show up. Initially, I thought he was just running late, so poured myself a weak vodka and sat in Chez Cleo listening to Radio Aphrodite's 'Party Hits' to 'get us in the mood'. Which was all working rather marvellously. I'd bagged up some bottles of Keo and a bottle wine, but as time passed, was sitting there like a plum and wondering how stupid I was to not get Pool Man's phone number to check our arrangement was still on.

Perhaps this happened. Perhaps that happened. Perhaps he's this. Or maybe he's that.

You twat, Amber.

I made myself a second drink. A stronger one. And muttered to the stars. And watched bougainvillea leaves swirl around the pool. And sang to cheesy party anthems. And fidgeted. And smoked.

And drank. And began to think, bollocks to Pool Man.

Then I checked the time for the zillionth time. And called for a taxi.

'Where to?'

'The sea caves.'

Fifteen minutes later, I heard the taxi rumble over the semi dirt road outside the villa.

I climbed in with my bags and dropped heavily onto the back seat.

'Hi. Do you know where there's a party going on at the sea caves?'

The driver turned in his seat to face me. 'Of course,' he said with a shrug. 'I take you.' His lined, postcard face creased into a smile and from the amused twinkle in his eyes, I felt as though I'd asked him what day it was.

As I settled into my seat, the driver looked at me in the rear-view mirror and held up a packet of Rothmans.

'Smoke?'

I glanced around and saw his window was fully open and the one beside me, halfway down.

'Oh! Is it okay?'

'It's okay. You want?'

I plucked out my own packet. 'I'll have one of these. Rothmans are too strong for me. These are a lot milder. Don't make me cough. But thank you.'

Again, those amused eyes. Christ. All I had to say was 'no thank you'. He wasn't after my life story.

'*Endaxi.*'

And off we rumbled. Down the hill, past other twinkles of villas, on to the main road below my villa, before cutting through a series of semi-dirt roads, across another main road, then pulling up at the end of a very long dirt track that got rougher and bouncier the further we went.

We were beside a restaurant. A basic, wooden building with customers sitting outside beneath pretty lamps and strings of fairy lights.

The driver turned and laughed at my expression of confusion.

'Is this right?' I asked.

He shifted in his seat and pointed to the right, away from the restaurant.

'Down there.' Then he stretched his hand out of the window and patted the air with a flat palm. 'Down, down.'

'To the party?'

'Yes. Down, down. Party.'

I wasn't entirely filled with confidence, but with the restaurant so close, decided if the party was non-existent, I could enjoy a few drinks there before working out a Plan B.

I paid the driver and thanked him.

'Down, down,' he repeated before heavily drawing on a fresh cigarette.

'*Endaxi.* '*Efharisto.*' And if I'd known the Greek for, 'I understand what 'down' means,' I may well have tagged that on as well.

I got out, watched as he pulled away, then walked towards where down-down was. As I neared, I heard the faint strains of voices and an outburst of raucous laughter.

Ooh... hello... this sounded hopeful.

I walked on, until I reached some large rocks with a sharp drop below. The spotlights on the perimeter of the restaurant grounds threw out a faint glow of green light, and as I adjusted my footing and leaned over, I peered down and caught the heads of a small group of people. I searched around and to my right, saw what looked like a well-trodden path between the rocks. As I reached it, I stood and paused for a few moments, suddenly feeling unsure about wandering into a party of strangers on my own. Despite the size of my last vodka.

I'd be having words with that bloody Pool Man when I saw him.

I flicked my thoughts back to the comment on X and used it to find the bravado I needed to go down-down.

'You don't win,' I muttered to myself. 'You. *Don't.* Win. Pool Man doesn't win. The gawpers. The knob-wipe trolls. The fucking arseholes after my story. And that murdering bastard *definitely* doesn't win. Come on, Amber! It's a party, not the fucking gallows! Grow some!'

So I did. And they were the size of a baboon's.

I gingerly picked my way down, carrying both clanking bags of drinks in one hand so I could use the other to rest on rocks to steady myself. At intervals, I looked towards the party – its guests now clearly visible as they sat or stood around in groups on the shingle – and grinned like a Cheshire cat at the few heads that turned my way. As I neared the bottom, I finally lost my footing and fell heavily onto my backside, before sliding forward with a leg bent at an awkward angle. With a wince, I waited for the sound of breaking glass as a lone bottle of Keo spilled from a bag and tumbled towards a rock.

10 out of 10 for an entrance, I inwardly groaned.

Miraculously, the bottle had other ideas; its momentum slowed and bobbled to a halt just short of the rock and remained intact.

'Are you alright?'

I looked up into the face of a smiling blonde woman in her twenties. Dressed in a bikini top and a long wrap-skirt, she stretched a hand towards me.

'Can I help you up?

I untangled my leg and took a moment to assess any damage or pain; I was fine.

'I'm okay, thanks. Just my usual party trick,' I began with an embarrassed half laugh. 'You wouldn't mind taking one of these bags off me?'

She stepped forward. 'Here, I'll take both.' I returned her smile as she reached for the bags. Jiggling them into one hand she once more extended the other. I gratefully took it, heaved myself up and brushed myself down.

'Still in one piece,' I laughed. 'Thanks.'

'By the way, I'm Petra,' she said. This one *definitely* had a Scandinavian accent and with her huge, Bambi-like blue eyes, enviable figure and long glossy hair, was absolutely stunning.

I pointlessly tapped my chest, 'I'm Amber.'

'Amber?' She rolled the word around as though experimenting with it. 'Pretty name.'

'Thanks. So's yours. Is it Scandinavian?'

'Yes! I'm from Sweden. There, it's not so much an unusual name.'

As she spoke, I retrieved the bottle of Keo and stepped towards her to take back the bags.

Petra offered them up and as I rested them on a patch of sand and bent to tuck the Keo back into its bag, I said, 'Oh? I've never heard it before.'

'Actually, in Greek, my name translates to rock or stone.'

I looked up at her. 'Stone? That's my surname!'

She tinkled an infectious laugh. 'Really? Well, that would make you Amber Petra.'

I straightened and cocked my head to one side. 'Maybe. Perhaps. I'm not sure!'

That laugh again. 'I agree. I think Stone sounds better for you.' Petra peered over my shoulder, as though I was secretly shielding someone, then scanned the pathway before looking up to where I'd begun my descent.

'Are you with anybody?' she asked.

'Ah. I was supposed to be,' I said with a shrug. 'But he didn't show up.'

Petra beamed me a dazzling smile. 'Men are such arseholes,' she said breezily as she took back one of the bags and linked an arm through mine. 'Come on, I'll introduce you to a few people.'

And like a vampire invited over the threshold – boof! – I was in.

It was all a swirl of friendly faces and very well organised. A postcard face hunched over an open fire, cooking skewers of meat and warming pitta bread. Beside him were a number of cooler bags which – as I found out later, contained large bowls of salad – presumably brought along by fellow guests. Large plastic bins were dotted around; home to various beers, wine and remains of those stubborn Cypriot ice cubes.

Carrying a paper cup of wine, I was swept around by Petra to meet some of the partygoers, with the first person being someone whose loud shirt I had already spotted from a distance; the smug expat.

'Okay. This is Roger,' Petra said sweetly. 'Roger, this is Amber.'

I gave his offered clammy hand a light shake.

'Oh, hello there!' he exclaimed. 'Now I've got a name to go with the face!'

As Roger began to twitter on about how he'd been coming to the beach parties on a regular basis since the beginning of time and occasionally accompanied by some *very* important businessmen from Nicosia, Petra made our excuses – with a convincing promise to return once introductions were completed – and led me away.

'He's very sweet, you know – but sometimes... ' she said, with raised eyebrows and a roll of her eyes.

'Do you think he really knows some *very* important people from Nicosia?' I asked.

'Oh, maybe,' Petra replied lightly. 'Perhaps some owner of a cabaret, which is basically another word for a brothel,' she added with a tinkle of laughter.

I looked at her, unsure. 'Really?'

'Well, I guess I was just joking about Roger going to a brothel. Or, maybe not,' she said with a broad smile. 'But cabarets, mostly, are brothels. Have you not been to Nicosia? I mean, do you live here? Are you on holiday?'

I told her how I was on an extended holiday, and to my shame, hadn't explored very much of the island. As the words came out, I felt embarrassed as to why I hadn't taken the time to stray far from my immediate area. It had been my pathetic intention to get into a writing routine – but instead, I'd fallen into a routine of doing nothing and achieving nothing, except a golden tan and getting drunk regularly. By means of justification, I blurted, 'It's a working holiday, really. I... er... write advertising copy for boring places like... finance companies and... stuff like that. I can work from anywhere – which is great.'

'Sounds interesting.'

It was my turn to laugh. 'Not really! But it pays the bills. What about you? Live here?'

Petra swished her hair over her shoulder. 'Yes, three years now. I'm working for an estate agent in Paphos, selling expensive – and not so expensive, property to Russians, Israelis... and the English, of course! I speak five languages so... you know... that helps.'

Along with your stunning looks and charming personality, I thought. It was easy to picture Petra schmoozing potential buyers and doubtless, earning herself some healthy commission on the way.

'Well, it sounds a lot more interesting than what I do,' I told her.

'Nonsense! Here, let me introduce to these people from Holland – they run a boat business for snorkel diving.'

The evening was turning out better than I could have dreamed. Petra used her considerable hostess skills to sweep me around a chunk of the guests who, either worked or lived in Cyprus. It was a real little community. I drank the regularly replenished wine. Kept to my working holiday story – which included telling an impressed – and (seemingly) ever-hovering Roger, that I used to work for Saatchi & Saatchi (I hadn't) and spoke to some interesting people from differing countries and walks of life. Before too long, I felt relieved Pool Man hadn't deigned to show up and was under no obligation to stay by his side. Although I had my suspicions things wouldn't have panned out that way.

After an hour or so, a Dutch couple – Johannes

and Eva – perky-looking retirees who had moved to Cyprus and held Pilates classes in the grounds of their villa – escorted me over to the postcard face for something to eat. By then, Petra had left me to it, after asking if I'd be okay and telling me to seek her out if need be. I sincerely thanked her for everything and told her I'd be fine.

The food was simple and delicious. I ate more out of politeness than anything else, not wanting to offend the old boy who seemed proud of the production line of food he'd obviously got down to a fine art. He'd beamed up at me once I'd shuffled along the small queue, and once he'd filled my plate with cubes of pork, pitta and salad and a wedge of lemon, I rather exuberantly experimented with, '*Bomba!*' – which, according to Johnny, supposedly meant 'that's great!'

The old fellow seemed highly amused. 'Ah! *Bomba! Bomba! Brávo!*' he repeated as he reached into a plastic tub of chopped parsley and liberally sprinkled it over my meal. For a moment, I fretted that Johnny had sold me up the river and '*bomba*' meant something entirely different – maybe something inappropriate or derogatory. But postcard face was happily serving his next hungry partygoer and seemingly nonplussed by my attempt at the local lingo.

As we sat down with our food on the uncomfortable rocks, I finally had the chance to draw breath and take stock of my surroundings for the first time; it'd all been a bit of whirlwind since my spectacular entrance; embarrassed smiles; offloading my drinks; being given a drink, then the rounds of introductions. I guesstimated there were about fifty people at the party. I noted some had been savvy enough to bring thick towels to sit on or, in one instance, a yoga mat – which had me wishing mine wasn't tucked away in my flat, back in England. As I picked at my food, I spotted little solar lamps dotted around the rocks and cave entrances which I hadn't noticed before, and became aware of music playing in the background. And unless I was mistaken, it sounded like party anthems from my mates at Radio Aphrodite.

The sea caves themselves were stunning, with the ones immediately behind us varying from deep recesses to small hollows. To my right, an imposing flat-topped rock extended into the sea, with four large arched hollows – the nearest, being the only one not immersed in water. The faint glow from the lamps made them look magical and mysterious.

The rocks we were perched on were rough and smooth by the same token and were formed into jagged tiers that led down to gritty sand at the water's edge. In the sea, dramatic rocks poked their heads out and made a scattering of mini-islands.

I was shaken from my observations by Eva's voice. 'Not hungry, Amber?' she asked, nodding toward the paper plate in my hands.

I gave her a sheepish smile. 'Sorry, but I wasn't

sure what to expect – this being my first time – so made sure I had a big lunch and a snack before I came.'

'Ah, no problem. I just wanted to make sure you're not feeling shy.'

I looked into Eva's kind face then beyond, to Johannes, who was happily wolfing down his food. As he munched away, he threw me an affectionate wink. They were such a lovely couple and from my first impressions, made a great match – which may or may not, have had something to do with their identically cropped grey hair. It gave me a warm feeling, to be in their company, and I enjoyed the laughter as they finished each other's sentences with little nudges or affectionate squeezes. I guess, with all our cropped hair, we could have been mistaken for a family. Ridiculous really... I barely knew them, but with their energy, intelligence and closeness, for a moment, I wished.

'Not shy at all!' I laughed. 'Oh! I forgot to ask... do I need to pay anything for my food?'

Eva leaned across and patted my hand. 'Don't worry my dear, there's nothing to pay,' she said as her face creased into a smile. 'Costa brings all the food and cooks because he gets pleasure from it. You know, he's a lonely widower and just enjoys having something to do and being around people. Sometimes, others bring food – but Costa likes things his way – you understand? So, if we bring something, we bring fruit – like today, I brought watermelon, which Costa will cut up later.'

I was quite blown away. 'That's incredibly kind of him. It must cost a small fortune, feeding us all.'

'Well,' Eva began, 'I think he likes to take his payment in the beers he'll drink after he's finished cooking.' She leaned into me conspiringly and whispered, 'Plus, he takes home all the booze that's left over. You know, I think he hides some of it when we aren't looking.'

'And don't be fooled by his appearance,' Johannes piped up. 'As the Cypriots say about themselves, someone can dress like 10 cents when they actually own an empire.' Then he gave me another wink to show his statement held no malice.

'It's true,' shrugged Eva. 'But I think Costa just likes to take them for fun.'

Johannes climbed to his feet and put his hands out for our plates. 'Any more wine?'

Content in their company, I sat a while longer with Eva and Johannes. We chatted. I drank more wine. The music became louder. And I watched as people began to dance on the sand or in the shallows of the gently lapping sea. I noticed a few had ventured a little further, and spotted Petra's bikini-clad body draped over a rock, her wet hair slicked back and looking like a glorious mermaid. Below her, I could see two Cypriot-looking men in the water, both eagerly vying for her attention.

I pulled my phone from my small crossbody bag and tapped out an email to Ball Bag with a squiffy squint. '*I've just seen a mermaid say sausages.*' Ping! Off it went. And didn't I feel chuffed with myself?

After I'd chatted some more to Eva and Johannes about their classes, Holland and living in Cyprus, I felt like getting off the hard rock and stretching my legs.

'Yes, yes – you must go and enjoy yourself!' said Eva, as Johannes gave a thumbs up behind her.

For a moment, I just wanted to wrap my arms around the pair of them and breathe in their kindness and loveliness.

Maybe we could adopt one another.

Instead, I thanked them for looking after me and told them I'd catch them later. As I got to my feet, I felt the effects of the wine and the earlier vodkas I'd had at the villa. I took a moment to let the slight feeling of vertigo pass, then weaved my way through the dancing partygoers to the water's edge.

I looked across and saw that Petra's admirers had joined her on the rock, and although she was too far away to hear, it was clear she was delighting the two men with her tinkling laugh as she coyly toyed with her wet locks. As I once more admired her body, I wondered if she'd be taking one of them home for the night. Or maybe both.

Lucky guys.

As I felt the first laps of water spill over my feet, I stepped in further and was immediately ambushed by a group of four squealing, middle-aged English women bounding into the sea. As they encouraged me to dance to 'Walking on Sunshine', one took my hand with a cry of, 'Come on!' and begun swinging and tugging it around. Whilst another got us to create a chain of linked arms and perform a shambolic can-can that didn't fit in at all with the song. Fuzzy with drink and caught off-guard, I was swept along by their antics.

But before too long, one of the women stumbled after an over-ambitious kick, and like a deck of cards, we all came tumbling down. Feeling myself begin to topple, I miraculously had the wherewithal to think about the phone in my bag and managed to propel my body backwards towards the sand, and in the process, dragged one of the women on top of me.

We all ended up in an unsightly heap, giggling, snorting and laughing like idiots, as I triumphantly held up my bag as though a prized trophy.

Once we'd clambered to our feet, I good-naturedly flapped away their cries to join them for more dancing, along with an offer from a dad-dancing Roger, whose straw hat now perched at a jaunty angle as he bobbed about between cringy pelvic thrusts.

As I squelched away in my wet sandals, I found myself wandering towards the large arch on the beach and smiling at how ridiculous my beachside collapse must have looked. My clothes were soaked, and as I picked my way over the uneven surface, I ran a hand over my skirt, only to find a rip in the back over my left arse cheek.

'Oh, *that's* stylish,' I murmured.

Once I'd wandered beneath the imposing arch, I was met by the sight of a small alcove with recesses scattered in the rock face. I'd no idea why I'd walked this way. Curiosity, maybe. I looked at the inviting sea and decided, as I was already wet, to get out of my sodden, uncomfortable clothes and take a swim. I moved across to a rock, peeled off my skirt and top and lay them on top of my bag on one of its shelf-like tiers. Then I groped about my backside in case my bikini bottoms had suffered the same fate as my skirt. They were fine.

As no one was around, I briefly wondered about doing away with my bikini, but instantly decided against it – if anyone came this way, I had no desire to offend them, especially as everyone had readily welcomed me with open arms and been so lovely.

I tightened the straps to my sandals and carefully went to the waters' edge. Without the solar lamps or glow from the barbecue, it was darker this side of the arch, although the half-moon offered a faint illumination that glinted off the sea. I stood for a moment and considered the poor visibility versus the amount I'd drunk and vowed not to go too far.

As I waded into the water, the initial chill soon dissipated and became more comfortable. Moments later, it was lovely. I swam breaststroke for a little while, keeping my head out the water as the strains of 'Club Tropicana' became more distant. Then I bobbed about for a bit as I trod water, breathing in the sea's saltiness and feeling the humidity in the air as I gazed up at the brilliant stars.

Wouldn't it be wonderful to live here, I thought. And have this on my doorstep every day.

Heaven.

I turned and swam slowly to shore and trudged my way back onto terra firma. As I gingerly picked my way over to my things, and wondered how yuk it was going to feel to put on damp clothes, a voice interrupted my thoughts and caused me to jump.

'Good swim?' I spun around to its source and saw a couple in their mid-forties or early fifties sitting by a recess I hadn't spotted earlier. As they climbed to their feet, I pressed a hand to my chest and took a few a deep breaths to calm myself.

'Sorry, did I scare you?' the man asked.

He was wearing a pair of shorts or swimming trunks that came halfway down his thighs and a pair of flip flops. His build was muscular and even from where I stood, I could see the thick, dark hair covering his chest.

'No, no – I'm fine!' I replied, light-heartedly. 'I just didn't know anyone else was here.'

The woman stepped forward. 'I have a clean towel, if you want to dry off.'

It sounded like a wonderful offer. As despite the warm sticky air, my flesh was prickled in goose bumps and yet to heat up from my swim.

'Are you sure?'

She waved me over. 'Come!'

I quickly retrieved my bag and clothes from the

rock and made my over. As I approached, they both sat down again and smiled as they watched me nearing.

'Here,' the woman said, as she handed me a large, thick towel. 'We always bring plenty. These rocks can be very uncomfortable. Let me take your things, I'll spread them out – see what we can do with them.'

As I dried myself off, I could feel their eyes watching me intently. I wasn't bothered – it was probably no different to my earlier assessment of Petra's body. And after all, we all love a look.

Once finished, I held out the towel to the woman. 'Thank you – that's a lot better!'

She waved her hand in the air. 'Keep it for now. The temperature's falling.'

The woman was right. It was probably as warm as a good summer's day back home, but with the fierce heat during the day, the nighttime drop to mid-twenty degrees could feel huge. As I wrapped the towel around me, the man patted the large picnic blanket they were sitting on.

'Come. Sit. Have a drink. Let's talk a while.'

Why not? I thought. Some more nice people to meet.

As I stepped towards the blanket and slipped out of my sandals, they shifted to make room for me and both hugged their knees up. And I saw that they had layered towels beneath the blanket as extra protection from the rough surface.

As I sat down and crossed my legs, the man reached into a cooler bag behind him and pulled out two small bottles of Carlsberg and a metal bottle opener. Both caps removed, he handed me a bottle then clinked his against it.

'Cheers,' he said, before taking a thirsty gulp.

'Cheers, thanks,' I replied. I turned the woman. 'Are you not having one?'

As I looked at her properly for the first time, I was quite taken by her striking looks. Wearing a black, strappy sundress that revealed an ample chest, I could see she had a solid-looking body and what some might describe as a 'handsome' face. Despite her masculine features and the crook in her nose, she really had something about her. With thick, black eyebrows and the darkest of eyes, she had a strongly defined chin and cheekbones, and full, wide lips. Her jet-black, short hair was slicked off her lightly lined forehead and seemingly still wet from an earlier swim. She looked like a dream sitter for an artist and could have easily been a model in a past life with her unconventional beauty.

She returned my gaze with an intensity that made me feel we'd both been studying the other.

'Later. Maybe,' she said, with a hint of amusement in her eyes.

'So... ' the man began, '... I'll get the boring pleasantries out of the way. I'm Omar and this is Hana. And you are...?'

I acknowledged them both with a small nod of greeting. 'And I'm Amber. And as everyone asks me this; I don't live here – I'm on an extended holiday.'

The man shifted into a cross-legged position. 'Okay. And what does Amber do?'

'I write.'

'And does Amber enjoy writing?'

I took a mouthful of drink and shrugged. 'Not any more.'

It seemed neither of them were overly interested by that statement, as Omar continued with his questioning. 'And have you been enjoying yourself tonight?'

I held my bottled aloft and grinned. 'I'm having the time of my life, thank you!'

Omar smiled and nodded. 'Ah. That's good. You see, Amber... the important thing about having the time of your life, is knowing and appreciating that you're having it. You get me?'

I did. I *actually* did. But like one of Lunge's brandies, Omar's Carlsberg was beginning to knock me for six. And now was not the time for a late-night philosophical discussion about such things.

Instead, I mustered a solemn face and replied, 'Uh-huh, yep. Very much so,' before quickly switching the conversation.

'So... Omar and Hana... they're not Greek names, are they?'

'Lebanese,' Hana said, before Omar interjected with, 'Not tourists. Here on business.'

'Oh. And what business does Hana and Omar do here?'

Hana lightly wagged her head from side to side.

'Import, export,' she said in a near sing-song voice that could have been construed as boredom.

'And do Hana and Omar enjoy importing and exporting?'

They both beamed at me as though I was a star pupil.

'Touché, Amber!' Omar said. 'Yes... Hana and Omar very much enjoy the import and export business.'

'That's good,' I said, before taking another mouthful of lager.

As a silence fell between us, I noticed Hana and Omar flick each other brief, unreadable glances. I shrugged off the feeling I was there to amuse them – but so what? Beginning to get warm with the towel wrapped around me, I slipped it to my waist, flapped two of its corners over my thighs and looked at Omar, who was absently watching his bottle as he twirled it between two fingers. As I took the opportunity to check him out, I could feel Hana's eyes on me.

I didn't care – I was hardly going to make a pass at her husband.

Yet – and just like Hana – he *was* handsome, with the same thick, black eyebrows and intelligent eyes. His full head of floppy, short hair was swept off his face and beginning to grey at the temples. He had weathered skin – much darker than Hana's – which had created smile creases in his dimpled cheeks and deep lines on his forehead. His nose was straight and strong, whilst his lips were neither one thing nor another. And whereas Hana's face was angular, Omar's was fuller, rounder, despite the small hollows in his cheeks. With his stubble and muscularly toned body, he looked rugged – like a real man's man.

Yet here he was, with Hana.

As though sensing my appraisal was finished, Omar slowly lifted his head and looked me in the eyes before leaning forward to rest a hand on one of my knees. Without breaking eye contact, his free hand stretched to place his bottle in the cooler bag before speaking.

'Do you want to play?'

I felt a catch of breath: I knew exactly what he meant.

Time stood still for a moment, yet somehow, I became alert to the faint strains of music emanating from the party. 'Relax' by Frankie Goes to Hollywood.

As the realisation hit me that this had been on the agenda from the get-go, Hana shifted position. I felt her palm cup my shoulder and begin to rub it in small circles. 'Is that nice?' she cooed, as the circles widened and travelled to my back.

A small smile crept across Omar's face as he began to alternate between lightly tracing a finger up and down my leg and smoothing the palm of his hand over my knee, reaching a little higher each time.

Their behaviour was a heady cocktail of predatory, danger and excitement.

As Omar softly asked again, 'Do you want to play?' Hana's hands massaged my back more deeply. I could feel her breath on my neck and as I acutely felt the sensation of their touches, a rush of blood flooded to my nipples and clit, making them swollen and erect.

'Yes,' I said, huskily, giving a small nod of consent.

Omar's eyes darted over my shoulder. Hana reached around and gently took the half-full bottle from my hand. I fleetingly wondered if it was going to be emptied and used on me, but could feel Hana lean away to place it somewhere behind or beside her.

Unsure what was about to unfold, my breath quickened into snatches of anticipation. Through the haze of alcohol, the situation felt surreal – but I'd somehow never felt so alive, or my senses so sharply attuned.

'Relax... ' Omar sang quietly, as he peeled back the towel from my thighs before circling his hands around each of my ankles and slowly uncrossing one leg then the other, then placing them wide apart on the blanket. Still looking me in the eye, he got to his knees, leaned forward, and in perfect synchronisation, lightly pulled on each of my bikini bottom ties, causing them to unravel at the same time and the fabric to slump and fold over, but still keep me covered.

Using two straight fingers like sugar tongs, he took hold of the material and unhurriedly lowered the front of my bikini bottoms to the blanket, as I felt the back of them fall away.

Omar broke eye contact for the first time and glanced down.

'You're clean,' he said, with obvious approval. 'Very good.'

Then he tugged at my towel. 'Bottom up,' he instructed. I pushed on my hands to support myself and did as I was told. Omar whisked the towel away, folded it neatly and placed it beneath me. 'And down... '

With the suspicion she was shifting into a preordained or familiar position, Hana snuggled up behind me, leaned my back into her body and planted her bended, open legs either side of mine. Her crumpled dress pressed into my lower back. She had obviously pulled down the top and hoisted up the skirt, as I could feel her hard nipples against my flesh and the warmth and moisture emanating from between her legs. Leaning further forward, she rested her chin on my shoulder and loosely placed her hands on my forearms.

Settled into a kneeling position, Omar grinned at me as his dark eyes glittered with a mixture of mischief, humour and expectation. A brief glance down revealed his erection straining against his blue swimming shorts.

It seemed we were all ready.

Resting one hand on the blanket, he crouched forward and smoothly slid a forefinger inside me.

Then just held it there.

Nothing.

Hana hadn't budged. And Omar was doing nothing. I looked at the top of his head, then down between my legs. I felt Hana begin to slowly rub my arms. And as I kept looking at the finger inside me and thinking, these were two total randoms playing with me, I felt a sudden release of wetness.

Omar quietly grunted – he must have felt it on his finger – but still, nothing.

Just as I began to think, is this *it?* Omar pressed the flat of his finger upwards. The move was practically miniscule, but in making it, his finger was now on the money shot – but still not moving.

It bizarrely crossed my mind, that if it wasn't for Hana's small strokes of my arms, we were forming some kind of fucked-up, trippy tableau and just waiting for an artist to wander along and paint us all.

Was this it? I thought again.

And then it began.

Tiny circular movements over my G-spot that would stop, pause, then start again. So slow. So gradual. Such a gentle touch. It felt nothing like I'd achieved with my toys back home. The lack of speed and roughness was excruciating but as horny as fuck. I could feel myself get wetter. I wanted to cry out for more. Faster! Deeper! But I was enjoying the ride too much.

Pressure on. Pressure off. Tiny little circles. Such tiny, filthy circles.

Such a wet Amber.

As I groaned for the first time, Omar's thumb pressed onto my clitoris and slowly rolled it around whilst maintaining the gentle circles inside. Fuck, I thought, this guy really knows what he's doing...

Then it stopped.

Omar withdrew his finger and used it to smear my wet over my clit. Smiling at me, he then sucked on the finger before sliding it back in, along with his middle finger. His thumb returned to its rolling work. The fingers; those miniscule circles; that tantalising pressure.

As though this stage was a signal to Hana – who had remained watching throughout – she lifted her head from my shoulder and reached up behind my neck to untie my bikini top. When it had flopped down at the front, she leaned back, loosened the tie across my back and gently pulled the top away before tossing it to one side. Cupping a hand over my forehead, she lowered my back against her body. As I became aware of her nipples once again pressing into my back, she reached down to mine and began to pull and twist.

I felt as if I could explode.

I desperately wanted some cock inside me. But then again, didn't. What Omar was doing was such a slow and gradual build-up, it was blowing me away. I imagined the scene through the eyes of a voyeur – not even caring if one was present – which only served to make me wetter and groan more loudly with pleasure. As it was, watching a stranger with his fingers inside me, only heightened my sensations.

Add Hana into the mix... it was simply indescribable...

Omar's steady rhythm finally had me climbing to the crest of orgasm. Then waver. And float. It was the most astonishing feeling. I felt like I wanted him to pick up pace. But the climb and subsequent hover in a pre-orgasm no-man's land was incredibly sensual. Part of me never wanted it to end.

Climb. Hover. Release.

Climb. Hover. Release.

As Hana gave my nipples a smart tug and began to kiss my neck, the climbing came faster, stronger.

My breathing quickened. I closed my eyes and felt the sodden fingers inside me doing their work. Hana was now roughly massaging my breasts and squeezing my swollen and deliciously sore nipples.

Climbing, climbing, climbing.

I felt my toes begin to wriggle. I was close. I began to pant and catch my breath.

Hana grabbed my chin, yanked it towards her and kissed me hungrily with her probing tongue. It was wet, sloppy and disorganised. Her free hand took a nipple between her thumb and forefinger and roughly stretched and twisted.

I finally exploded into the most extraordinary and lengthy orgasm that seemed to come and come in waves. As my body convulsed and twitched, Omar plunged a third finger deep inside and got to work with rapid thrusts. It was almost too much to take. I whimpered into Hana's mouth as she ran a hand through my hair. As our kiss continued – sloppier and with more urgecy – I felt as though I might drown in her mouth or pass out through the ecstasy.

Then the fall began.

My body began to slack. My breathing steadied.

And as the fingers were withdrawn and I felt my orgasm trickle from between my legs, I loosely kissed Hana back and let her taste my tongue.

And when we broke away, it was to find a naked Omar standing by our feet with an impressive erection.

I watched as Omar fucked Hana from behind. Her head was buried between my legs throughout and although the experience was highly erotic and pleasurable, it fell short of Omar's sensational expertise and not helped by the fact, my clit was still incredibly sensitive. I swung between wincing discomfort and enjoyment, rendering it impossible to come. In the moments before ejaculating into Hana with a staggered series of grunts, Omar looked at me with a filthy leer before closing his eyes for the final thrusts.

It was all very civilised afterwards. Bordering on indifference. I finished my lukewarm drink as Hana pulled up her dress straps and waded, skirt-hoisted, into the sea to clean herself up. Omar checked on my still-damp clothes and told me to keep the towel I'd used. Then, as Hana began to wander back, I dried myself off, put my bikini back on, and wrapped the towel around my waist as Omar began packing their things away.

There was no mention about anything that had just unfolded.

Seeing no point in hanging around, I picked up my clothes and bag and said goodbye.

Crouched over the cooler bag, Omar looked up, almost surprised to see me still there.

'So, did Amber have a good time?' he asked, distractedly.

'The time of my life,' I said with a smile.

'That's good,' he replied simply, before returning to his packing.

With her back to me, Hana was busily drying her legs and apparently content to for me to leave without a word.

'Bye, Hana.'

Nothing.

I began to walk away, but after a few strides, her voice filled the air. 'Don't worry about your scars. They suit you.'

I stopped in my tracks for a moment.

What a peculiar thing to say.

On such a fucked-up crazy night.

I laughed into the humid air.

And carried on.

12.

Amber Busts Out

The next morning, I felt surprisingly perky as I stretched on my bedroom veranda and plucked a few bougainvillea petals from overhead. As I pointlessly pressed them to my nose, I began laughing as I recalled the events of the previous night, when everything had been down-down alright...

'Dear Lord, where will it all end?' I said, as I released the petals to twirl their way to the jasmine bushes below.

Over breakfast, I watched my swallow friends get up to their usual stunts, and by the time my black coffee had kicked-in, I felt ready to tackle anything.

Aside from my writing.

As I reached for my cigarettes, I felt a jab of pity I didn't have the chance to see Eva and Johannes before leaving the sea caves. Despite having thinned out a little, the party was still in full swing when I passed under the arch but, sadly, their lovely faces were nowhere to be seen.

Rather than join in with the laughter and dancing, I just wanted to get back to the villa for a much-needed shower and needed to get a taxi arranged from outside the restaurant. And moreover, see if they were still serving drinks.

Initially, I didn't notice Petra – she was hidden by the group of partygoers she was dancing amongst – but as I walked by, she suddenly sprung out and tried to pull me towards their midst.

'Amber! Come! Dance!' she cried.

I laughed at her infectious enthusiasm and waved away her offer.

She looked me up and down.

'Have you been swimming?'

Yes,' I replied. 'Back there, through the arches.'

'Oh!' she said with surprise, as her eyes flitted over my shoulder. 'And did Amber have a good time?'

I searched her smiling face for any sign of hidden meaning and twisted around to see if Hana and Omar were in sight or heading our way to leave.

They were nowhere to be seen. And I was probably imagining things.

I left with Petra's business card and after her earnest and endearing efforts to get me to stay.

'See you soon!' she cried out as I began to walk away. 'Maybe? Maybe not?' she added, wagging her open-fingered hands from side-to side.

She was delightful. I mirrored her hands. 'Maybe! Hopefully!'

Petra flashed me a dazzling smile and twirled her way back into the heart of the dancers with her arms aloft.

As I wandered away, I smiled or said goodnight to some of the people I'd been introduced to earlier. And was pleased I managed to say *efharisto* and *kalinihta* to Costa, who I found sitting with a slumped Roger by the smouldering barbeque; backs against a rock and enjoying bottles of Keo. With his straw hat pushed to the back of his head, Roger looked thoroughly shit-faced, as he gave me a lopsided grin.

'*Bomba! Bomba!*' Costa cried good naturedly, raising his bottle.

And then I was climbing up the path and taking extra care my exit wasn't as spectacular as my entrance. Once at the top – and glad to see a few Cypriot stragglers still drinking outside the restaurant – I called for a taxi and half-wondered if it would be the same 'down, down' driver.

It was.

I took a drag on my cigarette and thought back to how embarrassed – or ashamed – I'd felt when telling Petra I hadn't seen much of the island. It was inexcusable, really and entirely my fault. When I'd first arrived in Cyprus, I had no desire to stray far and felt wary of being recognised. And aside from venturing out to buy essentials, I just tucked myself away at the villa, trying to tackle Susie and give myself the space and time to feel heal.

But after a while, being an island within an island wore a bit thin and rather than instilling a healthy writing routine, one of self-imposed isolation developed (the ever-chatty Pool Man aside). Which began to feel increasingly bizarre and ridiculous each time I heard happy and excited tourists passing by on their quad bikes.

I began to think about how privileged I was, to be able to stay in a beautiful villa on the Med for 3 months – something most people couldn't dream of. And what was I doing? Hiding away. So I called myself a dozy, fucking mare and took my first tentative nighttime venture into the village and into The Red Lion.

And guess what? The world still spun on its axis. No one recognised me. Or overly paid me too much attention. I got drunk. Smoked too much. Engaged in some polite conversation. Wobbled back to the villa. Then went back the next night and did the same.

A few nights later, I tried out Coral Bay where, aside from the incident with Missus Mouth Almighty, I was just a lone, pissed-up Brit perched on a bar stool. And one who needed to stop thinking they were centre of everybody else's universe.

I supposed it then became a matter of feeling guilty at not cracking on with the sequel that kept me going through the daily farce of sitting pointlessly at my laptop before slinking poolside or into Chez Cleo. Or maybe, it just suited me.

I watched as a swallow joyfully skimmed the pool's surface before soaring high into the clear, blue sky with a series of bobs and rolls. Shielding my eyes against the fierce sun, I followed its progress until it became a distant dot.

'Good idea,' I murmured.

It was finally time to bust out and get some sightseeing done.

Particularly as I was beginning to turn into the home straight of my Cyprus stay. And *maybe* (just maybe) a break from Susie would get my writing mojo back.

Yeah. Deffo.

I opened my laptop and embarked on a googling session. Which almost immediately confirmed my worst suspicions about Akamas: standard car rentals were neither insured nor allowed off-road. And having already promised myself I wouldn't pay out for additional rental vehicles, it was a non-starter.

Bollocks. I'd been keen to swim with the turtles.

Next time. Maybe.

After a while, I began to get dizzy with all the options, advice and endless TripAdvisor reviews. I just couldn't be doing with it all. As I peered at a map, I recalled Petra's mention of the capital, Nicosia – that'd do. Roughly a 2-hour drive. Totally doable. It'd be good to stretch Cleo's legs for a long drive, then I could come back through Troodos

Mountains. I just needed to get a wiggle on and get on the road.

Decision made, I closed down the laptop and gave my phone a quick check.

Ooh! A Ball Bag email... then I remembered messaging him from the beach party.

'Was she doing jazz fins at the time?'

Daft sod, I thought with a smile. I'll get back to him later.

With nothing else of any interest lurking in my inbox, I made the thunderbolt decision that X could go fuck itself; it was high time I got out of its toxic waste of space and took back some control by completely ignoring it. That much, I could at least do.

Trolling bastards.

I laughed at my bolshy resolution.

Who knew that slow and steady could get me *so* fired up?

Maybe I should get fumbled by randoms more often...

As things turned out, my intended 3 days of sightseeing morphed into two and a bit. I arrived at Nicosia full of beans and in goggle-eyed tourist mode, but the instant I got out the car, felt the additional inland heat hit me like a wrecking ball. I wandered around the pretty, pedestrianised Ledra Street area, admiring the old, shuttered buildings, cafes and bars – but not before plunging into the first tourist shop and coming out with a ridiculously large and floppy straw hat. I looked like an economy shepherdess in my shorts and vest, but didn't care – it felt good to be amongst so many people and I'd enjoyed seeing all sights and high-rise buildings on my drive into the city centre. I was somewhere new. Somewhere different.

As I finally reached the end of a long road, I saw a large group of locals and tourists looking hot and bothered, with some fanning themselves with passports, as they queued at kiosks manned by uniformed men and women. The signage told me I was at a check point and could have crossed over the Green Line and into the Occupied Area – if only I'd had the foresight to bring my passport with me.

Or at least the foresight to google some information about Nicosia before setting off.

Pffft. Next time. Maybe.

Instead, I cut through a side street and found myself at a paved area in front of an imposing Greek Orthodox church. Al fresco cafes were dotted about, and as it was more than time for some lunch and shade beneath one of the table's umbrellas, I gratefully plonked myself down on the first available seat.

As I enjoyed a cold drink and bowl of *louvi* (a mixture of black-eyed beans, tuna, cooked marrow, served with olive oil and a wedge of lemon), the church bells rang out the same time as loud, crackly chants piped through speakers in a language I didn't recognise. It was still going on when the young waitress placed my bill before me in a little silver dish.

As I dug about my bag, I asked her, 'Is that ancient Greek?'

'It's the Turks,' she told me with a shrug, 'they play their Islamic prayers when our bells ring.'

I'd wanted to ask more, but she was clearly busy as she briskly swept away to another table to take an order. The simultaneous bells and opposing prayers seemed bizarre, and only served to highlight how limited my knowledge was of Cyprus. I knew Nicosia was the only divided capital in the world and that Turkey invaded in the 70s, but beyond that, I knew very little.

After leaving my payment and a tip, I wandered down other side streets, away from the shops and hustle and came across graffiti covered, bullet-riddled and crumbling derelict buildings. Despite the shutters that hung forlornly at bowed angles and chunks of brickwork that had been blown away, it was easy to imagine how they'd looked in their former glory. Another turn saw me facing a guarding post, with sandbags and coils of barbed wire before it and two armed Cypriot soldiers, silently eyeing me with suspicion as I stood, unsure for a moment, in in my ridiculous, floppy hat. Armed and dangerous. Crudely painted signs left me in no doubt that I was to go no further and photos were prohibited. It was like another world, and hard to believe I was just a few minutes away from all the shoppers and diners enjoying their day out.

I let my eyes soak in the image, then turned around, took another side road and found myself on a street parallel to the one I'd first walked down. More cute restaurants and cafes, modern bars and shops that weren't quite doing it for me. As I trudged along, sweat ran freely down my back and I cursed my stupidity for choosing the one place on the island to explore even hotter than where I was staying. I literally felt like my insides were cooking and my head about to explode. Pulling out my phone, I checked the temperature – 37 degrees.

Yep. That'd do it.

With regret, it had to be goodbye, Nicosia. It was time get a cold bottle of water and head for the hills – or mountains, in this instance – before someone basted me. Or advanced with a large packet of stuffing.

It had been short, sweet and interesting – but far too bloody hot.

Troodos was a different prospect altogether. Thankfully, a lot cooler for starters. And full of pretty pine trees and vineyards, panoramic views and scattered villages and houses. With my hat relegated to the back seat, Cleo whimpered and complained at some of the steeper, windy roads – but she boldly pushed on. I stopped several times to breathe in the pine-filled air and admire the view, then randomly followed a sign and found myself in the dinky village of Kakopetria. With its mixture of old cobbled streets and wooden-framed, 3-storey chalet-type buildings, it wouldn't have looked out of place in the Swiss Alps.

From my snapshot of the place, it was utterly charming and delightful. On the second-floor veranda of a picturesque riverside mill, I enjoyed a dinner of grilled trout, and as I savoured the drop in temperature and first blushes of a sunset, I felt relaxed, yet invigorated, by everything I had seen and done.

Then it was time to get Cleo home, where, feeling too tired to go out, I spent some time in Chez Cleo; sipping vodka in the hot tub, then flopping on the cushions to look at the moon and twinkles as the crickets chirped away.

The next morning, I received a polite but rather indifferent response from Eddie. It was more or less, yeah yeah, whatever. It'd be great if you could crack on but, perhaps you're right; things will work out better when you return.

Initially, I wondered if he was being distracted by something – or someone – else. And had much bigger fish to fry. After all, he represented a large number of authors, and if the others were continually bellyaching like me, it'd soon get on anyone's tits. Particularly if all you were trying to do was get our work out there and make us all some money.

As I challenged myself to prove him wrong and make meaningful inroads with Susie, it crossed my mind that had been his intent all along with his 'whatever' email.

Probably. The sly old shark.

Either way, I'd meant what I told him – I would try my best. It just remained to be seen if my best was good enough.

I was more organised for my second day of sightseeing; I was off to the west coast – just under a one-hour drive – which would suit me fine after yesterday's 4-hour epic in Cleo. I sincerely hoped her hairdryer engine had enjoyed a good night's sleep.

Alas, it seemed not...

As, unfortunately for Cleo, one of the earliest parts of the journey involved a long, windy climb, and whilst it afforded me breathtaking, panoramic views over both woodland and coastline, she wheezed and belched and coughed and spluttered in complaint. For a while, I feared she might wave the white flag completely, but as the incline lessened, then levelled out, she said, 'Sorry about that,' swished her hair and happily trundled on.

On the way, I passed rustic roadside tavernas, abandoned armchairs and agricultural equipment, and stalls selling melons. I saw a garden centre, and clay ovens being sold kerbside, and drove past olive groves and a handful of villages, before finally getting my first sight of the west coast's sea and beginning my descent.

Once down at sea level, I stopped off in the small

town of Polis and had a wander through its cute pedestrianised streets. I browsed in a couple of shops selling local crafts, then took up the offer of fresh orange juice from a dinky, hatched window and sat beneath an ancient yew tree to enjoy my drink as I wrote a cheery message on the postcard I'd bought for Elena. Although Polis was utterly charming, it seemed I had walked the main tourist paths at its heart, and eager to get to my next destination, I got back into Cleo and made my way to the fishing village of Latchi, a few miles away.

At the picturesque harbour, I joined the throng of tourists milling about the waterfront restaurants – each with a staff member outside, beckoning me over for the 'best fish'. I almost felt dizzy with choice, particularly as all the menus on display looked pretty much identical. Spotting a prime seat in one of the smaller restaurants, I allowed myself to be herded in by a smiley Cypriot waiter and took my place at a table close to the water and bobbing boats.

Once I'd ordered lunch and a soft drink, I noticed other diners taking the opportunity to snap away with their phones as they sat at their tables or stood on the harbourside walkway. I could have throttled myself. Why hadn't I taken *any* photos since I'd been here? Particularly yesterday, when I visited Nicosia and Troodos? You total twat, Amber! I guess I just hadn't thought about it – what with barely straying from my village and the nightlife of Coral Bay, where it wouldn't cross my mind to take photos whilst perched on a bar stool. Who or what of? DJ Puny in a dodgy wig? Or maybe, the whole concept of taking holiday snaps hadn't been on my radar when trying to recover from everything that had happened.

Well, there was no time like the present!

I pulled my phone from my bag, smiled at the waiter who'd arrived with my drink, then got up and joined the others on the walkway to take photos of the boats and harbour. For some unearthly reason, I felt a little self-conscious – maybe because I was on my own (which I immediately doubted) or maybe, it was some form of misguided snobbery that I didn't classify as an average tourist due to my extended stay.

Come on, Amber. Get snapping. And your head out your arse.

Happy holidays. And all that.

When I'd finished my photography session, I returned to the table to find my meal waiting for me; a platter of calamari, grilled sardines, mussels and prawns, served with wedges of lemon, a bowl of salad and side plate of chips. It was more than I'd anticipated, so in true Cypriot style, took my time with it. As I picked away and admired the setting, I overheard some English tourists on the table behind me discussing their extreme disappointment over their visit to the nearby Baths of Aphrodite. According to the husband it was, 'barely more than a glorified puddle' and 'smelt rank'. Whilst the wife complained it, 'hadn't been worth the walk in the heat' and furthermore doubted anyone would want to bathe there, let alone a Goddess.

Mmm... I'd been hoping it looked marginally more impressive in real life than the online photos. Maybe not. And maybe I'd scratch my intended visit off the list. I could do without a whack of 'rank' up my nostrils with a belly full of fish.

Lunch finally over, (and already feeling bloated) I strolled back to where I'd bagsied Cleo a great spot near the harbour entrance. Here, the road swept left and had a few beach bars and restaurants. When I looked beyond, there was a palm tree-lined avenue running beside a long stretch of beach that curved outwards at its end, and was met by lush, tree-covered hills.

My home for the next few hours.

Noting the nearest part of the beach was rammed with filled sun loungers, I decided to get into Cleo and drive down the far end; it was way too hot to walk that far.

Floppy hat or not.

My time at the beach turned out to be blissful. I had the area to myself, so risked going topless, but kept my bikini top to hand should it suddenly become appropriate to put it back on. I untied my bottoms and positioned the fabric so it just about covered the essentials – I'd come so far to obtain an even, all over tan, and didn't fancy ruining it so late into my stay.

When I began to feel too hot, I took my increasingly swollen stomach for a refreshing swim in the sea. Or covered myself with the loose white shirt I'd brought with me and donned the shepherdess hat that was beginning to earn its keep. Just where *was* Chez Cleo and her shade when I needed her?

And when I was stretched out and listening to the soothing rhythm of the sea, I was taken back to all the crazy times on the beach at Brightlea. The guys at Brokeback. Olive Man. The old boys treating themselves to a tug. The many sights. The many characters.

And Luke.

Sigh...

Best not think about him. Or that beach. Which I doubted I'd ever visit again.

To distract my thoughts, I sat up and took some photos of the coastline and palm trees before settling back down again on my towel.

I ran a hand over my stomach. It was now incredibly distended and felt as though it was getting bigger by the second. Maybe I'd copped a rogue prawn. Or maybe it was the sugars in the orange juice. Or maybe... I'd just been a piggy and pushed my snout too far into the trough. Probably. I sat back up and inspected it; I looked as though I was 10-months pregnant. Glancing into the distance, I spotted a lone fishing boat. The way things were going, if I was spotted, they'd be pegging it over to fire a harpoon my way.

Or maybe not.

Either way, I was beginning to feel very uncomfortable. My skin was stretched taut over my belly and I was beginning to get a dull ache in the top of my stomach. I reached for my bottle of water and glugged down large mouthfuls. Maybe I was just dehydrated.

Jeez.

I checked the time. I'd been on the beach for almost 2-hours. Plenty. I reassembled my bikini, put on my shirt and gathered my things together. Then I drove back towards the harbour, parked up and went into the straw-roofed beach cafe I'd spotted earlier. I held little hope of the place stocking what I wanted, but after I'd sat down at one of the bench tables and studied the drinks menu, I was pleasantly surprised to see they had just what I was after. Peppermint tea. Ideal for bloating.

That'll do. Yes, please.

Ye of little faith.

The tea arrived in a tall, handled glass and with a sprig of mint. As I waited for it to cool, I took some more photos of the beach, catching the hills in the background and the distant spot where I'd been sunbathing. The fishing boat had wandered nearer to land, and into frame – making the shot idyllic. Then, feeling a bit arty farty, I took some photos of the large light bulbs that hung from thick, knotted ropes, and captured a passing speedboat as it cut through the sea in the background.

As I hunched over my phone to examine the

results, I felt someone's eyes on me.

I looked up and saw a plump lady in a yellow sundress two tables away. As she twirled the stirrer in her cocktail, she gave me a shy smile. I smiled back.

About to return to my phone, I sensed she was still looking at me.

She was. I scrunched my face in confusion, unsure if she was someone I recognised or knew, but couldn't place her. As I gave her an awkward half-smile, she tentatively raised a hand, gave a little wave and mouthed hello. She looked like an embarrassed pupil about to ask if she could go to the toilet.

I twisted to look over my shoulder on the off-chance we weren't having a comedy moment and she was gesturing to someone behind me. Finding no one there, I turned back around, only to find her coming towards me with her cocktail with an apologetic smile.

'Sorry,' she said, as she reached my table.

I scrutinised her face for clues as to who she was. Pale, freckly complexion. Natural strawberry blonde hair that was cut into a chin-length straggly bob and showed a few grey hairs. Her eyes were small and a weak blue. A stubby nose, and thin lips that seemed lost in her round face. I had no idea who she was.

With flushed cheeks, she asked, 'May I?' as she indicated to the bench seat opposite.

'Er... yeah,' I began. Then, 'Sorry. But do I know you?'

'Sorry,' she said, as she sat down and placed her drink on the table.

I sipped on my tea and eyed her over the glass. I wasn't going to say a thing until she told me who she was.

Cupping her hands around her cocktail, she nervously cleared her throat before speaking.

'Sorry,' she said once again. 'But would I be right in thinking you're Amber Stone?'

Oh, for fuck's sake, I thought. Here we go.

I raised my eyebrows and gave her a challenging stare. I'd obviously unnerved her as she began to gabble on in one long sentence.

'Only, I saw your photo in one of the tabloids the other day – a picture of you in one of the bars out here – and I don't remember the headline, but it wasn't very nice and I remember thinking at the time, that's not very nice and why are the papers always so horrible after everything you've been through, but the reason why I wanted to speak to you was to let you know that I'm glad you were brave enough to go to court, because my daughter was stalked and murdered by her ex-boyfriend – a bit like what happened to you and your friend – and I'm just so sorry for you... your friend... ... my daughter... and all the other women who have to... ... so when I saw you and recognised you, I just wanted to say hi, really, and say well done for being brave... they're just... such... *bastards*, these types of men and none of them should get away with it.'

It took me a while to absorb her words. I was so used to expecting something hostile or prying from the mouths of strangers who recognised me, she'd completely caught me off guard with her terrible story.

And then we were both so incredibly sorry.

I ended up talking to Carol for over an hour. We shared and sobbed and held hands. The story of her 22-year-old daughter, Jade, was harrowing but, sadly, all too familiar. One jealous ex. Numerous incidents of stalking and threats. No interest from the Police.

On the night Jade was murdered, her ex followed her to the pub where she'd been enjoying post-work drinks with colleagues. When she left, he approached her in the street and said he'd set fire to her parents' house if she didn't go back to his flat to 'talk'. Fearful he'd carry out his threat, Jade went back with him and was beaten to within an inch of her life. Hearing her screams for mercy, concerned neighbours alerted the emergency services.

With her eyes swollen shut and barely able to speak, Jade managed to say enough to the female Police Officer who leaned over her hospital bed to catch the faint words.

Two days later, Jade passed away from her extensive injuries.

Carol and her husband never came to terms with Jade putting the safety of their home above hers. No amount of counselling dulled the guilt and heartbreak. And the strain saw them divorce.

Carol dabbed at her eyes and smiled weakly. 'Did you find the counselling useful?'

It almost felt obscene to be catapulted back into my story, despite freely discussing certain aspects of it earlier.

'No,' I told her. 'I didn't.

I'd agreed to the offer. And due to the length of my stay, a pleasant and homely woman came to visit me in my hospital room. Despite her soothing, cooing noises, the session felt formulaic, as though she was rattling off questions and suggestions from a checklist she was unable to stray from, and which didn't entirely fit in with my experience. One size fits all.

And whilst suspecting she'd be the perfect fit for others, she sadly wasn't for me.

I recall wondering if I'd been landed with the runt of the counsellor litter, and should have checked her over for a lone star on her name badge.

Giving her the benefit of the doubt, I tried a second session. But about halfway through, her cooing drone began to grate and I half-wondered if she'd fully read my case notes. She told me how I was feeling. Or should be feeling. Which in no way correlated with the madness pounding away inside my head.

And with hands neatly folded on her lap, her sing-song voice told me not to blame myself.

There was no third session.

Carol explained she was at the end of a solo

week-long break and, like me, attempting to heal in a foreign land, away from daily reminders. When we said goodbye, we tightly hugged and I breathed in her scent of coconut oil and heavy sadness.

'You look after yourself. And be kind to yourself,' I told her, once we'd reluctantly released one another and stood, holding hands.

With tears welling, Carol's eyes travelled up to rest on my forehead scar.

'And you keep being brave,' she said, as she gently wiggled my hands and returned her gaze to my eyes.

We hugged once more, and that was that. Carol was off to start packing. And I was left to gaze at a stunning view and wonder what kind of world we lived in.

On the way back, I stopped off at a taverna on the outskirts of the village of Kathikas. Despite the peppermint tea doing its work, I was still full from eating the contents of the sea and had no desire to eat. *However*, I *did* have a strong hankering for an ice cold Keo.

As I hovered by the entrance, I asked the approaching waiter if I could just order a drink.

'*Endaxi! Endaxi!*' he beamed. '*Ela!* Come! Sit!'

I was ushered to a table and, once settled, immediately taken with the nearby olive tree and fountain that were illuminated by spotlights that changed colour. Overhead, heavily laden grapevines formed a lush and picturesque canopy. With my drink ordered and the hopeful offer of a menu politely declined, I had a bit of a jolt when feeling a cat wind itself around my legs, before lazily sashaying off to the base of the fountain to stretch out and lick its paws.

The photo opportunity was impossible to resist.

And I was in tourist mode again. God knows how many I took; with the lights changing colour every 10 seconds or so, a seemingly better shot arose, with the cat playing its part by adopting a series of endearing poses.

As I returned to my table, the waiter arrived with my drink, some lemon sponge cake and a small plate of grapes that had obviously been snipped from the vines above. Each was placed before me as though ordered, and realising refusal could offend or, more likely, be Lunge-like futile, I just said thank you, showed him my new teeth and felt grateful my stomach had settled.

Between picks at the food and sips of my beer, I looked around at my fellow diners. There were surprisingly few, but the closest were four Brits sharing a table; one pale, timid-looking couple, and a bronzed pairing who were dishing out advice on where to go and what to see. It didn't take a genius to work out which ones had recently arrived. As the sun-tanned couple warmed to their topic, their voices became louder as they imparted their words of wisdom, with the wife repeating fragments of her husband's sentences as though Mr and Mrs Timid had learning difficulties. And in some instances, talking over her husband to do so with confirming nods.

I tried to pay no attention, but my ears pricked up when Mister Suntanned mentioned the Baths of Aphrodite.

'Don't bother,' he instructed. 'It's a shitty puddle of water with a trickle of piss running down some rocks.'

The wife jabbed her loaded fork at the couple. 'Shitty puddle,' she confirmed, before putting the food in her mouth and chewing in a way that made her entire face mobile.

The Timids nervously glanced at one another before giving their lengthy and gabbled assurances they'd be doing *nothing* of the kind. It looked like a peculiar set-up, and I half-wondered if they were somehow being terrorised by the The Tans and possibly relieved of their holiday money in the process.

I had to refrain from laughing at my thoughts. But whatever was happening at that table, it seemed evident I'd saved myself a disappointing trip to see a shitty puddle.

As I popped another grape into my mouth, my thoughts drifted to Carol and her terrible story. Then onto to the fact my photo had appeared in one of the tabloids. I hadn't asked about the headline or subsequent copy – her 'not very nice' had been more than enough. I thought back to Surfer Boy and his crew in Sonny's and reckoned my initial instinct had been right; I'd been recognised and one of them had taken the photo and sold it for a few quid.

Nice one, lads. Cheers.

I let out a sigh. And supposed that's the way it'd be until the press found a new female pantomime villain who liked to get naked on a beach. Looked like I'd have a wait on my hands. Maybe the dreaded shepherdess hat would have to accompany me on all future forays. And I could complete the disguise by strapping on some ribbons and tying a floppy bow beneath my chin.

Mind you, with the size of that bloody hat, if a sharp breeze ever whipped beneath the fucker – that'd be me – boof! I'd be off like a hot air balloon and halfway to Turkey.

As the cat returned to perform figure of eights around my legs, I reached down to stroke it and marvelled at how I could even think up oddball things after my earlier encounter with Carol.

Survival, I guessed.

Mixed with exhaustion from the underlying feeling of sorrow people like myself and Carol had to live with on a daily basis. Enough to send anyone halfway around the twist, I thought, as the cat pressed its head into the palm of my hand with a contented purr.

As I broke off a piece of cake for the cat, Mr and Mrs Tanned were at it again.

'You need to be getting yourself down to Coral Bay. It's good down there. Cheap pints and karaoke.'

'Coral Bay. Karaoke.'

It was too much to resist. I let the cake tumble from my hands for the cat to greedily pounce upon, straightened, then loudly asked. 'What about The Taste of Bengal?'

'Bengal?'

'Bloody marvellous place. We fucking love it there.'

'Marvellous place. Love it.'

And we were up and running.

Another distraction created.

Bloody marvellous, indeed.

13.

Ball Bag and Lunge Get a Bit of What For

My third day of sightseeing didn't unfold the way I'd planned or wanted. It started off well enough, with a trip to the Tombs of the Kings in Paphos. I wandered around in the blazing heat wearing my dippy hat; I took photos; gawped; admired; learned and got *very* hot. Then I drove to central Paphos and strolled through the indoor market with an iced coffee and look of disbelief at the amount of tat being sold amongst charming handicrafts.

Then I was off to the busy harbour to turn down offers of boat trips, henna tattoos and the familiar invites for the 'best' fish restaurant in Paphos. I wandered down to the Byzantine castle for some obligatory photos. Then turned around and walked back, only to be pestered again by the same restaurant staff who'd had an unfruitful bash earlier. The whole vibe was a bit too busy for me; I kept being knocked and bumped into by unaware tourists and had one of my shins twatted by some silly mare in jumbo sunglasses who, for reasons unknown, was wheeling a small suitcase along the harbour front like an affected Z-lister film star. It was all a far cry from the relative calm of Latchi and as I had no desire to throw any more fish down my throat for the time being, it seemed pointless to hang around. I remembered the rustic roadside cafe I'd passed on the way into Paphos, with its handful of tables beneath vines. That'd do for a pitstop before setting off to the monastery in Tala I had chalked down for an afternoon visit.

I weaved between a couple of finger-pointing tourists and strode away to slap Cleo into life.

The cafe had an encouragingly limited menu; kebabs or traditional sandwiches. Four of the six tables were filled with Cypriot men happily chowing down and gabbling away about God-knows-what with intermittent hand gestures and loud outbursts. Before taking one of the free tables, I ordered a halloumi sandwich and cold drink at the kitchen's open window.

With my light breakfast seeming a distant memory, I was looking forward to some stodge after barely eating a thing the night before. When the sandwich arrived, in a twist of waxy paper, I ripped it open and happily wolfed it down. Then I lit a cigarette, watched the passing traffic, admired the overhead vines and gazed at the distant sea before suddenly remembering I hadn't checked out any of the photos I'd taken. Placing my phone on the checkered tablecloth, I went to my photos and began swiping with my free hand.

The Paphos photos looked fine and did the job; just a bunch of tourist snaps.

When I reached the pictures of the cat in front of the fountain – with the magnificent olive tree and lights that changed colour – I swept back and forth, trying to decide which one looked best, before swiping on. Then I was taken back to Latchi. Hanging bulbs. Beautiful beach. Beautiful trees. Pretty harbour. Boats. Blah blah blah.

Another swipe...

And I was greeted by the image of me and Spencer smiling, and looking daft and happy in front of the Sophia Classique plaque outside the caravan he was murdered in minutes later.

As I gasped and jolted in shock, I felt the blood drain from my face. I stared at the photo, unable to look away as my mind replayed the film of us returning from our boozy night out and posing for the pictures.

My beautiful Spencer.

What a great night we'd had...

That night...

A sudden pain in my fingers pulled my attention from the screen; my cigarette had burned down to the filter and in doing so, singed the inside of my forefinger. I tossed the butt in the ashtray and numbly inspected my finger before putting it in my mouth to suck on the burn.

As my eyes wandered back to the photo, a plate of watermelon chunks was placed next to my phone. I looked at the toothpick sticking out of one of the pieces, then up at the face of the Cypriot waiter who'd brought it over.

'My cousin, he grows them not far from here. On the house,' he said, with a warm smile. Then he kissed the tips of his bunched fingers with a smacking sound. 'Very nice.'

It seemed like the most innocent and charming thing I'd ever heard in my life.

I bit down hard on my finger. Wanting the skin to break. To taste my own blood. Wanting somebody else's brain.

Please. Not here. Not now, Amber.

But it was no good.

I took my finger away and managed to choke out, '*Efharisto*' before breaking down in uncontrollable tears, which were only made worse when the waiter rested a concerned hand on my shoulder

'*Signómee. Signómee*,' I gasped between sobs.

Sorry. Sorry.

Always, so fucking sorry.

And that was my sightseeing over for the day.

*

When I got back to the villa, I cracked open a fresh bottle of vodka, poured out a generous shot, added diet coke and made my way over to Chez Cleo, where I heavily plonked myself down on the cushions and glowered at my surroundings.

Where the fuck was Pool Man when I needed him? I could just about do with dishing out some grief to him about his no-fucking-show for the fucking beach party.

Fucking Pool Man barrrrrs-starrrred-eo.

With his stupid fucking sunglasses.

I raised my glass in toast. 'Bastards – the fucking lot of you!' I cried out, before taking a few hefty glugs.

Seemed I wasn't in the best of moods...

I extracted the bastard phone from the pocket of my shorts and grimaced at the raw memory of the scene I'd caused at the cafe, with my sobbing and snotting and wailing. The waiter who didn't know what to do. The old lady dressed in black, who shuffled over, patted my hand and spoke to me in Greek. The brandy I refused. The waiter escorting me to Cleo and asking if I was okay to drive.

How could I forget those photos were still on my bastard phone?

Or had I chosen to forget?

I toyed with the idea of calling Elena to let off steam. To whinge about the eternal hamster wheel of pain I was trapped in. The unexpected triggers that jumped out to fuck me over just when I thought I was making progress.

I took another mouthful and sighed. No – it wouldn't be fair on her.

It wasn't fair on me. But I didn't need to drag her down as well. Not after all the support she'd already given me.

I watched the leaves floating on the pool's surface, as they swirled and huddled by one of the skimmers but refused to drift in. Stubborn little shits. As a welcome breeze whipped across the water, it caused the cluster to bob and unfurl, giving it the appearance of a long-tailed blob. Or maybe a tadpole. Or another bloody lizard.

Long tail...

Yes!

Yes! Yes! And... yes!

I opened up my emails, pressed reply to Ballbag Derek's last message and tapped out a response.

'Jazz fins? Why not ask if she was blacked-up and singing Mammy? Fucking idiot.'

Another mouthful of vodka. A ceremonial twirl of my burnt forefinger in the air. Aaaaaand... send.

The regret and shame were instant.

'Oh, fuck,' I muttered.

I knew I was lashing out because I was hurting – but at Ball Bag? The one person who'd done nothing but put a smile on my face.

Really?

And going down the racism route? That was

a cheap shot of the lowest order. Besides, I didn't even know Ball Bag's heritage. Or anything, really. Location. Sexuality. The lot.

He was just an easy target for how I was feeling.

Oh, for fuck's sake, Amber.

And to call him a fucking idiot?

I mean, *really?*

I was the fucking idiot.

I stared at my phone, willing the email to bounce back with an undeliverable message. If only. Then I knocked around a mental draft of an apology email – but the words seemed shallow, insincere and in no way explained why I'd been so cruel or directed at him. Between mouthfuls of vodka, I stared at my phone some more, willing Ball Bag to reply with some obscure comical statement that would excuse or dismiss my disgusting behaviour.

Nothing.

I fidgeted and drank and got up to put Radio Aphrodite on. I checked my phone. Saw nothing. Felt worse. Fidgeted and drank and did a sweep of the pool to clear away the petals and debris. I went inside for a top-up. Put the pool lights on. Smoked and drank. And checked my phone.

A reply from Ball Bag.

'Oh, fuck,' I muttered, as my heart thumped in my chest. It took me several minutes and two large mouthfuls of vodka to open the email. I had no idea what to expect, but assumed it would be unfavourable and no less than I deserved.

But instead, it simply said, *'What's wrong?'*

I frowned at the message in disbelief.

How could someone be so gracious after I'd been so vile to them? *And* to show a degree of concern for me?

I had no idea how to reply. So I drank and smoked and fidgeted and walked around the swimming pool a couple of times to the backdrop of cheesy tunes. Then I picked up my phone and began to tap.

We emailed back and forth for over an hour. Sometimes our exchanges were quickfire. Others had gaps when I went for a wee, replenished my glass or stared at the stars whilst considering a response. I assumed the same could be said for Ball Bag. With the addition of scratching his ball bag between messages. Maybe.

Naturally, I kicked off with a lengthy and unreserved apology and stated that my behaviour had been inexcusable. Ball Bag told me to forget it and said he imagined it couldn't be easy being me. As the result of feeling overwhelmingly relieved by his response, I surprised myself by opening up a little. I told him things weren't too great and how I hated being recognised. He suggested a big hat. I told him I happened to be the proud owner of a hat the size of small planet and had recently misplaced my flock.

And it went on from there. Half-serious messages interspersed with daftness.

I asked him what he did. '*A gardener*,' he told me.

Ah ha, I thought, as I remembered his photo on X from the Chelsea Flower Show.

'Tricky work for a bulldog,' I suggested.

'Indeed,' he replied.

He asked if the Susie Convention was going ahead. '*Who knows?*' I tapped out. '*But if it does, I'll make sure I'm cocking my leg somewhere else when it happens.*'

'I don't like TwitteX,' I told him.

'Who does? I just use it to amuse myself, what with the day job being rather solitary. Gobby dahlias aside.'

'How do you cheer yourself up if you're feeling down?'

A lengthy wait...

'I don't know Amber. I can only presume my *feeling down wouldn't be the same as yours. I duff up disobedient hollyhocks. I sing badly to music I love. I stride through the countryside in ill-fitting trousers. And just for the hell of it, I cheat the self-service till at the supermarket. But if you ever want to offload, us bulldogs are well-known for being good listeners.'*

I had to laugh at that.

We emailed a while longer. I gave away a few innocuous scraps about myself – but nothing anyone couldn't easily unearth about me. I asked a few questions – but didn't probe. It felt good to yak to a stranger. Particularly one who didn't ask the wrong things, seem to judge, or force unwanted advice my way.

It was Ball Bag who brought our online conversation to an end.

'Sorry. Have to sign off. Gotta take myself for walk. These lampposts don't get covered in piss by themselves, you know.'

I was surprised at my pang of disappointment; I'd enjoyed our 'talk' – which had served to elevate my mood and calm me after my inexcusable behaviour.

'Okay,' I told him. *'I've got things to do as well. Those one hundred lines saying 'don't attack bulldogs' don't write themselves, you know.'*

'Ah. Self-flagellation. An overrated pastime in my book. Like I said, it's all forgotten, Amber.'

'Thanks. You're quite cool for a bulldog.'

'No I'm not. I'm just dying for a piss.'

'Enjoy!'

And that was that. I stared at my phone for a few minutes, wondering if there'd be a response. Nothing. Then I looked at my empty glass and realised I urgently needed two things; a refill, and to find a lamppost of my own.

In the end, I felt too drained to get a taxi and go into Coral Bay or make the walk into Ketra, so had a nightcap on my bedroom balcony before falling into bed and an exhausted sleep

What a day.

Pool Man rocked up the next morning. At the time, I was in my usual post-failing-to-write position (so much for the break...), lounging on a sunbed and listening to a caller whingeing to Sunshine Sam about the English breakfasts not having 'sufficiently plump' and flavoursome sausages. The caller further went on, (at some length) to describe the calibre of banger he regularly enjoyed at his local Wetherspoons back home and compared the Cypriot offering to something squeezed out by a constipated chihuahua. To his credit, Sam had a plucky stab at defending the merits of Cypriot sausages; citing the popularity of the heavily spiced traditional version and placating the increasingly agitated caller by conceding, that, 'maybe' Cypriot breakfast fayre could 'never live up' to the heady delights of Wetherspoons.

'Fuck the bloke off!' I bellowed.

But said bloke was having none of it, and countered by telling Sunshine Sam how him and his missus had recently bought a retirement home in Coral Bay and were now living to regret it.

'Because of the sausages?' asked Sam, with a note of amusement.

'Yes!' came the boomed reply. 'Because of the bloody sausages and it's too bloody hot!!'

'What a prick!' I hooted with a snort of laughter.

And suddenly – there was Pool Man. Reaching for his pole.

I lowered my sunglasses and peered over them.

'What happened to you? You were meant to collect me for the beach party,' I called out.

An indifferent shrug. 'Something come up.' He said it more like a question than a statement. He flashed a Jack Nicholson grin that matched those fucking sunglasses and began his sweep of the pool.

I watched him as he slowly made his circuit with the sun glinting off his lenses. There was something about his response that nagged at me.

'Did you set me up?' I asked when he neared.

Pool Man stopped in his tracks.

'Did you have a good time?'

That bloody phrase again.

'How do you even know if I went?' I asked, loftily.

Another shrug. 'Is Cyprus.' Then a smirk of amusement as though stating the fucking obvious.

I let my sunglasses drop back into place and nodded a few times as I considered his words. Maybe the cab driver was his cousin. Maybe Costa was his long-lost uncle. Maybe Omar and Hana were his swinging bezzies. And maybe Roger was his rogerer. And the beautiful Petra, his double O spy. I sighed heavily. I'd never know. And Pool Man wasn't about to tell me.

'Is Cyprus,' I agreed with a heavy sigh. 'You can carry on,' I added with a frustrated flap of my hand. As the words left my mouth, I realised how pathetic I sounded. Pool Man didn't work for me. And I was no lady of the manor dishing out instructions to her servants.

He stood in silence for a few moments, leaving me to wonder if my rudeness had offended. Then he raised a hand, flapped it in imitation and said, 'I carry on.'

The grin.

'Oh, *piss* off!' I said, light heartedly.

To my surprise, Pool Man released a short burst of throaty laughter, which transformed what I could see of his face into something resembling handsome.

He wagged a finger in the air. 'Piss off,' he said. 'Very good. Better.'

And off he went again with his pole.

And I was left with the tail end of Sunshine Sam's apology for the previous caller's bad language and the sincere assurance that Radio Aphrodite would *always* cut off abusive callers. I wondered what kind of on-air sausage or heat-themed scuffle I'd missed during my 'exchange' with Pool Man.

I'd never know.

Like I'd never know if I'd been set up.

Or if Pool Man's day job was cover for something much murkier.

Pool Man by day. Drugs mule by night. With half a kilo wedged up his crapper.

Bad Pool Man.

Or maybe he was a fixer...

It was time to get my sorry ass back to House of Lunge – it felt like I hadn't been for ages, and I had a real urge for a bit of quality food, a gawp at the soap opera and a swat at Lunge. But when I arrived in my normal sweaty state, and gnashing my teeth because all the outside tables were taken, he was nowhere to be seen. All the old boys were in situ, playing *tavli* with their usual good humour whilst, on the

TV above, a smartly dressed Greek woman leaned forward to hiss in the ear of (assumingly) her love rival – whose eyes darted about wildly and fearfully. The faithful violins struck up. And the screen cut to some muttering, open-shirted berk. As he paced a veranda with exaggerated looks of concern, he pressed the tips of his fingers to his forehead.

Da! Da! Daaaaaah!!!!!!

Still! No! Lunnnnnge!!!!

Instead, his wife shuffled over and didn't look in the best of ways. In fact, she looked exhausted, and I wondered if she was trying to cook and serve on her own. She wearily appraised me, gestured at the menu I'd picked up – but not studied – and glanced to the outside skies, as though wishing she could just fly away into the night and be done with it all.

Not wishing to cause any delay or put her through the bother of pouring vodka, I just said 'special', asked for a Coca Cola Light and smiled sweetly before thanking her in Greek. And off she shuffled, with me sincerely hoping she had someone else helping her in the kitchen.

Apart from the love rivals having a comedy hair-pulling session, as they rocked wildly from side-to-side (resulting in a dislodged earring and distinct shift of a lacquered wig), nothing of note happened while I waited for my food – aside from the rather impressive belch from a nearby German. I kept wondering if Lunge would suddenly make a guest appearance. Where was he? Maybe he'd been delayed by a 'breech birth' *difficulties* in the toilet. Or maybe he was getting his trembling leg over with one of the women unfazed by his wandering hands. Or those teeth...

Mrs Lunge appeared beside me with my drink and food, and plonked everything down without fanfare, before making her way over to the belching German's table to clear their plates away. It was impossible to tell how old she was, but from what I'd seen in Cyprus, they did like to work their women to a ripe old age. Or maybe, just being married to Lunge aged her.

Both, I suspected.

As per usual, the food was delicious with the 'special' turning out to be meatballs, bulgar wheat, salad, and butterbeans in a rich tomato sauce. Once finished, I was eager to leave as I wanted a proper drink and rightly or wrongly, didn't want to burden Mrs Lunge with more work. With her nowhere to be seen, I tucked some Euros beneath the side plate, added a generous tip, and made my way over the cobbles to The Red Lion.

Once there, I'd barely lowered my bum onto a bar stool before Roger's yoo-hoo voice filled the air with, 'Hiya, Amber!' I fixed a smile into place before turning to seek out his doughy features at the bar. As my eyes landed on his Hawaiian shirt and travelled up to his eager face, I saw Lunge sitting beside him. A whisky in his hand and his face heavily battered.

'Sally!' he croaked across the bar as his lifted his glass in greeting.

As I mouthed, 'What?' to Roger with upturned hands pointed towards Lunge, he hopped off his bar stool and made his way over to me. His little legs couldn't carry him fast enough.

'Hi Roger,' I said, as pulled up the vacant stool beside me. 'What on earth's happened to Lunge?'

Roger's face scrunched into confusion. 'Who?'

In that moment – and for the life of me, I couldn't remember Lunge's real name. Instead, I gestured towards Lunge who was contentedly sipping on his drink and having a bit of a natter to himself. 'What happened? He looks like someone's beaten him up.'

Roger's eyes glittered with the self-importance of being the bearer of news.

'They did', he replied knowingly.

And left it at that. I could have throttled the life out of the stumpy little toad as he sat there with a smug expression.

'So... are you going to tell me, or is it some big secret I'm not meant to know?'

And in the time it took Roger to adjust his position on the bar stool, lean conspiringly towards me and drag out the word, '*Well... ... ...* ', Johnny had made my drink, placed it in front of me and given the lowdown.

None of which came as any real surprise.

Two Finnish couples. Men go to next village for their evening meal. Women go to House of Lunge for a girls' night out.

Men finish their meal and rather than go straight

back to their hotel bar, decide to detour and pick their wives up on the way.

Husband A finds Wife A being fumbled by Lunge in semi-darkness of empty restaurant, whilst Wife B sits outside, smoking a cigarette and claiming she was just about to call her husband for help.

Husband A beats shit out of Lunge. A neighbour calls Police. Blah blah blah. Lunge doesn't want charges pressed. Policeman's his cousin. Doesn't want his wife to find out. Blah blah blah. Husbands and wives leave. All shouting at one another. Wife A says she didn't want him touching her, but still gets a clip around the ear. Off they go. Blah blah blah. Lunge spends night in hospital. Wife finds out. Big story. Blah blah blah. End of story.

'I'm friends with one of the top consultants at the local hospital.' Roger announced.

Johnny and I cast him dismissive glances.

'So, is he alright? Will he back at the restaurant? Has his wife thrown him out? I asked Johnny.

'Yes - he's alright. And his wife will forgive him – they always do,' he said with a shrug. 'So, yes, he'll be back at work when he's better. And when his wife calms down. She can't run the place without him. It's too much. Even with a Filipino helping in the kitchen.'

I took a mouthful of drink and couldn't believe my first concern had been for Lunge –rather than the wife who claimed she hadn't wanted him groping her. I glanced over at Lunge, who was glumly rolling his glass between his fingers and looking very sorry for himself.

'You're right,' I said to Johnny. 'It's not real life out here, is it?'

'You see?' he replied, before tapping the bar twice and moving away to serve some customers.

Roger edged a little closer.

'I don't think it *quite* happened like that,' he said with a touch of drama. 'But Johnny's given you the gist.'

'And who do you think is the real villain? The Finnish wife? Or... him over there?'

Roger looked me in the eye and got my meaning.

'Oh, Savva's a good enough guy – we go back years. Yes, very likeable chap. But... maybe he does love the ladies a bit too much.'

'He tried to touch my tits when I first met him,' I countered, using the crude term to drum my point home.

Roger brushed some imaginary fluff off his garish shirt. 'Yes, well... ' he began, '... he's certainly not everyone's cup of tea. I *do* understand that. But... ' he trailed off.

'But, *what?*' I challenged.

Roger smoothed his shirt over his paunch before speaking. 'There's plenty of ladies who *do* seem to like him.'

I let out a derisory snort. 'And the ones who don't? Do you think it's alright his hands are all over them?'

Roger blinked steadily at me as though I was

speaking a foreign language and kept silent. I was getting nowhere. As I took a mouthful of drink and wondered if it was even worth pursuing, the loud, shrill yaps of a dog filled the air. Turning to its source, I found a Jack Russell straining at its lease, whilst its middle-aged female owner struggled to contain the dog's eagerness to enter the beer garden.

'Tyson!' the woman screeched, causing heads to turn, 'Stop pulling and calm down!'

'Tyson?' Roger sneered from behind me. 'Roland the rat, more like.'

I swivelled on my bar stool to face Roger. 'Oh, I don't know,' I said lightly. 'The last time I saw one of those dogs, it was swinging off someone's bollocks after an altercation on a nudist beach.'

Roger's face was a goggle-eyed picture to behold. '*Really?*'

Enjoying the moment, I slowly reached for a cigarette and placed it in my mouth. I flipped open my Zippo, sparked it into life, then lazily lit up and blew a plume of smoke in Roger's direction.

'Yes. Really,' I said, flatly.

As Roger's face betrayed his struggle to believe or grasp the contents of my statement, I pulled out my phone, gestured it towards him and said in a bored tone, 'Sorry, Roge... got a few people I need to get in touch with... '. I turned my back slightly, which left him sitting there for a few uncertain moments before getting up and shuffling back to Lunge with a weak, 'Catch you later'.

As I went through the infantile charade of doing something *very important* on my phone, cries of, 'Sally! Sally! *Yiamas!*' boomed across the bar, followed by the instruction to join him, '*Ela!*' I pictured Lunge holding his whisky aloft with a drunken grin and his rank teeth on show; waiting for me to look up, acknowledge, smile and go over.

I ignored him. I had a bit of dissecting to do.

Instead, I tapped out a message to Ball Bag.

'Have you ever seen a Jack Russell swinging off a naked man's bollocks? I have.'

I pinged it off with a smile and wondered if the daft sod would believe me. I'd seen plenty of things in my time but, sadly, a canine/testicles combo was not one of them.

I live in hope.

14.

Ball Bags Indeed...

The days rolled by. I had miserable attempts at Susie. Swam. Sunbathed. And Pool Man did his silent sweeps in those fucking sunglasses. I had video calls with Elena and sent her more postcards. Sunshine Sam gave cheery tips about staying out of the midday sun and how to treat 'that pesky holiday diarrhoea'. One standout caller complained that the 'Elvis' performing at his hotel was nothing like the real thing ('some doddery old fart from Yorkshire with a stutter and a taxidermist's crow on his nut'). Whilst another asked who to complain to about the lizard that'd scuttled through her bathroom window and terrorised her whilst having a (said) bout of holiday diarrhoea.

I'd be missing Sunshine Sam when I returned to England.

I decided to bitch whip the life out of Cleo and

the floppy hat, and visited Aphrodite's Rock, the stunning Saint Neophytos monastery I'd previously missed out on, any number of pretty villages and took a trip to the idyllic Adonis Baths, where I swam below a waterfall with its backdrop of rocks and lush greenery. I dotted about here and there. And took photos of the turquoise sea at Coral Bay, horned wild sheep on a return trip to Troodos, and kindly old gentleman who, literally, let me take pictures of their postcard faces as they played *tavli* outside old coffee shops or just passed the time.

And amongst it all, (and to everyone's relief) the temperature finally began to drop.

I went back to House of Lunge, where Lunge was back in situ; subdued and in subservient mode, as Mrs Lunge circled with a suspicious eye. The food was still delicious. Lunge still called me Sally. And remained resolute in his attempts to polish me off with his gratis after-dinner brandies.

I got pissed at the Red Lion as Johnny served my 'usual' with or without request – but always with two taps of the bar. I got pleasure from seeing Roger's varying expressions as I told him more outlandish lies – but stopped short of chancing the Bond Girl story a second time.

And the wobble back to villa failed to get any easier.

Eddie emailed to ask the exact date I'd be back and had another plucky stab at getting me to sell 'my story'. And I had drunken, intermittent Ball Bag exchanges, which never failed to make me smile.

I had athletic and very satisfactory sex with a Lithuanian hotel worker I met at a boom-boom-loud Coral Bay bar. In the early hours, we went back to his hotel's pool for a meeting of minds. He stood in the water as I dangled from the low springboard, wrapped my legs over his shoulders and let his experienced tongue go to town on me. Ooh la la, indeed. Then we boinged around on top of the springboard; me on my back, legs swung over my shoulders, feet planted behind my head as he squatted over me and pounded away.

Boing. Boing. Boing.

God knows if any eagle-eyed (or binocular-wielding) hotel guests could see our shenanigans from their distant balconies. I hope not.

But then again...

My old mate – the 'down, down' taxi driver, took me to Sonny's and back a couple of times and, *obviously*, turned out to be a cousin of Andreas. Who in turn, asked if I'd enjoyed myself at the beach party with a mischievous smile. DJ Puny churned out his tunes. And sunburned tourists remembered the person they once were. Or pretended to be someone else.

I stayed away from X and felt all the better for it.

I flirted with the idea of going to The Taste of Bengal for the comedy value. But quickly dismissed it. One second later.

Thoughts of Spencer could swoop when I was

alone; having a nightcap in Chez Cleo or on my bedroom balcony, where falling bougainvillea petals had begun to form a carpet. And although my heart would twist with pain, for the most part, I stayed strong.

My hair began to look a mess.

I tried not to think about my return to England.

The days rolled by.

And suddenly, I was sorting out my laundry in readiness to pack.

I spent my penultimate night at House of Lunge, followed by a last hurrah at The Red Lion. Despite looking a lot perkier, Lunge still carried the air of a wayward puppy undertaking a course in house-training. But he greeted me like a returning hero, with cries of, 'Sally!' and steered me towards ordering the special; traditional *kleftiko* with roast potatoes and salad. A fitting (and filling) send-off. The old boys played *tavli*. Whilst the telly showed a heavily-ringed hand nudging open a bedroom door. As an aghast couple tugged up sheets with open mouths and wider eyes... the violins screeched their screech.

I didn't know what to say to Lunge after I'd drained the last of my monster brandy. I suppose part of me didn't want him giving me a 'goodbye' hug in case his hands got out of hand.

What a way to think...

Instead, I patted my stomach and kissed the tips of my fingers with a smack when asked if the food was, '*Endaxi?*' and replied with an enthusiastic, '*Bomba!*' that made him reveal his gammy teeth in a wide smile. Then, with his back turned, I got up and left with mixed feelings and the half-cooked reasoning, I'd probably see Lunge in the The Red Lion once he'd finished work.

As I entered the pretty beer garden, it was as though my planets had aligned for my final visit. The seas parted and a young couple hopped off their bar stools to adjourn to a table, making space for me at the crowded bar. And I was on one of those stools almost as quickly as eagle-eyed Johnny had made my drink and placed it on a Carlsberg coaster.

A smile. Two pats. And he was off to serve the next person.

The bar was the busiest I'd seen it, making me wonder if the more bearable temperature and late season prices were attracting a fresh surge of visitors. It certainly looked that way. Impossible to miss in his toucan-themed shirt, Roger was holding court with a seemingly awe-struck middle-aged couple. Maybe he was telling them how he was related to the Queen of Sheba or best friends with Boris Johnson. Or some other boring bullshit.

I sat with my drink and took in my surroundings with a feeling of mourning for a place I was yet to leave. Hopefully, I'd be back one day.

Yeah. I'd make sure of it.

I drank my drinks and smoked cigarettes. And developed selective hearing when Roger yoo-hooed me from across the bar. Then I gazed at the star-dappled black sky and breathed in the heady scent of a nearby jasmine bush.

It was hard to believe my time in Cyprus was nearly at an end. Had my trip been a success or failure? On the writing front, it had been a resounding failure, with my latest effort seeing Susie hang gliding naked over the West Cork coastline and looking for touchdown amongst an unsuspecting group of male ramblers. Desperate writing. Terrible.

But in terms of my recovery – and despite the wobbles and breakdowns – I felt I'd made progress of sorts.

'You seem miles away,' Johnny said, as he finally took the opportunity to wipe down the bar and change the ashtray in front of me.

I smiled at his open and good-looking face and gave a small shrug.

'I fly home in two days,' I told him. 'This will be my last night coming here.'

'Amber!' he cried with outstretched arms, 'Who am I going to make so many vodkas for?' I raised myself from my stool to meet Johnny's embrace halfway across the bar. As he released me from his tight squeeze, he cupped my head and gently pulled it forward to land a light kiss on my temple. And for an egotistical moment, I wondered why he'd never made a pass at me. The moment dissolved as Johnny roughly ruffled my hair.

'You're going to get your arse straight to a

hairdresser when you get back – right?'

As I lowered myself back down, I laughed and ran a hand through my hair in attempt to restore some sense of order.

I picked up my drink and raised it. 'It's top of the list. *Believe* me.'

'Good,' Johnny said. A smile. Two pats. And off he went.

I didn't see Lunge (or his teeth) again. And I think I'm pleased. Maybe there'd been some brandy-swilling stragglers at the restaurant. Or a crucial game of *tavli* had dragged on. Or maybe, he'd gone straight home to catch up on the dreaded soap opera. But that was that with Lunge. And I was Sally no more.

After I had my fill of vodka, I felt a drunken impulse to do something that had just occurred to me, wasn't thought through and was, in all probability, wanky of the highest order – but inexplicably, just seemed like a good idea at the time. I got my things together and made my way over to Roger – who had the same couple hanging off his every word. As I neared, I could hear, "Ambassador" and "dinner party" being rolled out in the same sentence. With apologies, I interrupted and squeezed past Roger's audience as he was mid-flow about something involving "outstanding asparagus". As I advanced upon him, he took a step back in surprise or trepidation, and when I cupped a hand to his ear and began to whisper, his face was everything I'd hoped it'd be.

When I'd finished, I patted him on the shoulder,

excused myself past the couple again and walked away. I ignored Roger's calls for me to come back. Instead, I raised both arms and wiggled my fingers in a toodle-oo farewell as the grin widened across my face.

At least he could now honestly claim that he'd met someone famous. Or infamous, rather. No mention of *that* night, but I had let him know I was a top-selling author, who had written chunks of her book on a nudist beach.

As I realised Roger might decide the Jack Russell story held some truth, I let out a snort of laughter. Well, at least it'd give him something else to tell his captives.

Mission completed, I returned to my bar stool and patiently stood beside it until Johnny had the chance to come over.

'You're leaving... *now?*' he asked, with a frown. 'Let me get you a drink on the house.'

I shook my head and thanked him for the offer; on top of Lunge's brandy, I'd *really* had enough.

'Will you be coming back to Cyprus?'

I honestly didn't know, so told him.

'I'll certainly miss this place,' I conceded. 'It's been really great.'

'Despite it not being real life?' Johnny asked with a raised eyebrow and smile.

'I suspect Cyprus has been good for me *because* it's not real life.' As the words spilled out, I realised the truth in them.

Johnny cocked his head to one side, 'Maybe'.

He looked at me with an unfamiliar intensity that I found unsettling. Unsure, and having already received a goodbye kiss, I put my hand forward for him to shake. Johnny let out a laugh as took it and pulled me closer to the bar.

'Just for the record, you're a very beautiful woman. And as for those green eyes... they're... not real life.'

Then he winked at me, 'Safe travels, Amber. See you next time'. Then he released me, patted the bar twice and walked away. Leaving me with my hand momentarily hanging in the air, my mouth open at his compliment, and once more wondering why we'd never got it on.

'Thanks for the Greek lessons!' I called after him. But he was already busy serving. And my voice swallowed up by the din of conversations.

On my wobble back to the villa, I waved my phone torch about and had a little natter to myself, as to why I'd been so remiss by not having sex with a Cypriot during my stay. Then I nattered back that it was probably for the best – after all, I had no idea if I'd ever return – and it just felt *simpler* that all my liaisons had been like ships passing in the night. And as I discussed *all of this* with myself at some length, I barely noticed the sudden gust of wind that swept over Ketra's hills and made my flesh prickle with goose bumps as charcoal clouds rolled overhead.

*

I was surprised to see Pool Man on my last full day. I hadn't really thought about it, but assumed he'd be rocking up once I'd vacated the villa, to get the pool spic and span for the next guests. Up until that point, my morning had been pretty productive. Most of my things were packed and I'd nearly cleared out everything from the fridge and cupboards. As a reward, I treated myself to a final swim and was busy adding to my deep tan when he arrived. I was initially unaware of his arrival, as I'd been pointlessly trying to calculate how much I'd spent on Factor 30 during my stay. I failed to work it out, but felt *positive* shares in a certain well-known brand would tumble once I got home.

When I caught him reaching for his pole and plunging it in the pool, I lowered my sunglasses and called over.

'It's *tomorrow* I'm going home! Shouldn't you be here *tomorrow* instead?'

That grin. The shrug. Those fucking sunglasses.

And off he silently went.

Leaving me to settle back down on my lounger, wonder why I bothered with him, and to listen to Radio Aphrodite belt out the aptly named 90's hit, 'Things can only get better'.

I could only live in hope...

When he'd finished his pool bumfuckery, Pool Man spoke. With a jolt, I opened my eyes and saw him standing about 10 feet away. His pole was nowhere to be seen.

'I'm going now.'

'O... kay... ' I replied, feeling unsure of the appropriate pool-themed etiquette for saying goodbye. As I groped around for something cheery to say, Pool Man did the unimaginable; he took his sunglasses off. And smiled at me. And had intelligent, attractive eyes. And was really quite handsome in his craggy way.

And... as I looked some more... he reminded me of someone.

Omar.

I noticed he was appraising me. But despite all the weeks of him seeing me naked, without his sunglasses on, I suddenly felt brutally exposed under his gaze. And what? Who? Was he Omar's cousin? Brother? What?

As I squinted up with a half tug of my towel to cover myself – and my head full of unformulated questions – the sunglasses were back in place, the grin returned, a finger was flicked off his temple and he left.

'Yeah... bye... ' I mumbled after him as I let the towel drop.

And that was Pool Man done and dusted.

Funny old thing.

Whoever he was...

... and what the *fuck* happened to his earphones from the first day?

*

An hour or so after Pool Man's departure, I felt unable to settle – a mixture of pre-flight fidgets, things still to pack, a desire to stay forever and another to just get it all over with and get back home. With reluctance, I gathered up my towel and sun oil, sighed at the view and turned off Radio Aphrodite with a genuine feeling of regret.

Inside the villa, I pottered about, put the poolside towels in the wash, waved an iron over the clothes I'd be wearing that night and for the trip home, packed away a few more things and pulled a couple back out.

Then it was time to shower, get ready, and hang up the towels as I waited for my non 'down, down' taxi to arrive. It took me to a seafront restaurant in nearby Chloraka, where it soon became evident, I'd misjudged the time of my booking to coincide with its 'stunning sunset views' by failing to consider the shortening days.

I had dressed to impress myself for my last night and wore a stretchy, strappy turquoise dress that brought out every inch of suntan I'd worked so hard for. And when I clip-clopped my way into the restaurant in the one pair of high heel sandals I'd brought with me, and showed off my new teeth to the waiter, I wasn't surprised to be given one of the prime tables at the front, where I could at least admire the final faint glows of the sun as puffy clouds loomed low in the sky.

After a starter of grilled calamari served with wedges of lemon, I tucked into a main course of *dolmades* – vine leaves filled with pork and rice – with salad and a pile of those irresistible chips. As I ate and gazed at the darkening sky, I found it hard to believe I'd be back in my Exeter flat in less than 24 hours, and probably having something crappy delivered for my dinner. Amongst so much more, I'd miss the wonderful Cypriot food.

I smiled when my polite refusal of the dessert menu resulted in a plate of syrup-drenched, deep fried dough balls being placed in front of me minutes later. I thanked the young waiter and blew the air from my cheeks as I picked up the accompanying spoon.

'Some people eat to live, but us Cypriots live to eat,' the waiter said proudly.

'So I've seen,' I replied. 'You certainly like fattening everyone up.'

The waiter gave the familiar shrug. 'Why not? Live for today, you can die tomorrow.' As he walked away, I mulled over his words for a few moments, gave a shrug of my own, and set my spoon to work.

Once finished at the restaurant, I went for a brief seafront walk to let the food go down. Unsurprisingly, my heels didn't prove to be best equipped for my intentions and after a while, I perched on one of the boulders by the promenade, lit a cigarette and listened to the hypnotic rolls of the sea. I wondered what life would be like on my return: the non-too-distant book launch, the subsequent book signing sessions, returning to work on Susie in earnest and the possibility of the convention going ahead.

And felt totally and utterly lost.

I stood and faced the sea and felt the warm breeze sweep over me. If only it held some answers. I shook myself out of my odd mood. 'Come on, girl,' I said aloud. 'Time for your last Cypriot piss-up!'

I'd always had it mind to spend my last night at Sonny's. And although The Red Lion was the first bar I'd ventured to – and despite Johnny's faultless hospitality – it was at Sonny's where I felt the most at home. Partly, because of Andreas. But also the fact there was more going on in there – which, in turn, gave me some much-needed distraction. Or relief.

So, Sonny's it was.

Andreas spotted me as I walked towards the bar and made a big deal about looking me up and down, before placing two fingers in his mouth for a mock wolf-whistle.

Flagging me over, he called out, '*Ela* Miss World!' then gestured with both hands to my usual corner.

I hammed it up by sashaying towards him, one hand on my hip and laughing because the feminist in me was a two-faced cow.

'Amber! You look like crazy good tonight!' he said, once I'd popped myself onto a bar stool.

I placed a hand on my chest, fluttered my eyelids and replied. 'Why thank you, kind sir – it's my last night, so thought I'd make an effort.'

With a degree of surprise, I saw genuine disappointment register on Andreas's face.

He threw his hands in the air. 'How is this possible! I thought you were going to live here forever!'

'If only,' I said with a laugh. 'I've done my 90 days, so now it's back to cold and miserable England.'

'Will you be coming back?'

'Maybe. I hope so.'

My first two drinks were on the house. Like The Red Lion, it wasn't my first freebie and came as a gesture of thanks for repeat custom, or when trying to gain loyalty from newly arrived tourists who were eager to find their 'local' for the holiday and came bearing beer vouchers.

As I sat on my bar stool, I recalled the feeling of expat smugness when my drink price dropped from 'tourist price' to 'local's price' once Andreas discovered the length of my stay.

Verrrry nice. But not something I'd achieved at The Red Lion – but with their keen 'village' prices, the occasional vodka 'on the house' was just an added bonus.

I drank my drinks, smoked a few cigarettes and watched a tired-looking DJ Puny spin his tunes for 80s Nite. I was glad to see he'd done away with his sweat-inducing props and instead, was seemingly channelling his inner Bros or Erasure by wearing a simple white t-shirt, with the baseball cap nowhere to be seen. It was the first time I'd seen his hair, which was thick, sandy-coloured and cut surprisingly stylishly. He looked like a different person. Better. Cooler. But ye gods, the lad looked knackered.

I knew some of the Cypriots could work a whole season without taking a day off – and supposed DJ Puny was no different – what with every nite being a whatever nite. Hopefully, everyone would be getting a breather before too long – now the season was beginning to wind down.

I watched happy tourists shake their stuff to The Eurythmics, Police, Pet Shop Boys, Simply Red etcetera etcetera. And snorted with laughter when an old boy's over ambitious move, saw him stagger towards a table and stumble headfirst between the legs of a shorts-wearing female about the same age as me. The surprise caused the woman to jerk the glass she was holding which, in turn, resulted in her cocktail slopping over the old boy's balding head, along with a tasselled foil cocktail stick – which comically attached itself to his pate like a sparkly octopus before slowly sliding off.

The woman took it all in good humour, and as the old boy used her knees as leverage to climb back up, I could see that his offer of a replacement drink was being laughed away. Then, as A-ha's 'Take on Me' filled the air, he was off again. Bouncing around the dance floor like a teenager and not giving a single fuck about his wet clothes or the imaginary cow he should have been milking.

What a legend.

With a smile, I picked up my phone and tapped out a message to Ball Bag.

'I've just seen a dance-crazed pensioner plunge headfirst between the legs of a cocktail wielding woman.'

And off it pinged.

His reply came within minutes.

'Are you at some kind of drug-fuelled foam party?'

With an abrupt bark of laughter that drew attention, I realised Ball Bag had no context without knowing where I was. I briefly toyed with telling him, but decided against it. We'd come this far – what would be the point when I was on the cusp of return?

'I'm sworn to secrecy. But this old fella is incredible. Doesn't give a fuck. He's just out there enjoying himself.'

'I hope that's me in years to come,' came the reply. *'I'll be dancing and farting my way down the aisles at Tesco and using my falsies as castanets.'*

I felt the grin widen across my face. Silly sod. I took a large mouthful of my drink and decided I couldn't be outdone. As I struggled to come up with a witty response, I looked across to the dance floor, where the old boy was waving his arms around and singing along to the chorus of 'Come on Eileen'.

The powers of vodka worked their magic.

'Never mind all that,' I wrote. *'When I'm old, I'm going to dye my hair purple, eat sausages and spend all my pension money at the bookies.'*

And off it went.

'Another drink, Amber?'

I looked at Andreas, who was pointing to my near empty glass. I quickly calculated how many drinks I'd had – including the couple at the restaurant – then thought of my flight time and that final bit of packing. With a heavy heart, I put my palm over the top of my glass as a signal.

'Sadly not, I'm afraid. My flight's in the morning.'

Andreas scrunched up his face. 'One *little* shot of tequila from me?' he pleaded as he pinched his thumb and forefinger together.

'Okay,' I replied, before reaching across to lightly rest a hand on his forearm. 'And *thank you* for looking after me.'

Andreas put a hand over my mine. 'Amber – it's been my pleasure.' As he gave my hand a squeeze, I half-expected him to wish me a safe flight. Instead, he said, 'And I hope your future is better.'

For a few moments, we held each other's gaze before I spoke.

'You *know?* About *me?*'

Andreas patted my hand twice, took his away and shrugged.

'A tourist showed me his newspaper because I was in the background of the photo.'

I lifted my hand from his arm and pressed my fingers to my lips in surprise. I knew exactly what photo he was referring to.

'You never said,' I half-whispered. 'I didn't see it, but I heard it wasn't nice about me.'

'Hey, you're life back in England – it's not my business. I'm just here to pour drinks and make customers happy. Besides, you seem like a very good person. A little bit drunk. A little bit crazy. But a good person. That's all I need to know.'

Andreas must have sensed I was building up to an emotional and dewy-eyed outpouring of sorts, as he sharply tapped the bar twice and brightly announced, 'Okay! Tequila time!' As I watched him fix a round of shots that included my Cypriot chums at the end of bar, I could barely believe he'd known the bones of my backstory for so long without previously mentioning it. He'd just let me *be.*

What a legend. Another one.

When the tequilas were divvyed out, I raised my glass and said a loud, '*Yiamas!*' to mirror the guys. A lick of salt. Down the hatch. A wincing suck on a lemon. And the immediate thought, 'Maybe this wasn't such a good idea,' as the liquid heat travelled down my throat and made my eyes water.

And then it was time to say goodbye.

'Make sure you come and visit again.'

'I'll try!'

'Ah! That'll be good. Very good. And what will you be doing back in England?'

I considered for a moment.

'Listening to lots of music from this century.'

And as if fully rehearsed, we ha-ha'd at the same time, before tapping the bar twice and pointing a finger at one another.

'Goodbye Andreas. And *thanks,* yeah?'

'Goodbye crazy lady. See you soon.'

I smiled warmly at Andreas, turned and clip-clopped my way towards the street. As I gave the dance floor a final glance and saw the old boy jigging away to Culture Club's 'Karma Chameleon' with shoulder-lifting moves, I glanced beyond and caught DJ Puny looking at me. With a grin, he gave me a thumbs-up and gestured at the dance floor, inviting me to join the other dancers. With a laugh, I waved a spread-fingered hand in decline. Puny gave me an 'at least I tried' shrug before a small wave of goodnight. Or goodbye. I returned the gesture and carried on with the hope he'd be getting a decent break soon and some of the local pork chops down his throat.

That lad seriously needed feeding up.

Once on the street, it seemed inevitable that the cruising taxi I flagged down would be my old 'down, down' mate. For old times' sake, I took one of his offered Rothmans and blew smoke out the back window as we drove in a comfortable silence, past the drag's neon signs and hillside lights towards the villa.

With my last '*kalinichta*' done for the trip, the taxi rumbled away. I went inside and took a few moments to decide where to have a tame nightcap. Chez Cleo or watching the twinkles from my bedroom balcony.

Twinkles. Had to be.

Decision made, I kicked off my sandals, grabbed a tray of ice cubes from the freezer and made my way upstairs. Clothes off. Wrap tied around my waist. Ice emptied into ice bucket. Mini fridge raided. And after the hit of tequila, a long and weak drink poured.

Out on the balcony, I stood at its end, breathed in the scent of jasmine, listened to the crickets and watched the flicker of twinkles from Ketra and beyond. As I sipped my drink and felt pleased at how my goodbyes had gone, a sudden shiver ran through me. That temperature was certainly dropping. I nipped back into the bedroom, slipped on the vest I'd worn earlier in the day, returned to the balcony and settled on the seat.

Another sip. A cigarette lit. A check of my phone. A smile at seeing a Ball Bag email waiting for me.

'Ha! Let's see what you've got in your locker, you daft old bulldog!' I opened the message with the expectation of a witty response.

Instead, as I read and then re-read, the seven familiar words on the screen, I felt shock, anger and above all, betrayal, jolt through me.

'Dear Lord, where will it all end?'

And there I had it: Ball Bag Derek was Luke.

How the *fuck* did I not spot it?

15.

All Change

As I toyed with the chunk of olive bread, I cursed my stupidity for getting so drunk. Speed drinking had not been a good plan. At all. *What a night*. What a headfuck of a fucking bastard night. And as if to match my mood, the Cypriot skies had chosen today of all days to start pissing down with rain.

I let the bread drop from my hand, took a gulp of black coffee and lit a cigarette.

'Well, that was a fucking waste of time, wasn't it, Pool Man?' I asked out loud, as I surveyed the layer of bougainvillea petals and debris floating on the pool. From my spot on the covered veranda, it was as though nothing looked recognisable with the heavy sheets of rain and overcast skies. It all looked as grim as I felt.

As I blew out a plume of smoke, I shook my head as I thought back to some of the key points from the previous night.

How I'd stared at the phone in my hand and trembled with rage.

How I'd paced the balcony, smoking and drinking as I tried to conjure up the right response.

And how, in the end, I just thought, 'fuck it' and dialled Luke's number. When it rang out to voicemail, there was no disguising the anger in my voice as I left a message, 'Luke. *Call me.* I *know* it's you'.

Then I paced. Smoked. Drank. And laughed hysterically into the night. Then I tried to fathom out if Luke had been using the 'dear Lord' expression first or if it had been me. But one thing was certain; he'd used those *exact* words when we spotted the canoeist with binoculars during our afternoon on nudey beach.

I poured myself another drink.

And then he rang.

For several moments there was a heavy silence as we waited for the other to speak. If it had gone on any longer, I would have half-expected the screeching violins to burst into life. But Luke broke cover first with a simple, 'I'm so sorry, Amber'. And before I could reply, he launched into a long, rambling and pleading speech to explain his actions – which left little or no room for interruption.

I paced and drank and smoked and pulled various faces, as Luke explained everything he'd done had come from a good place; from caring about me. That when I'd told him after the trial, I wanted nothing more to do with him, he'd felt unconvinced I really meant it. That I was still grieving. With my head all over the place. He had wanted to keep a connection between us, but didn't know how. And as I'd previously ignored his messages, he later found a way when discovering I was on X. He then created Ball Bag Derek, and once his account looked credible, followed me. Which was duly reciprocated the next day. He'd (rightly) assumed the majority of my posts were coming from someone at the publishers (suggesting he'd seen my drunken ones) and the only way he could get my attention, was by posting the kind of nonsense we'd previously enjoyed together. He hadn't entirely thought through his actions or knew what his end goal had been, but when I made contact, his overriding emotions had been of extreme pleasure matched with gut-wrenching guilt.

How could he tell me who he was, when we were messing around and having fun?

Particularly as he'd hoped our nonsense was giving me some respite from my – doubtless – ongoing pain.

And when we had our one serious exchange, he'd been *so* close to telling me – but decided the timing was all wrong. And then it was too late. And became impossible.

Until his earlier schoolboy error.

But now I knew. And hopefully knew nothing was done with malice or intent to harm. He still cared about me. Very much. And was whole-heartedly sorry. So very, very sorry.

Luke fell into silence. It had been quite a speech.

I examined the cigarette between my fingers. '*So*... was your schoolboy error intentional?' I asked. 'After all, you're hardly stupid'.

A long pause. A heavy sigh that travelled across the miles.

'... I don't believe that's what I did.' Then, 'Not consciously, anyway.'

'Mmm. And you don't think a text or smoke signal would have been better – to see if I was up to communicating, rather than having me believe I was enjoying a bit of banter with some random who only knew the headline bones of me?'

Another sigh. 'I know, I know... ' Luke muttered, '... I don't have anything to say in defence... I guess I was afraid of more rejection. And at least this way, we had contact. I just... *missed you*.'

I blew out my last drag, crushed the cigarette into the ashtray and looked at Chez Cleo's sodden drapes flapping in the wind. They looked ruined. Everything was ruined.

'We *can't*. I've *told you*. Spencer died because of *us*.'

The silence that followed was so thick, I felt I could I reach my hand into it.

'So... Mister Gardener... ' I said with faux breeziness, '... Kew Gardens and the pissing dog. Were you really there? Or was that another lie?'

A half-laugh that held no humour. 'There.

Doing a commission.' Luke said with a flat tone of resignation.

I began to reach for another cigarette but decided against it.

'Look, I have to go, now,' I said brusquely. 'I've got a flight to catch in the morning.' And just like Luke, the words were out there.

Accidentally or not.

'Oh? Coming or going?' Followed by, 'Sorry... I know it's got nothing to do with me.'

As I looked at the lashing rain, I decided it no longer mattered. 'Coming back. I've been in Cyprus for a while.'

'Did you... ' he began, before trailing off.

'Look, I really need to get going, Luke. I can't do this now. *Any* of it.'

'... Okay. Understood. I'll leave you to it. Safe travels, Amber.'

'Thanks,' I said, surprised at the warmth in my voice.

Maybe Luke took it as a thawing between us, as he quickly jumped back in. 'You know, Amber... I get that it's been 100 per cent worse for you... I really get that and can't begin to imagine... but it really affected me as well. Knowing it should have been me. What happened to Spencer. It's been... tough, you know? *Really* tough to process. And losing you as well... '

'I can't do this,' I whispered before ending the call.

As I stared at the pool and watched bobbing petals get battered by the rain, I realised my fingers were on my forehead, feeling their way around my scar.

I'd hoped I'd finished with all of that.

All of *that*...

There was an eerie silence when I entered the flat; it felt alien and as though I had been away far longer. With a final effort, I lugged in my suitcases and wandered into the lounge. There, on the coffee table, sat a neatly piled stack of post – courtesy of Elena – but aside from that, it looked exactly as I'd left it. The air felt still. Silent. And cold. The flat felt of nothingness. And emptiness.

Had it really been only eight hours or so since I'd ceremoniously left my floppy hat on the stripped jumbo bed and said goodbye to the villa and island I'd grown to love?

With a sigh, I wandered over to the central heating panel and put it on for a blast. Heat first. Close the curtains against the grey English skies. Then a black coffee. Unpacking. Washing machine on. Shower. Then order a god-knows-what takeaway, which'd doubtless taste like cardboard compared to what I'd been used to. TV. Vodka. Bed. Sleep.

It had been a long day. With a seemingly endless flight. Which I'd mostly spent with my head pressed against the window as I watched the island of lurve disappear from view, before launching into a one-sided argument with Luke that drove me half-crazy. Round and round. Then round some more. And each time finding a new injustice to tag onto my mounting list of grievances. Whilst bobbing away in the background, the root of my pain vied for my attention.

And as ever, finally succeeded.

Vodka. Vodka. Bed. Sleep.

A marvellous plan.

We broke from our tight hug. 'You look like a bloody scarecrow!' Elena said with a laugh. 'Albeit an extremely tanned one – Jesus, just look at the colour of you!'

I hadn't realised how much I'd missed her. As she tackled my scarecrow locks, we chattered away non-stop as though it had been years, and not a matter of a few months since we'd last spoke and had never hooked up on Zoom regularly. Elena thanked me for the 'old school' postcards – which she'd enjoyed and kept on a corkboard in her kitchen. Things with Adam were still good. Still exciting. And she surprised me by saying I'd had some great Susie reviews, and that I'd have to 'grow some' and have a look.

'I've not looked at anything for yonks,' I told her.

Elena leaned over my shoulder and smiled as she spoke to my reflection in the mirror. 'I know – you told me. But you should. The fans far outweigh the trolls. And they obviously love your mad Susie bollocks.'

'Bollocks, indeed,' I sighed.

Elena shook me gently by the shoulders. 'Can you roll up your bottom lip whilst you're in my salon, please? Not everyone is out to get you. Sure, there's some cockwipe trolls out there or readers who simply didn't get along with your work. But surely, every writer has to put up with that? So just give yourself a break for 5 minutes. New beginnings, eh?'

I reached up from beneath my gown and squeezed one of her hands. 'You're always right. That's why I love you. And I apologise for my default self-pity. It's just... my writer's block still hasn't buggered off and I'm due to speak to my publisher in the next day or so, and everything just feels so *big* – the launch, the book signings and all that. It's not so much if people don't like my work... although I guess that will always sting... but after everything that's happened, I'm not sure I can handle the unwanted publicity that'll come hand in hand with the book stuff. You know, the prying questions, the assumptions, the accusations... the *judgement*.'

'I hear you,' said Elena. 'So you'll just have to take back some control where you can, so you'll feel in a better place to face whatever comes your way. When you were in Cyprus, you mentioned you were thinking about selling that bastard flat. Why not start with that?'

I smiled up at her. 'Does your boyfriend know how wonderful you are?'

Elena gave my shoulders a final squeeze. 'I never stop reminding him,' she said with a wink.

As she straightened and got back to work, we kicked around some loose ideas for where I could move to. Maybe somewhere nicer in Exeter? Maybe somewhere coastal in Dorset, Devon or Cornwall? Rural was dismissed for being too remote. Bristol was a possibility. London a definite no go.

'Just get the agents around and get that bloody place up for sale – you'll feel better once you're somewhere new and will probably start writing again. Something with an inspiring view to get your creative juices going,' Elena instructed, as she added the finishing touches to my cut.

'I will,' I promised. And meant it. The whole idea of getting shot of the flat had been picking up traction during my final weeks in Cyprus, and now, with Elena's enthusiastic approval, I felt more than ready to take the plunge and set the wheels in motion.

'Glad to hear it. And with a bit of control back, maybe you'll feel better equipped to tackle these book events. You should be enjoying them, Amber. Not filled with dread. I guess, people will be curious about you for a while yet, regardless of how you're feeling – it's just human nature – so you'll have to somehow learn how to live with it, or it'll take you over and you'll be spending your days hiding beneath the duvet, wherever you live. You've worked for this, Amber, so enjoy it! The good and the bad!'

'You're a good friend,' I told Elena in a thick voice, as emotion welled up behind my eyes.

'Oh, stop that, you dozy mare, or you'll start me off. Here, let's wave a hairdryer over you, get some wax on, then I can pack you off into the streets to fend for yourself.'

'God, you're heartless woman.'

When my hair was done, I tilted my head from side-to-side and admired it in the mirror. After the *just about* passable results in Coral Cutz, I was back to me again. And when I left the salon, with Elena's words and advice still ringing in my ears, my new haircut felt symbolic of the changes I wanted to make in my life.

'Drinks sometime?' I asked Elena after I'd paid.

'Definitely. Let me see when I get some free time and I'll message. You take care, right?'

'Great. And you take care, too. And by the way... cockwipe... excellent word choice. Think I'll nick it.'

'You're welcome!' Elena trilled with fluttering eyelids.

'Oh!' I said, plucking the spa vouchers from my handbag, 'These are for you, as a thank you for keeping an eye on my flat. It's *really* appreciated.' And as Elena examined the vouchers in her hand with a look of surprise, I turned and walked out of the salon. I didn't need any thanks. I was the grateful one.

I strode past the burger bar that was once The Grub Shack, giving it neither a thought nor a glance.

Then picked up pace as ideas for getting some control back into my life began to formulate. I felt buoyed and excited.

Flat. Eddie. Or maybe, Eddie first. Flat second. And Luke? What to do about him? Anything? Nothing?

I'd chosen not to speak to Elena about Luke and his deception. It was too recent. Too raw. And despite having some time to absorb Luke's words and understanding that, he too, had been affected, his ongoing duplicity couldn't be dismissed or simply brushed aside. He had falsely gained a degree of my trust whilst working on my own recovery. And the gain of our online relationship had been entirely tipped in his favour. He was getting what he wanted from it – as was I on a superficial basis – but, ultimately, I was entirely unaware of its reality.

We'd not been on a level playing field.

Advantage Luke.

Advantage Ball Bag.

It was as simple as that.

I had reached Cathedral Green. Home to the art gallery where I'd first met Clarke. I felt surprised and glad to see it was no longer there and had been replaced by a speciality loose tea and coffee bean shop.

Things move on. They always do.

As I continued on my way towards the flat, over the cobbled street and past students enjoying some late autumn sun on the grass beside the cathedral,

I noticed two women and a man walking slowly towards me, staring and talking behind cupped hands. They looked like office workers and to confirm any doubt of what they were talking about, one of the women lightly touched a crooked finger to her forehead before all eyes returned to me.

Panic flickered across their eyes as I marched towards them with open arms and a wide grin.

'Yes, it's me!' I said loudly, before performing a full twirl which came to a halt in front of the trio.

With satisfaction, I saw their faces flush with embarrassment. 'Oh, I'm sorry,' stammered one of the women. 'We thought you were someone else.'

I lowered my arms and laughed. 'That's the kind of lie only a mother would believe,' I told her. 'Still, at least you've all got something to put in your diaries – meeting big, bad Amber.' I waved my opened hands and performed a naff, horror film, 'Woooooaaaahhh!' before flicking a salute off my temple. 'Enjoy the rest of your day!' I cheerily wished them. And off I went.

Feeling pretty pleased with myself.

'So, have you got your shit together now?' There was no malice in Eddie's question and I was strangely appreciative of his bluntness.

'Well, head-wise, I'm feeling a bit more... grounded... if that's the right word. But on the writing front, it's the same – nothing doing. *But...* I'm putting the flat up for sale and feel hopeful of getting my writing back on track once I've got away from here. Somewhere *new*. Then I'll feel ready to get my Susie hands tap-tap-tapping away. I'm sure of it.'

During the silence that followed, I considered my lie. The truth was, Susie had packed her bags for good and pissed off. I no longer felt any connection to her. And didn't feel convinced that forcing myself to do a sequel would bear any worthwhile results. It certainly hadn't to-date.

'Forgive me for saying this,' Eddie began in a measured tone, 'but first, you had to get away. Now you have to move. For all I know, you'll move and there'll be something else stopping you from writing. The convention's going ahead in Brighton next February, which would provide the perfect platform for giving a rough release date for the sequel and garnering substantial interest. We've invested time, resources and money – so please excuse my scepticism that another obstacle might present itself in one form or another.'

As I heard his words, I bit on my lower lip; I had no idea what to tell him. Eddie had been the only one to take a risk with Susie and given me exactly what I'd sought.

At the time.

Yet I'd begun to have an unformulated hankering to write something different to a disastrous chick lit. Something a bit more 'heavyweight'. Less of a joke. Despite how well it paid. As though reading my mind, Eddie broke me from my thoughts.

'I take it you've seen your royalties payment?'

I had. The money had dropped into my account the day after I arrived back in England. The sum had been quite remarkable, and I'd felt sure there'd been an error. But one of Eddie's team sent me a statement report of sales a few hours later. Everything seemed present and correct. Yet still unbelievable.

The money was most welcome. After all, I'd been living off Spencer's inheritance, and despite there being a substantial sum left, I felt relief when seeing I'd be more than capable of finally supporting myself. Spencer's money could be there for emergencies or spending on something fittingly special.

'Yes, I have,' I told Eddie. 'It was... erm... quite a shock.'

'Well... get your arse into gear – with no more fucking around, and there'll be plenty more.'

'It's just been... *difficult*... you know?'

'Look, Amber... I'm not quite the monster everyone believes me to be. Just do it in bite-sized chunks. Chapter by chapter. Then when each one is done, send it over and I'll get the editorial team onto it. If you're struggling, they'll be able to give you advice, pointers – that kind of stuff.'

'And galvanise me into life with encouragement?'

A snort from Eddie. 'Something like that.'

A thought suddenly occurred to me. 'And once the sequel's done, would you then be expecting a series or would I be able to do something else?'

'Well, it depends what you've got in mind. I mean, you're not considering... '

'No,' I said firmly. 'I'm not sure yet what I'd like to do. Just something less *crappy*.'

'I'll save you the dodgy Yorkshire accent, Amber – but where there's muck, there's brass.'

'Maybe so,' I conceded. 'But I'd rather not go to my grave known as the woman who invented a daffy mare with a bastard perm and large blouse collection.'

Eddie sighed. 'Unfortunately, you'll be remembered for a lot more than that.'

'Yes... I expect so,' I conceded.

'Look... do this sequel with the help of my team. We can make as collaborative as you like. Once that's done, you can give me an outline of what you want to work on next, and let's talk. No more Susie. No series. Just a change of direction. *If* I think it's a good one. And viable. Of course. What say you?'

His suggestion seemed a reasonable solution: I knock out a 'wind assisted' sequel; Eddie makes money; I make money; I wave ta-ta to Susie the traitor; I get a bit of time to work out what my next direction might be; Eddie makes money from that; I get to feel like a 'real' writer.

Win-win.

'Okay. That sounds like a brilliant compromise. Thank you. And I don't have to go to the convention?'

'I'd prefer if you did. But it's entirely up to you.

Last I saw, there's a plan for a giant inflatable Susie to stand outside the hotel entrance. It'll probably get covered in seagull shit. But there you go. Where's there's muck... '

'Or bird shit,' I suggested. 'And Susie's launch?'

'Yep. All happening three weeks today. In Exeter. We were going to do the London flagship store first... but Exeter... well, that's where you're from. Made sense.'

'Ha! You mean, it's where I'm most well-known.'

'It's good business sense, Amber. Exeter, London, then the rest. You should already have a full list of all the national book-signing dates.'

I did. I'd received the email from Eddie's office when in Cyprus. I'd seen the heading in the subject matter, but for reasons unknown, hadn't looked at it. Instead, I'd wandered down to my sun lounger and allowed myself to be distracted by yet another of Sunshine Sam's callers rueing their visit to The Taste of Bengal.

Reasons unknown. Who was I kidding?

'Yeah. Got it,' I told him. 'Just need to look at it again,' I lied.

'You do that,' Eddie said. 'The Exeter one will have a few of my other authors there to give a bit of self-serving support – along with industry professionals, who'll be giving you some press. And of course, there'll be the great unwashed, expecting a reading, a brief Q&A session and their books signed. The usual stuff.'

'Usual to you,' I replied, as I fought back a feeling of trepidation.

'You'll be fine, Amber. A touch of nerves is normal. Get the first one under your belt and the rest will be a piece of piss. Oh! And before you go, I see you've been missing in action on X.'

'The truth?' I asked rhetorically with a sigh. 'It makes me unhappy. I don't even want to look at it. It's toxic.'

'Well, I can't disagree with that, although I'm not sure how long your enigmatic approach can continue. Readers want their writers online. Simple.'

'Well, judging by the figures, it doesn't seem as though it's affecting sales,' I countered. 'Unless they're lower than you'd hoped?'

Eddie whistled through his teeth. 'That they're not, Amber. That's for sure. I don't know... maybe there's something in your perceived aloofness and cloud of mystique. Look, we can talk about this again, and in the meanwhile, my team can carry on posting stuff. Just crack on with those bite-sized chunks so we can get something out next year. Then... we'll see what ideas you have for something else. Just no more of this... *bollocks*... okay?'

'That's my plan. No more bollocks,' I said, meaning every word. 'And Eddie... *thanks* for putting up with me while... '

Eddie cut me off midflow. 'To be honest, Amber, you're a total fucking nightmare. Look, I'll see you in 3 weeks' time. And for the love of God... get bite-sizing before I lose the will to live.'

'Will do!' I laughed. But he was already gone.

'I love your plan, you big old, scary shark,' I said aloud to no one. 'It's a plan and it *might* just work.' And just like that, I felt revitalised to get stuck back in with Susie. It all felt less *daunting*. A bit of support from HQ sounded ideal and would hopefully get me over the finishing line sooner rather than later. And then? Freedom to write something else.

'But,' I added, with a finger raised in the air, 'don't go biting the hand that's keeping you in gold cufflinks, Mister Hirst.'

And as I hummed 'Mack the Knife', I browsed online for a local estate agent.

Check me getting my shit together.

16.

A Voice from the Past

'So, it's up for sale?' asked Elena.

I clinked my wine glass against hers. 'It is, indeed. Some shiny-faced child in his starter suit came around a couple of days of ago. Told me the market for one-bedroom flats close to the city centre is going through the roof. Along with the prices. Jeez... I can't believe how much it's gone up in value.'

'Well, congratulations!' beamed Elena. 'It's all coming together!'

'Thanks, it does feel like progress. And thanks for kicking me up the arse about it,' I replied before taking a sip of my wine.

'Maybe we could celebrate by using the spa vouchers – I didn't get the chance to thank you. And of course – you shouldn't have – there was no need.'

I leaned over the table and squeezed Elena's hand. 'There was *every* need. You've been solid since day one. Throughout *everything*. And thanks for the offer, but maybe take someone else? Adam? Or another girlfriend? I've got a lot on – what with trying to get this sequel out and decluttering the flat for the move.'

The candle on the wine bar table flickered across Elena's face. She looked more beautiful than ever. Serene and content. And Adam was obviously having a positive effect on her. For an uncomfortable moment, I wondered if the light was being unfavourable to my scar. Compared to Elena's unflawed complexion, I briefly felt like the ugly sister. I quickly swiped the thought away. It was too ugly.

'Okay. Understood,' she said with an affectionate wink. 'So... any ideas about where you want to move to?'

I blew out a huff of air. 'Nope. Still mulling over various options. But the child estate agent said he'd be able to find a rental if the flat sold and I was still faffing. Hence wanting to clear out some stuff, in case I need to travel light.' With a smile I added, '*Especially* if all he can find me is a space in his crèche. Besides, I think a declutter would be *good*.'

'Any clothes and you run them past me first.'

'That's a given.'

Elena traced a finger around the rim of her wine glass. 'I've never asked,' she began, 'but the flat... does it not remind you... of *him*?'

I didn't need to think through my answer. 'No. It doesn't. Ever since... summer last year... it just feels *empty*. I think I was so traumatised when I returned from hospital, there wasn't space for anything else. Then, after the trial, and despite going straight back to the flat from the court, it was just like a *shutter* had come down on any thoughts about him. Everything was consumed with my grieving for Spencer. Thankfully, it's quite incredible how rarely I think about Clarke. Maybe I don't want to give him the satisfaction. But I suppose a decent shrink could tell me why.'

I gave a shrug of my shoulders to signal the end of the topic. But maybe Elena saw it in my hardened expression.

She clapped her hands together smartly. 'So! Luke! Any thoughts about getting in touch now you're back?' she asked breezily.

Ah. I'd forgotten she knew nothing about the inner workings of Ballbag Derek.

We ordered another bottle, and I took Elena through the whole sorry saga.

She sat in silence and listened intently until I'd finished.

'Okay. Let's break all this down.'

'Into bite-sized chunks?'

'Exactly,' replied Elena, as she swilled her wine glass in thought. 'So... *before* what happened, were you enjoying Luke's company? Yes or no?'

'Yes,' I confirmed with a nod.

'And you thought there was the potential for a long-term relationship – the same as Luke said during the trial? Yes or no?'

'He's a great guy.'

Elena wagged a finger at me. 'Yes or no?'

'Yes.'

'And you don't want to reignite things, because you believe it'd be disrespectful to Spencer's memory? Yes or no?'

Suddenly tiring of Elena's squiffy game, I told her, 'It's more complicated than a simple 'yes' or 'no'.' I sighed heavily and pushed on. 'Spencer died because of our relationship. When I was feeling vulnerable, Luke lied to me and deceived me. If I got back with Luke, it just wouldn't feel... *right*. I'm not even sure if 'disrespectful' is the right word – but as in the same way I felt betrayed by Luke, I feel like I would be betraying Spencer. You know... a bit like, hey-ho – at least we're alive and happy.'

Elena put her glass down and counted on her fingers. 'One... Spencer died because of Clarke – no one else. Two... Luke only tricked you as he didn't know how else to reach out. For which he's apologised. Three... I just don't buy it. It's only you stopping you from getting back with Luke. Aren't words like 'disrespect' and 'betrayal' just a smoke screen for something else? Wouldn't Spencer *want* you to be happy?'

I looked directly into Elena's eyes as I slowly spoke. 'Spencer would want to be alive.'

As Elena nodded her understanding, she reached over and took one of my hands.

'Just give the poor guy a chance to fully explain,

without you cutting him off. You know, it must be a complete headfuck knowing that someone died when it should have been you.'

I lifted Elena's hand and gave it a small kiss before letting go.

'So much for our cheery drink,' I said with downturned lips.

The smile that creased on Elena's face broke into a laughter so contagious, I found myself joining in. And like a couple of idiots, we laughed until tears rolled down our faces.

'This is why I don't drink wine,' I said, once the laughter had subsided. 'And I don't even know what we were laughing about.'

Elena dabbed at her eyes with a napkin. 'Look, just hear him out. Okay?'

'Yes. No,' I said, as I performed robot hands with a squiffy grin.

'Oh, for fucks sake,' laughed Elena as she took a playful swipe at me.

The child in the starter suit was nothing if not keen. In fact, a bit *too* keen for my liking. The flat was marketed almost instantly, causing a flurry of viewing appointments. We'd agreed that I'd make myself scarce for each of them, to allow potential buyers to nosey around in peace and give a better illusion of space. All of this would have been marvellous, had the child not brought people around earlier than the appointed time.

I was hunched over my laptop the first time it happened, smiling at a brief email from Eddie. It was giving me contact details of his new editor – who would be offering support for any chapters I sent over. Her name was Vegas Deauville. Beside which Eddie wrote, 'I know she sounds like an out of work drag queen – but trust me, she's shit hot'.'

Hearing a key turn in the front door, I looked up to find the child ushering in two potential buyers who looked even younger than him. They gripped each other firmly as they stepped over the threshold, with their faces filled with such apprehension, I fleetingly wondered if they thought they were being taken to the gallows. Once inside, the peered around as though seeing one of the seven wonders of the world.

I snapped down the lid of the laptop and jumped up.

'Oh, you're early!' I exclaimed to the child.

As the couple wordlessly shuffled towards my bedroom, he called out to them, 'I'll be with you in a second!' Once they'd disappeared from view, the child turned to face me. 'Yes, sorry about that,' he said. Then – and rather astonishingly, he raised his right hand and waved it about as he clicked his fingers in quick succession. 'It's a fast-moving market and I like to keep on top of it.'

'Hmmmm... are you *sure* they're serious buyers? They look like they've just bunked off from school.'

'Don't let appearances deceive you, Amber.' And

that was me told. By a child in his first suit.

Oh, the shame...

I reached for my coat and bag, and when I turned to say goodbye, the child was gone. And all that was left, was his voice drifting in from the bedroom, making mention of dual aspect windows and storage space. I tugged on my coat and left them to it. Hopefully one of them had bought some marbles along and they could make an afternoon of it...

Don't mind me, you shitty little squirts. Lollies in the freezer. Cola in the fridge.

It took me a while to see a pattern forming. The key in lock. The expectant and hopeful faces peering in. Followed by a confused frown when invariably spotting me on the couch. (Although I did have one frantic and hasty 'wipe and go' episode when happily sitting on the toilet and hearing the child's cheery, 'Here we are, then!' ring out from the lounge.) I later challenged the child about his 'premature entry', but all I got was more finger-clicking and explanations that it was, 'dog eat dog out there' and that he liked to, 'move fast'. The worst thing about our exchanges, was the fact he spoke to me with the strained patience of a parent explaining something simple to a sulky child.

Which was made all the more unsettling, as I held the firm belief *he* was the love child of Gordon Gekko and David Brent...

When I was prematurely invaded for the fourth time, I decided to adopt a new strategy; get the fuck out of the flat 45 minutes before a viewing. The old one – where the child was supposed to update me of any earlier intrusion, clearly wasn't working. By that time, I'd had a young male office worker walk in to find me muttering to myself and jabbing a finger in the air, as I worked on the sequel. Then a couple in their thirties, who looked at me in horror as I burst through the bathroom door after the 'wipe and go' debacle. And finally, a single woman who clapped a hand over her mouth after squealing at me in recognition. Enough.

'You're *not* selling to her,' I hissed into the child's ear as I passed him on the way out.

After the ninth viewing, the flat sold above asking price when a bidding war broke out between a female lawyer, the horrified couple and the squealer. Thankfully, I had no need to step in regarding the squealer, as the lawyer outbid all comers and I was only advised of outcome when the child called me with the news.

'A female lawyer sounds good,' I told him.

'She's chain-free. Just left her husband. So, if all goes smoothly, you'll complete in about 3 months' time. Maybe a little longer, what with Christmas and New Year slowing things down. So February time. There or thereabouts. Job done.'

I thanked the child, put my phone down and looked around the flat. It was really happening. I'd be leaving the place where so much had happened.

Good. And good riddance.

And somehow, I had to find somewhere else to buy or rent, work on the sequel, do the launch bumfuckery thing and the round of book signings. Then there'd be all the paperwork for the sale. As I felt a wave of anxiety rush through me, I became aware of my increased heartrate. I stood up, took in a deep breath through my nose, held it for 3 seconds, then breathed out slowly through my mouth. And repeat.

'Bite-sized chunks, Amber,' I told myself once my breathing had steadied. 'Take control. Tick things off, *one thing at a time*.'

With my hands on hips, I wondered what I should do first. Surely I should be doing *something*. Shouldn't I?

'Okay... let's work this out. Bumfuckery isn't today or now. Somewhere to live can wait until next year in case the sale falls through. I can rent if need be. Storage and cheap hotel the worst scenario. Paperwork for flat is immovable. Deal with as and when. But not here yet. Sequel. First two chapters are with Viva Las Vegas. Waiting to hear back.'

I began to pace the lounge. 'What else? What else?'

And as the light bulb finally went off, I channelled my inner child and performed a series of flamboyant finger clicks as I waved my arm around.

'Declutter! Start packing! Yes! Yes! I have the ability and *furthermore* the *know-how* to do it *all* of that! Let's go, you scatty mare!'

*

'Christ. You never think you own much until you start having a clear out,' I murmured, as I threw another old handbag on the bed. For twenty minutes I'd been making two distinct piles of unwanted clothes and accessories. One for Elena to cast her eye over. The other for the charity shop. I thought back to how little stuff I'd taken with me to Cyprus and how, despite spending most of my days naked, one large suitcase and a holdall had been enough for 3 months. And at no point, had it crossed my mind to top up my wardrobe whilst out there. Floppy hat aside. It just hadn't seemed important to me at the time. As I slid hangers to and fro, I struggled to understand why I ever thought I needed so many clothes, as in the grand scheme of things, they seemed so trivial.

I peered down at the rows of footwear smirking up at me from the bottom of the wardrobe.

'Vegas fucking Deauville – what depths of hell do we have here?' I exclaimed, as I sat down on the carpet and crossed my legs. I plucked out several pairs of shoes and sandals and inspected their condition.

'Keep. Charity. Charity. Keep. Maybe Elena... need to get her shoe size.'

I put my keepers to one side, separated the others and repeated the process until only my boot collection remained.

'Holy moly,' I said with a sigh, as I tipped a pair

of knee-high boots towards me. 'Just how many feet do I think I have?'

As I pulled out the boots, my eye went to the sturdy cardboard box that had been concealed behind them.

And immediately recognised it as one of Spencer's boxes of belongings I'd tearfully pushed to the back of the deep wardrobe that filled an alcove.

How on earth had I forgotten? Or was it just another case of selective memory?

I put my hand to my mouth for a few moments, then reached past the dangling hemlines and trouser legs and pulled out each pair of boots before tossing them to one side. I stared at the exposed, taunting boxes for what seemed like an eternity, then leaned forward and heaved the nearest one out.

Doubt flickered though my mind; was I strong enough to do this?

Then I thought about everything I'd been through since Spencer's death and began ripping away at the brown tape. Once done, I took a deep breath and pulled back the flaps.

I've no idea how long I spent browsing through the items. Some were familiar and evoked fond memories. Others, I'd never seen before – presumably gained after our split. There was an iPad, two laptops, a pair of cufflinks I bought Spencer for an award ceremony we'd attended for his work, and an expensive gold watch he'd inherited from his father.

There was a mountain of luxury brand aftershaves and skin products, along with an exquisitely made tan satchel that must have cost a fortune. I felt quite blown away by the estate agents tasked with clearing out his flat, who hadn't thought to get a little light-fingered in the process. Maybe the commission for the sale had been enough. Or maybe, the back story as to why the flat was being sold tugged at their finger-clicking hearts. Possibly a bit of both.

I vaguely recalled telling them to get in touch with the charity Spencer supported for under-privileged photographers, to see if they wanted the larger items, such as tripods and lighting umbrellas – along with Spencer's collection of cameras. Hopefully, that had unfolded. And when I delved further and found a pile of hardback books about photographers Spencer had admired, I vowed to post them to the charity to see if they were of use.

I was doing okay. A wobble at the cufflinks. A smile at his cherished watch.

I pushed the box away and tugged out the other. This one felt lighter and I could hear shifting and rattling from within as items appeared to be loosely packed. With a tut I wondered if the agents hadn't been so wonderful after all.

Once the box was open, it became evident Spencer's framed photos and awards had neither been bubble wrapped nor tightly packed, causing them to slide about or clatter against one another when moved. I gingerly lifted them out one by one for examination. Like the first box, only some of the items ignited familiarity.

As I admired a print for a high-end perfume, I was struck by the model's devil-may-care attitude whilst still looking elegant and stunning. Spencer sure knew how to get the best from his models, I thought with a smile. As I continued, I began to wonder where the large-framed photos had got to. They would have been too big for the boxes – but maybe Spencer had given them away or auctioned them for one of his favourite charities at a fund-raising event. To my surprise, I found I wasn't bothered, and a bit like my clothes; it wasn't important. Possessions had never been his thing. Our thing.

Once all the framed items had been taken out, looked at and set aside, all that remained was a bulging, document wallet at the bottom of the box. I picked it up, opened the flap and looked inside. It was a pile of loose photos. Some from fashion shoots. Others, scenes of London. Or character studies: the shouting market trader drumming up business for his fruit and veg stall; a squinting beggar with his filthy hand raised for money or a frail pensioner, stooped over a tartan shopping trolley as she wheeled it home. And so many more.

As I flicked through, I came across photos of men. Lovers, I assumed, from the look in their eyes. Windswept smiles on the Embankment. Laughter as autumn leaves were scooped into a stiff breeze. A knowing gaze over a restaurant table. Naked, erotic shots, in both colour and black and white. Lovers, indeed. All of them handsome. And a match for Spencer's good looks and athletic body.

The erotic shots were mesmerising. Whether they were stretched out naked on a bed in varying poses, or partially covered with a sheet. Stroking themselves. Full on erect. Or laying on their side in bed, seemingly post-sex and looking at Spencer lovingly through his lens. Just as I recognised the similarity to one Spencer had taken of me, I flicked to the next photo. And there I was.

In fact... there seemed to be the majority of the 'Amber and Spencer' collection as I remembered it. I flicked through the photos quickly before I could delve too much into my emotions. The sex toys. The masturbation. The sex. The cum. The laughter. The one of our toes touching post-sex – which Spencer had used for his proposal. And others. Me in Camden Market, cupping cold hands around a steaming coffee. Walking ahead in Regent's Park and pointing at something in the distance. Sitting cross-legged on Spencer's floor and happily smiling up at him without a scrap of make-up.

There were more. Dirty ones. Clean ones. Photos of the both of us. Shots from our wedding day.

And beneath them all, an unsealed envelope with my name written on the front in Spencer's distinctive, loopy handwriting.

With a trembling hand I picked it up and stared at it.

As my heart began to thud, I reached inside, pulled out the sheet of paper and carefully unfolded it. And after a steadying deep breath, I began to read.

My Darling Amber

I've tried to imagine the confusion you must feel now you know who (or what) I really am. I have no words to express the deepest sorrow I feel at the hurt I have caused.

We often spoke about the importance of freedom. And I had no option but to set you free.

Free to live the life you deserve. Without my subterfuge and duplicity.

If it could have been any other way – believe me – we'd still be together. Til death do us part.

You have been my treasure and love during the most special years of my life.

And nothing would make me happier than you becoming someone else's.

Freedom, Amber. Always freedom.

Never forget.

A large part of my heart will never heal from losing you. But I will fill the rest with joy and laughter.

Please do the same.

With my eternal love

Spencer x

I expected the all-too-familiar tears to tumble freely down my face. But instead, I rubbed my thumbs over the paper and gently rocked backwards and forwards as I softly repeated the chant of, 'You beautiful, beautiful man'.

I don't know how long I sat on the floor, holding that precious sheet. But when I shook myself from my thoughts, I looked around at Spencer's possessions scattered around me. It seemed so little for a life. But yet, so much.

It crossed my mind that whoever was responsible for packing away the items must have a had a field day when they saw the erotic photos. Ha! Spencer would have found that hysterical, I thought with a smile. And as for my letter? I was just grateful they didn't throw it away. If they read it – who cares? It was part of my life now. And so very precious. As it had no date, I had no idea when Spencer had written it or even if he'd intended to send it. But he'd taken the time and effort to compose those powerful words and put them down on paper. He'd meant them. And that was all I needed to know.

He'd set me free.

The beautiful, beautiful man.

I carefully repacked everything except for the letter. Then I pushed the boxes back into the wardrobe. They were keepers. Decluttering or not. And when I found a new place to live, some of Spencer's professional shots would be going up on the wall. Maybe a couple of the two of us, smiling into the lens during happy days out. I could handle that. I wanted to handle that.

I bagged up the clothes I'd sorted earlier. And put the footwear back into the wardrobe to divvy out another day. Then I carried the letter into the lounge, set it down on the coffee table, picked up my phone and made the call.

'I'm ready to listen,' I told Luke when he answered.

And when I said where I wanted to meet, he asked, 'There? Are you sure?'

'I'm positive,' I told him.

When we'd finished our brief conversation, the tears finally came. Incredible boulders of tears. Full of heartbreak, loss and love.

And release.

And hope.

Spencer, you beautiful, beautiful man.

17.

The Ghosts of Our Sins

'Just over here will do,' I told the taxi driver. 'Outside the pub'.

I paid the driver and as he drove away, I smiled up at the hanging sign of The Flabby Mermaid in all her glory. Before going in, I took a moment to look up and down the road that had been my daily trudge in the heat, seemingly several lifetimes ago. How different it looked on a November afternoon. The seaside tat shops were all shut, and aside from the distant flickering sign for Cod Almighty, it seemed virtually everywhere else had also closed for the season. Spotting a middle-aged couple in quilted jackets heading my way, I wondered if they'd had a walk on nudey beach or maybe ventured over the cliff top. If they'd been hoping for a sly peep at some ageing knobs, then they'd certainly come in the wrong weather.

As I mounted the steps to the pub, the sudden thought of wrinkly bits hibernating for the winter put a grin on my face. But as I pushed my way through the heavy swing door, it quickly vanished when I looked around and disappointment washed over me. I hadn't expected it to resemble anything like the heights of summer, but all I was greeted with, were two seated couples staring forlornly out the window in silence with untouched drinks, and an old boy perched on a bar stool, nursing a pint. Behind the bar stood a lanky lad, head down and scrolling through his phone. No Jen. No lads. Just the grimness of a seaside town in the winter.

I'd been planning to have a drink, but now it seemed like a bad idea. As I turned to walk away, a loud voice boomed out.

'Oi! Blondie! Is that you?'

I turned around and saw Fucker Frank coming out of the Men's toilet and hoisting up his trousers. I felt ridiculously pleased to see him. He walked towards me with open arms.

'Fuck me – I thought it was our old Bond girl. Come on, girl – let's have a look at you!'

He gave me a tight hug before holding me at arm's length and examining my face. 'Dear oh dear, you have been in the wars, haven't you?'

I laughed at his refreshing audacity. 'Yep. You could say that.'

'Life, wasn't it?' Frank asked, his tone now serious.

I nodded my confirmation. 'Minimum of 25 – unless hell claims him first.'

'They won't be letting that bastard out. Ever. He'll probably get done over in there, anyway.'

'We live in hope,' I said sweetly.

Frank put an arm around my shoulder and used his free hand to pull my head towards to him. With a loud smack, he landed a kiss on my scar.

'Come on, girl. You're still a dazzler – let's get you a drink.'

As we approached the bar, Frank's voice once more filled the air. 'Oi! Droopy bollocks! How about getting your head out that phone and pouring some drinks? Fucking parched, here.'

'No more Jen?' I asked, as Droopy reluctantly put his phone down.

'Gone, I'm very sorry to say,' Frank said. 'She's got bar work in Torquay for the winter, serving all the coffin dodgers. What you having? On me.'

The order placed, we incredulously watched Droopy make the drinks. He was painfully slow and ponderous, as though the combination of glass, vodka, mixer and ice had never been requested before.

'Don't worry about the ice!' I called over, when it seemed to be getting a step too far.

'See what I have to put up with? I could write bloody War and Peace in the time it takes to get a drink in here. A two-toed sloth on Prozac could knock them out quicker.'

Drinks finally made, Droopy placed them before us with a scrunch-faced sarcastic scowl before ambling back to his phone.

I took a mouthful of my drink before settling on a bar stool, whilst Frank remained standing, clutching his pint to his chest.

'So how have you been?' I asked.

'Me? I'm signed off sick, innit? Waiting for my compensation claim to happen.'

'Oh, I'm sorry to hear that – what happened?'

Frank shrugged. 'Nah, it's alright. I was asked to lift some boxes and wasn't told how heavy they were. Put my arm right out. Can't do nothing with it.' As he put his pint to his lips, he indicated to his raised arm with a nod.

I should have guessed. 'Looks like you'll live. Anyway, how's everyone else?'

'What? The Lads? Same old. Same old. We did wonder if we'd be seeing you around this summer. But then, what with... you know – we weren't sure. Mind you, from the colour of you, you look like you've been abroad or something?'

'Yeah, things got a bit much, so I spent some time abroad. I just needed to get away.'

Frank wiped the back of his hand across his mouth before speaking. 'I don't blame you, Blondie. Old Stevie boy told us about seeing you in court. Sounds like it was a real shit storm – but at least it's done and dusted now. And that bastard's tucked away.'

I looked at Frank and briefly wondered how it must feel to live in such an uncomplicated world. And suspected it was marvellous.

'Yep. All done and dusted. How is Stevie, by the way? Still with Freya?'

'Yeah, the soppy git's shacked up, loved up and getting married next year. He only gets to mooch out on a Friday night – but he seems happy enough.' Frank nudged my arm with his drink. 'Here, did anything ever go on between you two? You and Stevie? We all thought something happened that night he gave you a lift back?'

'No, nothing happened,' I said lightly. 'It was just like he said in court – he dropped me off and that was that.'

Frank didn't look convinced. He tilted his head and looked me in the eye for a few moments before speaking. 'If you say so, Blondie.'

As I drained the last of my drink I avoided his gaze. 'Right then, Frank. I'm afraid I have to go. Places to be and all that. Thanks for the drink. And it's been really good seeing you.'

It was touching to see the disappointment register on his large face.

'Oh? Right you are, then – thought you'd necked that a bit sharpish. Well... guess I'll be seeing you around. By the way, did you hear they've taken that caravan away? It's just an empty plot now.'

I hadn't. In fact, I'd purposely told the taxi driver to bring me through the alternative route to avoid passing Brightlea Sands. Despite feeling stronger in so many ways, I didn't feel ready for that. And possibly never would.

'Good. Done and dusted, then,' I told Frank in the language he understood.

'I reckon so. Okay, give us a hug.'

As we squeezed each other tight, I breathed in his cheap aftershave and wondered why I enjoyed the company of this gobby, foul-mouthed, straight-talking lump. And when we released and smiled at one another I realised that, sometimes, there's a time and a place for that kind of person. Particularly, if beneath it all, they've got a big heart.

'You take care of you and that arm,' I told him with a smile.

'What this old thing?' Frank said with a grin, as he raised it in the air and swung it from side-to-side in a loose figure of eight. 'It's been giving me nothing but gyp.'

'You're a terrible man, Fucker Frank.'

'Harsh, but fair, Blondie. Harsh, but fair. And you stay out of trouble, right, or I'll be coming for you!'

Pecks on the cheeks. A round of goodbyes. A disinterested glance from Droopy Bollocks.

And out I walked.

I passed a lone amusement arcade still trading as I made my way down towards the seafront. It stood deserted and sad, as its bright lights and squawky sounds did nothing but chew up energy. Like the old boys' knobs, the place would be better off hibernating for the winter. I imagined firing one of the toy rifles at the power box with a loud ker-boom! and putting the whole place out of its misery.

It was terrible how these places struggled so much out of season. No government support. No regeneration plans for the area. And no wonder that Jen had hot footed it to pastures new, where she'd be guaranteed work over the coming months.

As I strode on, The Captain's Table came into view. Last visited on Spencer's last night alive. When we'd had such a blast. Full of the joy and laughter he'd talked of in his letter.

A much more fitting way to remember him.

As I approached, I saw that the A board in the street had no mention of any theme 'nite' and instead, offered a 'Winter Warmer Deal' of two meals for the price of one. The faint strains of an Abba song rang out from within, and I could spot the heads of a few customers dotted about, possibly taking up the offer of a cheap meal out.

As I recalled how Spencer and I had thrown ourselves into the boisterous karaoke session, I drew upon my predetermined resolve not to have a wobble. And then there'd been those outrageously named cocktails we'd shrieked about and drunk so many of.

Just keep remembering the good things, I told myself, as my mind wandered to the fun we'd had dancing.

I was so immersed in my memories, I paid no attention to the approaching footsteps, but turned when hearing Luke's voice.

'Amber?'

Standing a few feet away from me, he wore a long overcoat with the collar upturned and an uncertain expression.

'I thought we were meeting at the front – but if you prefer to have a drink instead?'

I took in his tired face and gave him a small smile. 'No, I'd like to see the old haunt. If that's okay?'

'It's fine.'

We walked side by side in an uncomfortable silence. Both carefully maintaining some distance between us. When we reached the sea front – by the crazy golf that had closed for the winter and the near-empty car park, we ground to a halt. I looked out in the fading light towards the sea and breathed in the salty air.

'I was surprised by your call... ' Luke said. His words hung in the air as though he wanted to add more but didn't know how or had decided against it.

I kept my eyes on the sea. 'And you want to know what changed my mind?'

'Well... yes.'

With a shrug of my shoulders I gave him his answer. 'Let's just say a couple of people drummed some sense into me.'

'They sound like very good friends.'

I turned to face Luke. 'The best.'

As a strong breeze whipped across the water, we stood looking at each other.

'You look well,' Luke said.

'Thank you. Nothing like overdosing on a bit of Vit D.' I took in the couple of new lines etched on Luke's handsome face. 'And you look done in. Come – let's walk before it gets too dark and you can tell me everything.'

From the grateful look in Luke's eyes, it seemed he was more than ready to talk. To me. Or possibly, anyone.

'But how are *you*?' he asked with concern.

'You first,' I replied. 'That's why I'm here.'

Along the seafront we walked, then over the pebbles and towards the jutting cliff, where the tide was conveniently out. I let Luke talk without interruption. Until we hit nudey beach and the reveal of a sensational sunset that had been hidden behind the cliff. Purples and pinks and greys slashed across the sky with streaks of gold. We stopped in our tracks.

'Wow... ' I murmured in admiration. 'That's really something.'

'It certainly is. Winter offers up the best sunsets to amend for the rest of its nonsense.'

I smiled up at Luke. 'Pity you haven't got your paintbrushes with you.'

His gaze remained on the sunset but said nothing.

I looked along the beach. To the spot where I'd descended on my first day. Then further along, to where I'd sunbathed that very same day and met Luke. And as I peered into the distance, I could roughly work out where Brokeback Bay was. Easier to spot in the dim light was the distant cliff Luke and I had walked around for our afternoon of fun.

'Look! You can just about the see the scene of the crime!' I said, as I stretched out an arm and pointed.

A hollow half-laugh escaped Luke's lips. 'Indeed. The ghosts of our sins.'

As he stood with his hands plunged deep in his coat pockets, his expression was unreadable.

We only walked a little further. The light was rapidly fading. The breeze getting chillier and beginning to bite. Luke stopped what he'd been saying to suggest we turn around and get a drink to warm ourselves up. He'd been in full flow before then. So I told him that'd be great.

I took a deep breath as I entered the Captain's Table and was immediately grateful that, like Flabby's, it was barely recognisable from my last visit. We found a booth table tucked away in a corner, Luke got the drinks and sat beside me. And for twenty minutes or so, he continued to let it all out. Whilst working his way through the two large whiskies he'd bought himself.

He looked at me with a mixture of apology and defiance when he finished speaking.

'There you go,' he tagged on. 'Nothing remotely close to the abject hell you've been through, but it's been a bit rough, nevertheless.'

I leaned over and took one of his hands in mine.

'Thanks for listening to my bleak outpouring,' he said. 'It was incredibly gracious of you – given the fact we should have been talking about how you've been doing.'

'Well, we can touch on that later, if you like. I just... had no idea how *crap* everything's been for you.'

Luke gave my hand a squeeze then released it. 'Enough of this morose talk!' he said, as he slapped his palms on the table. 'I take it you still smoke? Let's go outside for a puff and then you can tell me all about Cyprus, that book of yours and... whatever else you fancy telling me.'

I'd almost forgotten how much I loved his soft Irish accent.

We ended up staying in the pub for another two hours. And as the drinks went down, our conversation flowed easier.

I gave Luke some edited highlights from Cyprus, and when I told him about the nickname, House of Lunge, it amused him so much, he threw back his head and roared with laughter. And in an instant, the old Luke was back. With a sparkle in the eyes full of grey and blue flecks. I told him about some of the good days and the bad. The triggers for my grief. The desire and determination to feel stronger. The belief I was gradually making some inroads to healing.

Luke listened intently. And told me he was glad I felt I was making progress.

Then I spoke of my inability to write in Cyprus. My love of the island. The copious amount of mind-numbing vodka I'd drunk. The view from the villa. Sonny's. The Red Lion. The beautiful bougainvillea. The skimming swallows. The amazing food. And, of course, the twinkling lights. But nothing about the sex I'd had.

I leaned towards Luke. 'You want to know one of the things that put the biggest smile on my face when I was out there? I met a young lad called Josh one night. In one of the bars on the main drag. Lovely lad. About twenty. He *bizarrely* thought he recognised me from a film, so I gave him some cock and bull story about being an ex-Bond girl. Which *incredibly*, he fell for. Anyway... amongst all that... he just asked me outright about my scars. Just like that! Which I didn't mind at all. Felt kinda refreshing. And do you know what he called me because of my scars? A sexy pirate! A beautiful, sexy pirate. Quite choked me up. And the shame is, he'll *never know* how much I needed to hear that.'

For the first time, Luke allowed his eyes to rest on my forehead scar. Then, he gently cupped a hand beneath my chin and tilted my head about as if undertaking a thorough examination of my face.

'You know, Amber,' he said, 'I think that lad was definitely onto something. You're a beautiful, sexy pirate sitting in The Captain's Table pub. It's perfect. Josh is a very wise young man. He speaks the truth.'

With our heads so close together, we suddenly

locked eyes. I felt surprise at the lurch in my chest as our eyes creased into affection and, for a moment, I wondered if Luke was going to kiss me. Instead, he smiled and said, 'I reckon this place should offer you a job as their poster girl. You'd make a killing for them. Or at least a few chests of gold coins.'

Then his hand left my chin and went back to his glass.

'So what about this sequel and book launch?' he asked, after taking a slug of whiskey.

Unsure as to what had just unfolded – or indeed, if anything had – I matched Luke's slug of drink, took a moment, then told him.

When I finished speaking, Luke gave me a brief summary of what I'd just said.

'So... you don't particularly want to do the sequel, but you're just churning out a Susie version of some of the things you did in Cyprus and hamming it up.'

I gave Luke a nod before he continued.

'And you're not keen on this launch and book tour – particularly the Q&A sessions –and want to write something more *meaningful*.'

'That's about the strength of it. It's just amazing... after all my writer's block, knowing I can now just pass some half-arsed crap over to someone else has taken away the absolute feeling of *burden* I'd associated with Susie. Funnily enough, the editor emailed me this morning with her feedback and thoughts for *moving forward*, and better than any of that; a heavily tidied-up version of what I'd sent her.

And now I'm banging it out, there's no stopping me. It's just blah blah, Cyprus, blah blah, add water and stir. In fact, if I carry on the way I am, it'll be done before I move.'

'Oh? You're moving?' asked Luke with surprise and uncertainty in his voice. 'Anywhere nice?'

'I haven't decided yet,' I said truthfully, as I twirled my glass in my hand. 'I just thought that it would be good to get away from that flat, you know?'

'It'll be grand. I'm sure you'll sort it all out for the best,' Luke said evenly. I couldn't tell if he was indifferent, playing it cool or something else entirely different. Furthermore, I had no idea how I'd wanted him to react.

I looked across to the large blue and white lifebuoy above the bar. The outside was trimmed with thick rope and its centre filled with a clock face.

'I guess we should think about ordering some cabs,' I said. 'Otherwise, we'll be fighting over a horse and cart if we leave it too late. Unless you're getting a bus?'

'Dear Lord, no,' said Luke.

'Don't you mean, 'Dear Lord, where will it all end?'' I said with a crooked smile.

Luke ran a hand through his thick hair and sighed. 'I know, I know. What was I thinking?' He turned to look at me. 'As I said, it was the only dumb ass thing I could think of to have some contact. I'm an idiot. That's what I am. An idiot who was missing you. And missing *us*.'

Luke looked at me with a steady gaze.

There it was again, that thump in my heart. And confusion swirling around my head.

I cocked my head to one side. 'You know what? I *really* miss my online relationship with Ball Bag Derek... '

Luke leaned forward and reached for my hand. 'I'm still here, Amber.'

'I *know* you are,' I said as I squeezed his hand. 'So... let's go back to that. I think it'd be a good place to begin again.' As Luke opened his mouth to speak, I silenced him with a fingertip touch to his lips. 'It's been a long time, Luke. Much water under many bridges. And I'm sure tonight's been as much of a head fuck for you as it has for me. So... and to quote one of the few phrases I learned in Cyprus; *sigá sigá.* Slowly slowly.'

Luke lowered his head and frowned. I remained silent while he considered my suggestion. I knew it wasn't what he'd wanted to hear. Or rather – I presumed it wasn't. A part of him still seemed so damaged. And here I was, still fighting my own battles.

The seconds ticked by. Then Luke lifted his head.

'Well, I reckon this old bulldog's still got some life in him yet,' he said with a wink.

As we waited outside for the taxis, I had to ask Luke something that had been playing on my mind.

'You know, with everything you told me earlier… how on earth did you manage to be so bloody funny with those posts and messages?'

With pressed lips, he gently shook his head before looking up to the winter sky.

'I don't know,' he answered with a sigh. 'I guess it's the age-old thing; people hide behind humour to disguise how they're really feeling. It's something we're both guilty of,' he added with a brief glance. 'But despite everything that was going on, I guess I wanted to sprinkle a few smiles on your face after what you'd been through. And maybe lift my own spirits in the process. And when you took the bait and we began messaging, it just felt so *good* to have that connection again. And like you, I enjoyed our light-hearted exchanges – despite the deceit. Was it self-serving? Undoubtedly. Did it all stem from a good place with no ill intent? Very definitely.'

Luke smiled down at me. 'Am I forgiven?'

'Just this once,' I said with a smile. And meaning it.

'Thank you,' he silently mouthed.

As the wind whipped in from the sea, I began to shiver in the thin jacket I'd inappropriately selected for a seafront walk.

Luke opened his overcoat. 'Come under here for a bit to keep warm – the taxi shouldn't be too long now.'

I gratefully stepped forward and let Luke envelope me in the heavy cloth. My arms wrapped around his waist. Our faces were inches apart.

'Thanks for listening. Giving me a chance to explain and all that.'

'Anytime, Luke. And I mean that. *Anytime.*'

The flecks glittered in his eyes. 'Can I kiss you?'

I scrunched my face into a confused expression.

'Well, I'd rather you pissed up my leg, if it's all the same to you.'

A dazzling smile turned into a joyous laugh.

There was my old Luke again.

He raised his hands and cupped my cheeks as he looked deep into my eyes. Then he slowly slid one hand further until its fingertips found my scar. With the lightest of touches, he traced a finger up and down its full length whilst maintaining eye contact. It felt an incredibly intimate moment. And one full of trust.

'You're a beautiful, sexy pirate,' he said huskily before wrapping me in his arms and kissing me.

I melted into him. It had been such a long time, I found myself hungry to taste and explore his mouth. And when we finally broke, I was more than aware of his hard-on pressing against me.

'I see that you're not feeling quite so bad after all,' I said, teasingly.

'And I see that you're still a dreadful woman,' Luke countered. He peered over my shoulder. 'Looks like the first taxi's here. You have it – I'll take the second one.'

'We'll message, right?'

Luke nodded his response. 'Everything will be at your pace, Amber. Slowly slowly.'

As the taxi driver beeped his horn with impatience, we tenderly pressed our lips together in a goodbye.

'Laters, bulldog!' I called out as I climbed into the taxi.

'Laters, pirate!' came the reply.

I watched Luke wave me off as the taxi pulled away and when he was no longer in view, I settled back in my seat and became aware of the ache and pulsing between my legs. I peered out the window and saw a wicked smile reflected back. Maybe I'd be unearthing those sex toys when I got back home.

Dear Lord etc etc...

18.

It's a Dog's Life

'So everything's back on?' Elena asked.

I hugged my knees up on the couch and gazed out the window as I spoke into my phone.

'Of sorts. We're going to start with texts and emails, maybe a call here and there and see how it goes. You were right; he's been struggling. And I think both of us just need to be... I don't know... careful... and feeling a bit stronger, I suppose.'

'And the catfishing?'

'All explained. All forgiven.'

'See? You were right to give him a chance!' Before I could reply, I could hear someone calling Elena's name. Her next appointment had arrived.

'Must dash. Full head of highlights and gossip to attend to. Catch you later!'

'Byeeeee!'

I placed my phone back on the table and thought

about my call with Elena. About how I'd only given her the barest scraps of information about Luke. Anything more would have been breaking a confidence. What Luke had told me was private and personal. And extremely brave of him to share.

As for me, I felt confused and conflicted after the hours spent with Luke. Before meeting up, I was practically positive I'd want nothing more to do with him after we'd spoken. Then he talked. I listened. We both spoke. The drinks flowed. We laughed a little. Things felt more *familiar.* There was the sensitive way he tackled my scar insecurities. And that kiss.

Yet amongst it all, the 'real' Luke had only popped his head out a number of times – the majority after a few drinks. Otherwise, he'd seemed a little distant, a little damaged – his eyes uncharacteristically dull and lifeless – and as though protecting himself. But after listening to his story, I wasn't sure I could blame him.

I thought back to his words.

About how his commissions had unfairly dive-bombed once word of his connection to the trial spread. The talks, the tutoring and mentoring sessions – all but gone. The sales that I'd hoped he'd gain due to his notoriety – the opposite happened. It was only thanks to a London-based friend who 'didn't give a fuck' that saw him get some work at the flower show and a modest commission in the Peak District. Other than that, he was practically an outcast. With the grapevine loving every second of gossip about the 'respected artist' who 'hung around' a nudist beach on the pick-up for sex. Word even got back to Luke that the terms "pervert" and "Jimmy Saville" had been used in the same breath as his name. The annihilation he'd felt had been total.

And on top of all that, he had to deal with a torrent of online abuse.

Devastatingly, some of it attributed varying degrees of blame for Spencer's murder. Some of it related to his perceived nudey activities. Most of it was about big bad me. Or rather, Luke's relationship with big bad me.

He spoke of the mental torture and guilt about Spencer's death. Knowing it should have been him. That Spencer's life was snuffed out instead of his. And the harrowing thoughts about that night, when his unanswered texts had been happily sent as Spencer lay dead and I was on the brink. The nightmares were relentless.

At one point, he'd stood in the howling wind on the edge of a Dartmoor quarry and thought the only release from the pain would be to jump. The coward in him couldn't go through with it and, instead, he crouched into a ball and sobbed like a child.

And was the point he decided to seek counselling. Which plugged some holes. Put some sticky tape on. Was still work in progress.

The thought of trying to have a relationship seemed impossible. On his trip to the Peak District, he went on a dinner date with his female client. But nearly had a meltdown and when badly losing his temper as she took a selfie of them and proceeded to post it on Instagram, whilst cheerily saying, 'Well, this should give the ex-husband something to think about'.

As Luke tried to snatch her phone a terrible scene unfolded. Luke was filled with panic and fear that history would repeat itself, and a jealous ex would be coming out the woodwork to do harm. He couldn't believe how stupid his date had been by seemingly goading her ex-husband. And in no uncertain terms, he got his point across.

Date over.

Another client lost.

And throughout all of this, the only person he wanted to speak to was me. Who'd been through it worse. And might understand.

But more than any of that, he missed me. Missed what we had. And hoped we'd be able to have it again one day.

Luke told me it had been a 'total kick in the guts' when I rejected him after the trial. He had no expectations of us picking up our relationship where we'd left off. But I had firmly shut the door in his face on the hope of resuming things further down the line.

But as he later mulled over our meeting, my words and demeanour failed to entirely convince him that was what I wanted. All he knew, was that everything was brutally raw. I was hurting. I was grieving.

So, when he discovered how Just Susie was

taking off, he simply couldn't resist the opportunity presented when discovering my online presence. And the rest was @ballbagderek history...

I stood up and walked to window. As I peered out at the flats across the road, I remember how I'd felt once he'd told me everything.

I'd no idea. I'd been so wrapped up in my own grief and pain, the thought of Luke struggling hadn't even touched my radar. Dealing with my own recovery had been my number one priority. And even if I'd known, I wouldn't have been strong enough to carry Luke as well as myself, when feeling so fragile.

Yet, when he'd told me his *story,* amongst all the differing emotions I felt, the dominant one was guilt. I'd never *really* stopped to consider how Clarke's case of mistaken identity would affect Luke. Let alone his reputation and livelihood. But it had broken the man talking to me. The same man I'd so readily dismissed at court.

I'd contributed to his pain.

And now, a day after our meeting, the guilt I refused to show Luke was turning into anger.

That cunt, Clarke, had claimed a third victim.

And he didn't give a fuck about any of them.

I went back to the couch, picked up my phone and took a deep breath.

'*Earth to Bulldog? Earth to Bulldog?*' I tapped out in a text. '*It was good taking you for a walk yesterday. Who knew a canine could neck so much whiskey? Tsk. Tsk. xx*'

And off it pinged. A hand reaching across the 18 miles or so.

I tossed the phone to one side. How was a worthless piece of shit like Clarke still breathing in air when lives were being ruined on an almost daily basis by people like him? I thought back to Carol in Cyprus. Her daughter murdered by someone just like Clarke. Off they go to prison. Leaving their victims to flounder in torment, without a care in the world.

As I felt the rage begin to build, my eyes rested on my laptop. Before Elena's call I'd been ploughing through correspondence from the solicitor handling the sale of the flat. As I cast a look around it seemed – just like that – the mental block I'd had about associating Clarke with my home had been blown to smithereens.

The sale couldn't come a moment too soon.

With an angry shake of my head, I picked up my laptop and got to work on helping things move as quickly as possible. All the while chewing over my thoughts and getting more and more wound up.

Solicitor dealt with, I went to the kitchen and poured myself a strong vodka and diet coke with trembling hands. I *never* drank in the flat during the day, but yesterday had been tough, along with the effort it had taken to show no distress when hearing Luke's words. I didn't want him to think he was upsetting me; the time we had was all about him offloading. After all, I had Elena for support.

Luke – no one that he wanted to open up to – apart from his shrink.

And now... having had the chance to analyse everything he'd said without the distraction of him being present... it just made me feel so fucking *helpless* about these inhumane *creatures* who caused such devastation with its far-reaching ripple effects.

I swallowed down a large mouthful of drink and felt grateful for its warmth as it rushed down my throat with an immediate hit. And with a feeling of contempt, I took another two gulps.

For so long, all I'd felt was guilt, sadness and grief.

And now? Rage. Pure, unadulterated rage.

Which somehow felt better.

I threw back the rest of my drink and made my way to the bedroom to get some more packing done.

Just take control wherever you can, Amber.

But as I reached for an empty cardboard box and cast a look at the shitty English weather outside, my mind was still a smouldering volcano.

'Sorry for slobbering over your face last night, but you were hard to resist. Must have been that perfume. Just love the smell of chicken and gravy xx'

Ballbag Derek was back in the house!

I smiled at his text. '*It took two showers, five flannels and man-sized box of tissues to get all your drool off. Bad doggie. You okay?*'

'Yeah, not too bad, thanks. Nothing like a bit al fresco unburdening to lift the soul.'

'I'm pleased to hear that, Luke. I've been packing, plotting and scheming and putting the world to rights.'

'Watch out world!'

'Ha! You bet! Just working on some sequel bollocks, so best crack on.'

'Not a problem. I'll leave you to your bollocks. I'm sure they're very impressive.'

Without thought, I began tapping a flirty response about preferring to work on his bollocks – as though we were back in that summer, so very long ago. Christ. How easy did it feel to slip back to how things used to be?

Instead, I wrote, '*Pure gold. Which is why I carry them around in a trolley. Okay, catch you later. Don't forget to call if you need me xxx*'

'Understood. And thank you x'

I'd slowly and gradually managed to calm myself down from earlier. And after endlessly talking to myself as I hurled things around in the bedroom, a few things were settled in my mind. But not what I wanted to unfold between Luke and myself. Despite our kiss and almost going into autopilot with a flirty message, I felt we both needed to tread carefully. One way or another, there was a lot at stake – our mental health included.

Sigá sigá. We'll see how it goes.

I cast my eyes over my latest offering to Vegas. It was terrible. Truly terrible. The whole thing to-date was far worse than the original – but I didn't care. Just let her tart it up, along with the rest, and get it all over and done with. Then I could cast my net over something new. Something of *substance.* Maybe some contemporary women's literature. Or something of that ilk.

That'd give Eddie some bigger fish to fry.

I just hoped I had what it took to change my style. To get away from the drivel I was known for and become a serious writer to be reckoned with.

But as I scanned through what I'd written, I began to have my doubts.

Jesus...

... Susie has a late-night consensual grope with the man himself at House of Lunge. As the fumbling hots up, his new dentures somehow get dislodged and bounce off Susie's exposed knocker before clattering across the floor. Whilst, above their heads, an embracing couple peer out of the TV screen in goggle-eyed shock as the violins begin to screech...

... Susie gets herself locked in Bengal Nights (didn't think the legal team would approve of the real name) *when the sudden onset of a dicky tummy saw her camped out on the customer toilet until staff re-opened the next afternoon. As she emerged, ashen-faced, dehydrated and reaching for assistance, Susie was promptly handed her bill and a request to put a review on TripAdvisor...*

... Susie runs naked circuits of her apartment's communal pool, when a lizard interrupts her toilet activities by scampering through the bathroom window and terrifying her as she is mid-wipe. To the horror of the

poolside families, Susie trails a length of toilet roll from her backside as she squeals her way through the sun loungers...

... Susie embarks on some springboard sex with a Romanian labourer she's picked up. But as she attempts to unfurl and lower herself into the awaiting Romanian's mouth, a strap on her M&S padded swimsuit gets entangled, causing it stretch beyond recognition and half-throttle Susie to death. As she is left dangling, gagging and wheezing with her emergency Velcro gusset flapping open, the nonplussed Romanian gets stuck in...

And so on and so on.

Working title; 'Susie Does Cyprus'. Described as a 'Romp in the Mediterranean'.

Just a series of diluted anecdotes and held together by the flimsiest of storyline threads.

But Vegas was doing her magic. Eddie seemed happy we were chugging along. And I'd be getting to say ta-ta to the Susie I once loved.

Poor Susie.

19.

Skipping Around Puddles

The days trickled by. The flat sale chugged along, as did my writing. I'd boxed up as much as I could. Taken bags of stuff to a charity shop. Given some clothing to Elena. And exchanged messages with Luke most days. We were getting along just fine and doggie dandy. He told me he was making progress with his counselling sessions, and I couldn't have felt more pleased.

And throughout it all, Eddie's shark muzzle remained in place.

He called one day, to remind me I had to visit the printers during my London trip and sign stacks of Just Susie before she went to the distributors. He thought he was sweetening this chore by offering to put me up in a smart hotel and having dinner with him and industry *others*. He had no idea how little I cared for any of it, but as he seemed in good spirits, I thanked him and said yes. All was going swimmingly in Eddie's world as launch day approached. And I liked that muzzle just where it was.

I repeated my concerns about the Q&A session; I had no desire for any quizzing about my personal life and/or what happened to Spencer. But he assured me he'd be on hand to fend off any unwanted or inappropriate line of questioning. Despite hearing myself say I felt reassured, that nag was there again. As though things could be beyond my control.

Control... that word again.

A couple of days before the launch, I had a phone call from the child, asking if the female lawyer could pop over to do a bit of measuring up. Late afternoon. Today. If possible. As I was intending to be at home, working on Susie, it wasn't a problem. 'Awesome,' the child said before signing off. I shook my head in disbelief as I put my phone down. Then – and just for the hell of it – I clicked my fingers about in a wild dance before blowing a lengthy and satisfyingly loud raspberry.

From the countless forms and correspondence about the flat's sale, I already knew the name of the buyer, so when she later knocked at the door, I was ready to greet her.

'Tanya! Hello!' I said to the smartly dressed, plump lady who stood holding a briefcase. As I stepped as aside to let her in, I couldn't help but admire the vibrant red, wavy hair that fell over her shoulders. It reminded me of the Pre-Raphaelite paintings I'd stare at in awe when visiting Tate Britain, so very long ago.

'Hello Amber. Good of you to let me come over.' Glancing over my shoulder, she spotted the open laptop. 'I hope I'm not disturbing you?'

I waved away her concern. 'No – it's fine! Nothing that can't wait. Would you like a coffee before you start?'

As Tanya smiled and told me that'd be lovely, I noticed her green eyes. How unusual to see ones so similar to mine, I thought with mild surprise. And what a compliment they were to that gorgeous, red hair. I made the coffee, told Tanya to feel free to wander around, then left her to it as I sat with my knees hugged up on the couch, sipping my coffee and pointlessly trying to make myself as unobtrusive as possible.

She began in the lounge. Tape measure out. Notepad at hand. Then onto the kitchen, the bathroom and finally, the bedroom. Once finished, she popped back into the kitchen to pick her coffee from where she'd left it and wandered into the lounge.

'Well, that's me done,' she announced before draining the remains from her mug.

'Oh? Okay. Got everything you need?'

'Yup. I'm thinking of getting white shutters throughout, so just wanted to get a ballpark quote before I totally fall in love with the idea.'

I swivelled my head to look at the lounge windows. 'Do you know,' I said, before turning back to look at Tanya, 'I think they'd look brilliant. I'm happy to let in anyone who needs to do a more thorough measure up, if that'll help?'

Tanya tapped her notepad. 'Thanks, but these should do for now. But if I decide to go ahead, that'd be great.'

'No worries.'

I watched Tanya as she took her mug back to the kitchen. When she returned to the lounge, she picked up her briefcase and tucked away her notepad and measuring tape. As she fiddled with the clasp, she spoke without looking at me.

'Just for transparency... I know who you are.' She glanced up to gauge my reaction. I threw her a shrug with raised eyebrows in suggestion of '*aaaaaand?*'.

I suspect it was due to her job that her composure didn't waiver.

'I work at Exeter Crown Court,' Tanya continued, 'and *obviously*, your case was familiar and discussed between a lot of my colleagues. Myself included.'

I remained silent and allowed her to carry on.

'And... unfortunately, we see too many of these cases coming our way. Violence against women. Stalking. The results of obsession... '. Tanya left the sentence hanging as she looked at me intently with her head cocked to one side. 'You know, after the emergence of the #metoo phenomenon, there was hope there'd be a decrease in these crimes, but sadly, they just seem to be on the increase. Or women are feeling more emboldened to report them. Anyway,

I just wanted to say how sorry I am. And that you were incredibly brave – going to court... amongst all that... hostile media coverage. Sadly, a lot of women drop the charges rather than have their day in court. Whether it's through fear or guilt or any number of reasons. But you went through with it. The world could do with more victims like you, so more men like Clarke get locked away for a very long time.'

I swung my legs around and sat up.

'I just don't see it like that,' I said. 'I'm not *brave.* First and foremost, it was a murder trial and I don't think I'd have been allowed to not attend. What happened to me was terrible. Terrible, but *secondary* to what happened to Spencer. I had no choice. So I went.'

Tanya took a step towards me. 'You're right, of course – there's no option to drop charges in a murder case. But along with your evidence, your day in court saw justice. You stood in the dock with that man sitting just yards away. Please don't tell me that's not bravery.'

My mind flickered back for a moment. 'Not sure about that. But, you know, for so much of the whole thing, it felt as though I was on trial.'

'Don't women always?' Tanya said with a sigh as she reached into a coat pocket. She pulled out a business card, walked across to where I sat and handed it over. 'There's somewhere I need to be, but here's my card. Maybe you could phone or message, so I've got direct contact details in case I need that measuring up done? If that's okay with you?'

I turned it over in my hand before smiling up at her. 'Consider it done. And I don't think you need to worry about me stalking you.' As I got up to show Tanya out, she let out a half-laugh. 'Don't start me off again! We all need to club together to try and solve this horrendous problem.'

'Sorry Tanya, I'm no crusader. I don't rattle a tambourine for anyone. I'm just trying to get by one day at a time.'

'Well, that's a shame, but I obviously wish you well in your recovery.'

As I held the door open, I felt a wave of regret at her imminent departure and had a sudden thought.

'I've... er... got a book signing thing on the High Street this Friday evening... if that's of interest?'

Tanya looked at me blankly as her forehead creased into a frown. As the words had left my mouth, I felt self-conscious and the need to fill the ensuing silence.

'I mean... if you'd like to come along. There's er... wine and... er... nibbly bits... industry people... and er... '

As she tightened the belt to her coat, Tanya smiled at me kindly. 'Sorry Amber, but it's not my thing.'

'I'm not sure it's my thing either,' I said before laughing too loudly, as a rush of embarrassment coloured my cheeks.

After we'd said goodbye, I returned to the couch

to slump head in hands in cringe mode. And when I finally spread my fingers and peeped through, I saw Spencer's letter on the table where I'd left it.

'What a twat I am,' I groaned. 'Ooh! Nibbly bits! If you'd like to come along! And maybe I'll rattle my fucking tambourine for you! *Tambourine...* give me fucking strength!'

I roared with laughter. And wondered how hysterical Spencer would have found it.

'Get you with your invite to your fancy book signing with nibbly bits! Who do you think you are? Bleeding Cleopatra, wheeling a hostess trolley around?'

I could almost hear him saying it.

I laughed some more. And when I'd calmed down, I picked up his letter and held it tightly to my chest in deep thought.

'*Brave*,' I muttered with a shake of my head. 'I'm not brave. Angry? Yes! I'm fucking livid. But not brave.'

I carefully placed the envelope on the coffee table, smoothed over it with a palm and looked at Spencer's handwriting.

Brave...

Maybe I was...

'I've got something to tell you,' I informed Luke.

'Oh, mercy – this sounds ominous.'

It was our first phone call after a few weeks of messaging and instigated by me. Luke had been pleasantly surprised to see my name light up his phone, and after a bit of chit-chat, told me about his recent counselling session and the further progress both he and his counsellor believed he'd made. And that somewhere at the root of his recent uplift, had been my forgiveness for his deceit. As I tried to interject with something like, 'It's all forgotten,' he uncharacteristically talked over me.

'So, I think it's important to allay any concerns you might have – or get – about my recovery being dependent on you. And that it's clear, your most welcome forgiveness merely provided a springboard for leaping over a few obstacles in my progress. Everything I'm doing in these sessions is purely for me. And I am well aware, that the only person responsible for my happiness, is me. After all, neither of us knows what will or won't unfold between us in the future – and for all I know, you might drop out of my life again at some point. So I'm determined to rebuild my life, one way or another. And... I guess that's all I wanted to say.'

It was good to hear the resolve in his voice – along with the words.

How different – yet similar – our journeys were.

'You'll get there, Luke,' I said with warmth in my voice. Then I lightly tagged on, 'and it's good to know you're not the sort of dog who'll be clinging to my leg and dry humping it as I try to hoover the lounge.'

Luke laughed softly. 'Yep, there's nothing like a

whimpering and clingy man to drive a woman away.'

'Quite so.'

I also liked his springboard analogy, so nicked it for the reason for my phone call.

'Nothing ominous,' I told him, 'but I thought it was high-time I told you about my own springboard.'

Luke listened in silence as I gave him a loose overview of Spencer's letter. Of how it had served to lift me from the ocean of guilt and complex feelings I'd been drowning in. And given me permission to go out there and get on with life. Which included the decision to meet up at Brightlea.

'He sounds like an incredible man.'

'He was,' I replied with a sigh. 'And despite how strange this might sound, I think the two of you would have got along.'

'Very sadly, we'll never know – but I'm sure you're right. It's just a shame he'll never be aware of the... *relief*... or *release* he's given you.'

I took a moment to consider Luke's words before speaking again. 'You know, since finding it, I've always regarded his letter as a gift to me. And it's certainly had a more positive effect than any of the counselling I received.'

'Oh?' Luke said with surprise. 'You had counselling?'

'Yeah. Not long... *after*. But it wasn't for me. Each to their own and all that.'

'Indeed,' replied Luke. 'And *thank you* for telling me about that letter. I understand how personal it is. But it does explain your change of heart about seeing me. If you love someone... etc etc.'

'Yeah, Spencer was all about freedom and living life to the full,' I said with a smile.

'Amen to that.'

'So,' I said, suddenly wanting the subject closed, 'if you don't mind my asking – I've been rudely wondering how you're getting by without an income? Selling your body in deepest Shaldon to the blue-rinse brigade?'

'Ha! If only!'

Luke spoke briefly about how he'd taken to selling some of his art online, to people who seemingly didn't know, or care, who he was.

'It doesn't pay anything like the galleries, sadly – but it'll do for now,' he concluded. 'Anyway, onto brighter things; tonight's the big night, isn't it? Good luck!'

'Thanks,' I replied. 'I'm really not looking forward to it, but I'll be brave.'

'Well, that's one thing you certainly are. You'll smash it, Amber.'

We finished our call shortly after, and I was left to stare once more at Spencer's loopy handwriting in front of me.

'Am I brave enough?' I wondered out loud.

I slumped back on the couch and laced my fingers on top of my head.

One way or another, it was *definitely* going to be a big night...

*

It was drizzly and cold as I made my way towards the High Street in my wide-brimmed hat. I skipped around puddles from an earlier downpour and weaved through the flow of people making their way to the month-long, Christmas market on Cathedral Green.

As I took in the glitzy decorations that draped across the streets or hung in shop windows, I thought back to where I was a year ago. I had come so far. With a deepening sense of resolve, I pushed on and soon found myself on the High Street. Keeping to the opposite side of the road to the large bookshop, I walked on until I stood facing it.

I hadn't entirely considered what to expect, but when I saw the long queue outside and mass of bodies inside, I felt shocked. And more than a degree of fear. I stepped back into the doorway of the fashion outlet behind me and peered across the road. Glasses of wine. Head-rocking laughter. Industry professionals, maybe. Or other authors.

And then a glimpse of Eddie. Cupping the elbow of another suited shark as he leaned in to speak to him. Smiles all around. A light slap on the back. And by the looks of it, trebles all round. An outstretched arm to bring someone else into the fold. And there she was; Viva Las Vegas Deauville. With the outrageous black bee-hive hairdo I'd seen online. Air kisses. Guffaws. A check of her watch. A frown.

Sensing eyes on me, my attention was diverted to a bespectacled young man standing in the queue. He was looking at me inquisitively with scrunched recognition beginning to form on his face.

I tugged at the brim of my hat and took a deep breath.

It was now or never.

Pulling my phone from my coat pocket, I dialled the number and watched Eddie break from his conversation to answer. As I spoke, I could see his thunderous expression as he bobbed about trying to spot me outside. But I was already head down and darting around the corner.

Which was where he met me a minute later.

The scene that unfolded must have looked straight off the set of my Greek soap opera to the little old lady who sat hunched over her bags at the bus stop across the road.

Eddie's explosion of rage. His shouting. His pacing. The exasperated, flapping arms. The exposed shark's teeth.

Me trying to calm him with 'down, down' hands.

Eddie walking away for a few paces, only to return and jab an angry shark fin towards me.

Hands on hips as he finally listened to me with a bowed head and tapping foot.

Dawning realisation. Understanding.

His ringing phone switched off during our fifteen-minute conversation. Nods. Answered questions. And finally, a smile. A tight hug. A brief examination of his damp suit.

And off he went. Slicing his way through the water to clear up my shit.

I realised I was trembling. And needed a drink. I walked away from the High Street and into the first available pub. Large vodka, please.

Then I sat down in a corner and with shaking hands, phoned Luke.

When I finished the call, I placed my phone face down on the table and thought about the confusion and shock in Luke's voice. Then I sat for a while with my fingers pressed against closed eyelids as I realised what I'd done. And in the hope that I'd made the right decision.

Why was bravery so utterly, fucking *exhausting?*

20.

With Some Bite-sized Chunks

'It's just like the walkthrough video – yes?' Petra smiled at me expectantly as she waited for my reaction. I stood in the open plan kitchen-living area and nodded my response with a wide grin.

She walked ahead to the large sliding doors that led out to the pool area and opened them. 'And here is the best bit.' I followed her and stepped outside into the sunshine and familiar scent of jasmine.

As I took in the unobstructed views of the coastline and the pool directly in front of me, Petra stood on her tiptoes and pointed. 'From how you explained it, I think that's the roof of your old villa down there!' I followed the direction of her finger and squinted into the sun.

And there it was. Just a glimpse of the red-tiled roof belonging to what had been my home for

3-months. I found myself smiling at the thought of Pool Man being down there and cheerily dragging his pole around.

How similar yet different this villa was. The living areas were practically the same, although this one wasn't split level and had no bar. Outside, the pool and the covered seating and dining areas were at the front, rather than the side. And sadly, there was no Chez Cleo. Three bedrooms rather than two. One downstairs. Two upstairs. The master with a spacious ensuite. Two additional bathrooms to service the other bedrooms. And a wide wraparound balcony that offered the same mesmerising, panoramic views – just from a higher vantage point.

To both sides and beyond the swimming pool area, there was a gravel garden dotted with lemon and pomegranate trees; a row of three, towering palm trees; a stunning olive tree; bushes, plants and large, stone ornaments. And the villa walls were festooned with bougainvillea along with climbing jasmine that framed each outer door.

'It looks even better than the video,' I told Petra after we'd finished our tour.

Petra's face beamed her delight. 'You're happy?'

'Very happy,' I told her.

'You know, it's a shame I couldn't push the price to less than €300,000 for you – but then you wouldn't have been able to get your residency. But it's still a very good price.'

It was *more* than a very good price. And I had no

idea how Petra had unearthed such a bargain that also met the threshold for gaining 'Residency by Investment'. It was the most perfect use of Spencer's money. And one he would have undoubtedly approved of.

'You've done a brilliant job. Thank you.'

'Awww. That's my pleasure, Amber – I hope you'll be very happy here.' With a check of her phone, Petra began to speak quickly. 'I'm sorry, but I have to run now. Appointments. Busy. Blah blah blah. Okay, okay... your keys are on the kitchen table. If you need anything, call me. Oh! And when you're ready, I have some clients – a couple of Nicosians and some Russians. You know. Rich, rich. Money, money.' And with her tinkling laugh, she rubbed together the fingers of one hand as she began walking towards her car.

I couldn't help but grin as I followed her. 'She'll probably wind up richer than half of them,' I thought in all seriousness.

A hug. Pecks on each cheek. Petra climbing into a mink-coloured Mercedes CLK. Engine starting. The driver's window lowering and Petra's head popping out.

'Just so you know... the beach parties start again next month! June until the end of October. We'll have fun – yes?'

Before I could answer, she pulled away with a cheery wave and two honks of her car horn.

I walked back into the villa, closed the door and

took in the surroundings of my new home. Petra had worked wonders – despite the previous owner wanting a quick sale; fully furnished, an unbelievable price and that magical view. And in a few days' time, boxes of my other belongings would be arriving. But for now, it was time to lug my bulging suitcase upstairs and unpack.

'Sally!' cried Lunge with a full display of his horror teeth. I let him give me a hug and was relieved to note that he kept his hands to himself. Behind him, the old fellas played *tavli.* Whilst above their heads, a bejewelled and heavily-eyebrowed, middle-aged woman advanced upon a bare-chested and terrified Greek Adonis. As he pressed a knuckle to his mouth and his back deep into the bedroom wall, the woman shrugged off her fur coat to expose her bare back. And the violins screeched their screech.

It was good to be back.

'Amber! You're here again! Can't keep away, eh?' A kiss of cheeks across the bar.

'It's good to see you,' I told Johnny. 'How could I stay away when no one makes my drink like you?'

A point of a finger. 'Ah ha!' Two taps of the bar. 'Drink first. We'll talk later.'

My vodka placed before me as I lit a cigarette.

'This one's from Roger.'

I blew out smoke and looked across the bar. Panama hat, jungle-themed shirt, an overly eager wave followed by a grinning thumbs up.

'Thank you,' I silently mouthed as I raised my glass towards him.

Johnny leaned on the bar. 'You know, he told me you're some kind of famous writer and all that.'

'I'm afraid it's the *all that* I'm best known for.'

As I took my first mouthful of drink, I threw Johnny a wink.

I had an invisible pool man. He came early morning. Before I got up. Before it got too hot. Petra had made all the arrangements. Apparently, he's called Brian. And originally hailed from somewhere 'up, up' in England. He could be Scottish.

I missed my meaningful chats with Pool Man of the Grinning Sunglasses variety.

My boxes arrived from England. There were surprisingly few – all things considered. I took out the prints I'd had framed in Exeter; a couple of Spencer's fashion shots; the one of our toes touching; a black and white, hot and sweaty head shot, taken post-sex – where we couldn't have looked more in love if we'd tried – as we hugged and smiled into the lens held at arms' length.

And there was a press photo of Spencer that I'd initially overlooked, when rifling through his boxes back in Exeter. Taken by one of the Sunday supplements, it was of his head tilted towards a cloud-streaked London sky as he laughed with those familiar crinkles around his eyes. He'd just won another award and the accompanying article highlighted his meteoric rise and achievements.

He looked so full of life. Embracing life. Excited to taste and experience every little bit of life. But also finding amusement in the awards and prestige he cared so little about.

It was *so very* Spencer.

I took to the prints to the spare upstairs bedroom, where they'd be finding a home on the walls.

As for his letter, it already lived happily in my dressing table drawer. To be looked at often.

With gratitude. Dear memories. And love.

Always with love.

The sound of crickets. The smell of jasmine. Beautiful bougainvillea. Sunbathing. Swimming. The delights of Sunshine Sam. Those views. That heat.

It was almost like I'd never been away.

21.

Is Anyone Sitting Here?

When I walked into Sonny's, I was feeling pretty damn fine about how I looked. Along with my smokey eyes, I was wearing a strapless tube dress I'd forgotten I owned, but had unearthed during my decluttering session in the flat. With a swirly, abstract design, it was a mixture of aqua blue, yellow and black. And was one of the few patterned items of clothing I owned.

DJ Puny did a quick double take when he spotted me. Then, with a brief smile, he raised a hand and gave me a wiggle-fingered wave. He looked a lot fresher than when I'd last seen him. And possibly a few pounds heavier. Hopefully he'd enjoyed a winter break and managed to have a bit of a munch. The baseball cap was back in situ and back-to-front, and he wore the 'Choose Life' t-shirt made famous by Wham back in the 80s. And as A-Ha's 'Take on Me' played to the smattering of filled tables, it didn't take a genius to work out what theme nite it was. I gave him a cheery wave back and made my way to the bar, where I found Andreas at the far end, deep in conversation with the chain-smoking Cypriots.

Just as I'd settled on my favoured bar stool in the corner, one of the Cypriots nudged Andreas with his whisky glass, then used it to gesture towards me with a few muttered words.

'Amber! You crazy woman!' As Andreas walked towards me with outstretched arms, I stood on the bar stool's footrest to greet him with a hug. We squeezed each other tight and I breathed in the thick scent of the oil in his long hair.

When we broke from our embrace, Andreas appraised me admiringly. 'You look beautiful!' he exclaimed. Inside, I purred; it seemed the extra effort I'd made with my appearance hadn't been in vain.

'Thank you. You don't look bad, yourself. How have you been? Did you close over the winter?'

Andreas held up four fingers. 'December, January, February, March – shut.' At the last word, he swept his hand away from him for emphasis. 'A big group of us went off to Thailand for a long rest and lots of fun.'

'I bet!' I replied with a laugh.

Two taps. 'Let me get you a drink.'

As he walked away, I cast a look around. It was so much quieter than my last visit. But I guessed, give it another few weeks or so, and the whole area would be swarming again.

When Andreas returned with my drink, he placed it before me and asked, 'So, how's everything back in England? I don't get the English newspapers – but have sometimes wondered about you.'

I obviously knew what he was referring to.

'Things are a lot better, thanks. Sort of. Well, I did something new. Something different. Some crazy stuff.'

Andreas threw his hands in the air. 'Of course! Of course! Crazy stuff! What else does Amber do?' Then in a serious tone, asked, 'But you're okay – yes?'

'Yes. I'm fine,' I assured him with a small nod.

'*Endaxi*. And how long are you staying this time?'

I took a long slug of my drink then smacked my lips together. 'Could be long, long time,' I replied with an arched eyebrow.

'*Bravo!* Good news for me! Good news for my profits!'

About to give Andreas a witty response, his attention was taken by the arrival of a bewildered-looking couple advancing upon the bar. I shifted back on my bar stool and once more took in my surroundings.

As I gazed around, I thought, what a whirlwind this past year has been.

So many highs and lows. And big decisions. And changes.

Including the move from my flat into one the child had found me on a rolling monthly contract.

Small and boxy, but with views of the River Exe that helped me finish the sequel that had taken longer than anticipated.

How sadly indifferent I felt when I wrote those final words.

My mind wandered further back to December. To my London trip to sign copies of Just Susie at the Vauxhall-based printers and later, hook up with Eddie. Out and about, I'd been spotted by a few eagle-eyed fans and after answering some innocuous questions, I wound up signing another author's novel, a notebook and two refillable coffee cups with dedicated inscriptions. With understanding, they respected my decision to decline photos having taken with them and we happily went our separate ways.

Unfortunately, it was a different story when recognised under the harsh lights of a tube train. A young and seemingly drunk, young couple had a very different set of questions for me.

Spencer. Nudist beach. Scars.

Yada yada.

Tight-lipped and maintaining a blank expression, I silently willed them to leave me alone. But as their interrogation became increasingly loud, intrusive and offensive, the girl pulled out her phone and began filming me. With a glare, I stood up and roughly pushed past them before squeezing through growingly curious commuters and getting off at the next stop.

I was still being filmed as the train began to pull away and as I stood, shaking with rage, I took a small and infantile satisfaction by giving them the finger with a broad smirk before they finally disappeared from sight.

Later that night, Eddie dabbed a napkin to his mouth before telling me, 'Highly unpleasant – but hardly on a level with what happened to Salman Rushdie.'

Pick the fish bones out of that, I'd thought, as I pressed my wine glass to my lips.

I've no idea if that footage ever made its way online. I still hadn't touched social media since my last Cyprus trip, and still relied upon Elena for a loose overview when, or if, she felt inclined.

Of course, the whole irony of the London trip was that boxes of the signed books wound up at the Susie Convention a month later. Apparently, it had been a roaring success, with stalls selling blouses, permed wigs, saucily messaged pebbles, stethoscopes, homemade cakes and slogan-bearing badges and t-shirts (with 'I'm Wellard' and 'The Sea is No-one's Mama' being of particular note). Whilst on-stage, scenes were camply re-enacted and excerpts theatrically read aloud. There was a Susie quiz, a lively panel debate about what Susie should do next, and the whole thing was rounded off by the highlight of the day – a Susie lookalike fashion parade.

It didn't need a genius to work out this event

would be supported by a strong contingency of drag queens. But what no one had bargained for, was the unsightly fiasco when an unsuspecting Vegas Deauville – who'd been representing Baulsach Publishing and selling signed Susie copies – had been practically wrestled onto the stage in her prim claret-coloured blouse and orderly slacks.

Despite her vocal and writhing resistance...

'Loving the beehive, honey,' one of her fellow contestants whispered, as Vegas found herself standing in line and holding up a numbered card.

She came third.

Eddie had sounded most enthusiastic when I spoke to him later. 'All the books sold out, we got hundreds of names to put on our mailing list for the sequel, and Vegas ended up going out on the town with the drag queens – inflatable Susie in tow, and wound-up singing, 'I am what I am' in some godforsaken basement bar.'

Good old Viva Las Vegas. A star is born.

With contained laughter at the thought of her on stage, I raised my arms above my head, stretched and savoured the delicious warmth on my flesh.

It really was wonderful to be back.

And as for anyone else who recognised me... I'd just jolly well deal with them on an individual basis. And based on their attitude.

I'd be *okay*.

I finally felt excited and hopeful about the

future. And ready to face whatever challenges this new chapter of my life had in store for me.

Bravo Amber!

I lowered my arms and dipped into my bag for a glance at my phone before pulling out a cigarette. About to place it in my mouth, a wide grin spread across my face as Rick Astley's 'Never Gonna Give You Up' filled the air. I thought back to when I'd seen Luke at The Captain's Table and how the song had blared out surprisingly loud and for the second time.

'This is what hell must sound like,' he'd said with a shake of his head. 'Hearing this pile of shite going round and round on an endless loop for all eternity.' With a smile, he'd raised his glass in toast. 'Dear Lord, save us all from Rick Astley and his inane warbling.'

'Amen to that,' I'd agreed, as we clinked glasses.

My mind wandered back to the Boxing Day walk we'd had along Teignmouth seafront. Both content to let Christmas quietly slip by unmarked, it had been our first opportunity to talk face-to-face since my bombshell phone call.

Oblivious to the wind and spray, we made our way along the promenade and back. Deep in discussion. Answering his questions. Posing my own. Both being brutally honest. We finished up sitting on a bench, with Luke nodding in understanding as I began to wind things down and summarise.

How long ago that seemed. In fact, being back

in the Cypriot heat and amongst the neon lights of Coral Bay, it felt like a lifetime ago.

I drained my glass, set it on the bar, nudged it forwards for Andreas to see, then picked up my lighter. Just about to spark it into life, I heard a voice.

'Is anyone sitting here?'

I slowly put down my lighter and the unlit cigarette. With the beginnings of a smile, I turned around.

'You made it,' I said simply, as I tried to sound casual despite the betrayal of my beaming face.

'Well, you know me,' Luke said. 'Nothing was going to stand between me and a bit of Rick Astley action.'

As I laughed at his answer, he dropped his duffle bag to the floor, slipped off the backpack that hung from one shoulder and ran a hand through his hair as he looked around and took in the unfamiliar surroundings. And when his gaze landed back on me, I could see those magical flecks dancing in his eyes.

'Too soon? Too public?'

'For what?'

'This,' he said, before cupping my face and kissing me deeply.

We didn't stay too long at Sonny's. Two rounds of drinks. An introduction to Keo and Andreas. Luke's friendly exchange with him about how crazy I was. Culture Club, The Police, UB40, Wham (et 80s al) and the suitably inebriated Dad Brigade finally lumbering towards the dance floor.

It was time to go.

Luke seemed distracted and incapable of hiding his tiredness when I tried to give him a guided tour of the villa. About to lead him outside to the pool area, he suddenly asked if he could have a shower to freshen up.

Once upstairs and his bags were dumped in my bedroom, I'd pointed Luke towards the en-suite and handed him a towel.

With his head tilted to one side, he asked, 'Will you join me?'

For a moment I considered the offer as we stood, facing each other with curls of knowing smiles. But I wanted to delay the inevitable a little longer. I'd been ready for Luke since that kiss outside The Captain's Table – I could wait some more.

'I thought I might unpack some of your things while you're showering – if that's okay?'

Luke threw me a tight-lipped smile as he nodded. He knew exactly what I was doing.

'Let's leave all that nonsense until tomorrow, eh? How about a fixing us a drink?'

'Not a problem. Keo alright? Or do you prefer whiskey?'

'Well, I suppose I'd best get better acquainted with the local stuff.'

'Sounds a plan,' I replied.

Yet to source a mini bar for my bedroom, I went

downstairs to get the drinks. Once made, I took them back upstairs, out to the balcony and put Luke's on the circular table with two chairs beside it.

Then I leaned against the balcony rail, breathed in the sweet smell of jasmine and gazed out at the twinkling lights.

I let out a contented sigh. 'Everything's going to be alright,' I muttered to the stars before sipping my drink.

I wasn't aware of Luke coming out of the bathroom, but when he stood behind me and wrapped his arms around my waist before kissing the nape of my neck, he didn't catch me by surprise.

As he squeezed me tightly, his warm body pressed against mine and I could smell the scent of my shower gel. His hard-on was impossible to ignore.

Resting his head on my shoulder, Luke asked, 'So are these the famous twinklies you told me about?'

'They are, indeed,' I replied. I squeezed one of Luke's forearms before rubbing my palm along it with sweeping movements. 'What do you reckon?'

He lifted his head and softly kissed the back of my neck again as he tightened his grip and pushed his groin towards me. And there it was. Another throb of my aching clitoris. Another release of wetness. I'd been in a heightened state of sexual arousal all day, which repeated masturbation had only seemingly made worse. I was swollen and wet and beyond ready. It had been far too long.

'I think,' he murmured into my neck before

straightening, 'they're nearly as beautiful as you.' Luke leaned back, hooked his thumbs inside each side of my dress and smoothly pulled to it down to my waist. As he cupped both hands around my breasts, his fingers sought out my hardened nipples.

He pressed into me again, his breath heavy against my ear. 'Oh God, Amber, I don't think I'll be lasting too long tonight.' Pushing my dress further down, he ran his hands over my exposed stomach before returning to my breasts – to roughly massage and twist on my nipples. The readiness I felt was almost unbearable.

I arched my back and with my free hand, cupped the back of his neck and laughed into the warm, night air filled with the chirps of crickets. I twisted around to face him. 'I think I'll be lasting even less,' I told him with a smile before stretching to put my glass down. As I wrapped my arms around his neck and looked into his beautiful eyes, I added, 'But it doesn't matter – we've got all the time in the world,' before kissing him lightly on the lips.

Luke's eyes travelled over my face.

'Then I'll die a happy man,' he said, before swooping me up in his arms and carrying me towards the bed.

I began to giggle. 'I feel like a damsel being rescued from a burning tower'

'Hush now, wench,' Luke said, before throwing me on the bed. As he unwrapped his towel and let it fall, he added, 'For one night only, let's go vanilla and see if we can last more than a few minutes.'

'Ooh er,' I said with a laugh as Luke climbed onto the bed. The tip of his swollen cock was already glistening. Between us, this would surely be over in seconds, I thought. But I didn't care one bit.

I left Luke to sleep in the morning. I looked at his peaceful face resting on the pillow; limbs akimbo, the sheet twisted around his waist and one leg, and got up and went downstairs. I cut off a chunk of olive bread and some slices of watermelon, made a mug of black coffee and took them to the poolside veranda table and sat down.

As ever, I took a few moments to take in the view with a feeling of gratitude and disbelief. As I looked towards my old villa and wondered who was currently enjoying it, two swallows skimmed across the surface of the pool – the first I'd seen since my return.

'Well, *hello* to you!' I said, with a smile as I shielded my eyes and watched them soar into the clear, blue sky.

While I picked at my food, I couldn't help but feel acutely aware of the delicious soreness between my legs, and thought back to the sex with Luke. The vanilla sex I usually hated. So gentle and slow. But for once, it had felt right. After he'd tugged off my dress and thrown it to one side, I'd stretched out, waiting for him. I remembered laughing at his grin that could rival a Cheshire cat's as he drew up my knees before spreading both of my legs.

'You have no idea how long I've wanted to do this,' he'd said throatily, before burying his mouth into me.

And as I squirmed and gasped, I had no idea how I didn't come straight away.

I'd returned the compliment when Luke straddled me on his knees and edged his way towards my face. Propped up on my elbows, I slowly licked the pre-cum juice off his cock before adjusting my position to lick along its length as I cupped and massaged his balls.

'Oh, Dear fucking Lord... ' he'd whispered with closed eyes.

I took Luke in my mouth and after he'd rocked into me a few times, he let out a whimper and pulled out.

'Sorry... I just need a few seconds,' he said apologetically with a boyish look on his face.

I laid back and reached up my arms. 'Come here, you big old brute.'

Supporting his weight on his elbows, Luke laid on top of me and we began kissing. But before too long, what had started out as tender, exploratory kisses, transformed into a frenzy of hunger.

I could bear it no longer. 'Get inside me,' I said, hoarsely. Above me, Luke's face creased into a slow smile.

As he retreated along my body, he stopped to roughly suck on each nipple before trailing his tongue down my stomach. Getting into a kneeling position, Luke slid a hand beneath me, lifted my bottom off the bed and using the palm of his free hand as a paddle, landed it between my legs with three or four swift smacks that smarted in the best possible way. Then, without pause, his palm roughly and briskly rubbed back and forth between my legs, with his spread fingers causing the most delicious friction.

'Vanilla,' I said, between breaths. 'I thought we were doing vanilla tonight.'

'You don't like it?'

Between gasps I told him, 'I fucking love it – you know I do. But... just *get inside me,*' I pleaded.

Luke stretched out above me and rested on his elbows once again. Our eyes locked on each other, and through my anticipation of what was to come, a flood of warm emotion rushed through me as I looked into Luke's eyes. It had been right to leave things until now. Of that, I was certain.

Still maintaining eye contact, Luke shifted position and slid into me. His pupils flared wide for an instant as we both gasped.

'Oh fuck... you dreadful, dreadful woman,' he murmured, as he slowly began to move rhythmically.

We never once looked away from each other. Even when my orgasm began to build, and my splayed arms reached out for my fingers to twist the edges of the pillows or sheets. Just a deep study into the other's soul, that felt full of wonder, as much as intimacy and longing. It was really something else.

I'm positive Luke felt it too.

As he kept it slow and deep and grinding – and despite the overhead ceiling fan – I could see the sweat beginning to form on his forehead. The concentration to not come was etched on his face. But as his groans increased, and as the tempo picked up, I looked into the glittering eyes as he bore into me and knew he wasn't far away.

I hooked my legs up around his waist and heard him catch his breath as he paused for a moment, before thrusting deeper and faster. Wrapping my hands around his neck, I pulled him towards me as I began to climb and climb, almost feeling dizzy from the need of release. I could feel Luke's panting breath on my face and as I felt myself about to go, I reached up and pressed my parted lips against his as I groaned my orgasm into his mouth with a series of shudders, that clamped and released Luke's cock in contractions. With a deep, guttural sound, two rapid thrusts were followed by a ramming third, which remained plunged inside as I felt the pulsing explosion of Luke's cum pump into me.

It felt totally, fucking filthy. And divine.

As we caught our breaths, our lightly touching mouths broke into smiles and then grinning laughter.

Afterwards, when Luke had taken me in his arms for a cuddle, he'd joked about it being a miracle he'd lasted more than five seconds.

'Yes, it was the best minute of my life,' I informed him.

'Oi. Enough of that,' Luke said with humour as he gave me a reprimanding squeeze.

'But seriously,' I began, 'is it just me, or was that really… *intense?*'

Luke looked at the spinning ceiling fan as he considered his reply for a moment. 'It was pretty off-the-scale, to be honest. I don't know if it's because it's been so long. Because I've been thinking about being with you for so long. Or I was just drowning in those green eyes of yours. Probably all three.'

As we gazed at each other, I could see his eyes beginning to close. After a few moments, they briefly fluttered before succumbing to sleep. I ran a hand softly through his hair.

'*S'agapó*,' I whispered, before gently kissing his temple.

I listened to Luke's deep breathing, and about to close my eyes, he groggily spoke. 'Saggy what?'

Typical, I thought with a smile.

'Nothing,' I replied.

'No, go on, tell me. Saggy what?'

'Okay. Sag-a-bore.'

'Sag-a-bore… is that right?'

'That's it. Bang on.'

'And what does that mean, for crying out loud?'

I landed a smacker on his cheek. 'I'll tell you when you're older.'

'Hmmm… '. And then he was asleep.

*

I pushed my plate away, picked up my coffee and stared at the light bouncing off the sea. We'd come so far. Me and Luke. From the phone call on that drizzly night in Exeter – when I'd broken the news of my plans. To our Boxing Day walk – when I embellished upon the scanty details previously offered. And then talked about *us.*

About how I wanted him in my life – but not quite yet.

He needed to be sure he was better. And I needed to deal with the flat sale and the sequel and general *life* without any trip-ups or meltdowns. I was already getting a bit better at handling the occasional gawpers and their favourable or unfavourable comments. And although the pain I felt about Spencer would never go away, the knife that was lodged in my heart, no longer twisted as deeply or as brutally as before. But surprising things could still trigger me and set me back. And the tears would return. But each and every time, the thought of Spencer's letter saw me wiping my eyes and promising him I was determined to enjoy my life.

So, I told Luke I'd like us to carry on as we had been. Messaging, phone calls and meeting up once in a while for a walk or a drink – when we'd always ended up kissing passionately. Invariably, Luke would tell me what a dreadful woman I was. Invariably, I would make a bad dog gag in response.

And each time I saw him, he told me he was feeling stronger. Better.

He almost didn't need to tell me; I could see the improvement for myself. He'd become more laissez-faire about things. The work that had dried up. The slur on his reputation. But his biggest progress was beginning to believe he wasn't responsible for Spencer's death.

I guess, like me, there'd always be the odd wobbly day.

He'd jumped at the chance to join me in Cyprus. Late spring, early summer, I'd told him. Let's just be really special friends in the meanwhile.

Let's not *mess this up*.

We'd talked so much during those months and gotten to know each other so much more. Private things. Personal things. The lot.

The plan was for Luke to spend his 90 days here with me in Cyprus. Then pop back to Shaldon – either with or without me – to check on things back home before returning for another stint. We'd take things from there.

We were both excited. I had my plans. Luke his; to start painting again.

And, of course, *us*.

And throughout those months of finding out more about the other, and the laughter and the walks and the drinks, there was always the undercurrent of sexual tension and the thoughts of us finally having sex.

It certainly hadn't disappointed...

I drained my coffee and smiled. I was feeling great. Better than great. And today was the day I'd be getting to work. I was finally ready. And raring to go.

I tightened my wrap, went upstairs and looked in on Luke, who was still sleeping deeply. I decided to leave him – he'd had a long day yesterday. The flight had been delayed for five hours. The baggage reclaim painfully slow. He'd had a late night.

Quietly opening the door to the spare room, I put on the aircon, closed the door, then took a moment to admire what I'd done with it. Spencer's framed photos were dotted around the walls, with my favourite – the press release photo, hanging behind a small table I'd taken from the lounge, which would now function as my desk. With dual aspect sliding doors that led to the balcony, the desk was positioned so I could sit with my back to wall and look at out the view. With Spencer watching over me.

I walked over, kissed the tip of my finger and planted it Spencer's face.

'Today's the day,' I told him with a smile, before sitting down and firing up my laptop.

Despite all the notes I'd made, I was finding the first line elusive. I'd written several before deleting them and was looking at my latest effort with a critical eye when Luke wandered in, scratching his head, yawning and wearing a pair of creased shorts. He smiled at me dopily as he made his way over and bent to give me a hug.

'Ah, you're hiding in here. Please don't tell me I've lost a day sleeping,' he said, as he squeezed me and kissed the top of my head.

I leaned into him and rested my cheek against his hand. 'Nope same day. And without wishing to sound like my mother – you must have needed the sleep.'

'Ha! That I did. And I could probably do with some more. So... is this it?' he asked with a nod towards the laptop screen.

'Yeah... I know what I want to write, but I just can't decide on the opening line. What do you think?'

Luke leaned forward and read aloud. '*This is the story I thought I'd never tell.*' He mulled it over for a few moments before speaking. 'Well, it sounds about right, doesn't it? I mean, I'm no expert... but that's pretty much bang on, I reckon.'

He rocked me gently in his arms as we both looked at the screen in silence.

'Then, that's how it's going to begin,' I said, finally. 'Thank you. And you're still sure you don't mind being in it?'

Luke straightened. 'I've already told you, it's no bother. I'm part of it all. Besides, nothing can be worse than what's already been said about me. And never mind, thank you – will you just look at this place in the daylight!' He released me and walked towards the sliding doors to peer out.

'Well, why don't I fix you some breakfast and then we can finish the tour?'

Luke flapped a hand at me. 'No, no, don't let me stop you from working. If there's food and coffee downstairs, I'll find it. You just crack on – I fancy a lazy day.'

'You're sure?'

'I'm sure. I'll have me a nosey around, unpack my stuff and contemplate my navel for a while.'

'By which time I should be done – I just want to do a couple of hours – I'm certainly not going to spend all my days locked away in here. Just bite-sized chunks at a time.'

Luke came back to plant another kiss on me.

'Well, I'll leave you to it and go exploring. Maybe get a bit of sun on my bones.' About to walk away, he scratched his head and said, 'By the way, what was that you called me last night – saggy arse or something?'

I laughed and slapped his backside. 'That's right, flabby bum. Now get away with you!'

'Charming,' Luke muttered with shakes of his head. 'A man travels two thousand miles and all he gets is abuse.'

'Abuse, yes... ' I said, before raising a finger in the air, 'but *also* a space for painting in the downstairs bedroom.'

A wide grin. 'Is that right? *Well...* on that note, I'll leave you to it and go check out my domain.'

I smiled as I'd watched him go. I was looking

forward to telling him about the clients Petra had lined up for him. And seeing his face – he had no idea. I'd met up with her a few days earlier, when she'd generously taken time from her busy schedule to help me find a car. No Cleo this time – she talked me into a racing green Mini convertible to whizz around the island in. One previous owner. Barely used. It was more than I'd intended to spend, but looked like fun. And fun was what I was all about now.

The clients were ready as soon as Luke was. Petra had shown them examples of Luke's work from his website, and whilst some had a particular subject in mind, most of them just wanted some original and expensive artwork to show off. By the sounds of it, there was a ready-made queue of commissions just waiting for Luke to reignite his passion.

Let's see what he thought of his working space first.

I returned my eyes to the laptop screen, hovered my fingers over the keypad and began to type.

It was finally happening.

22.

Dancing's All About...

Of course, Eddie had wanted to throttle the life out of me when I told him I wasn't going to my book launch and signing event. At one point, he'd bared those shark teeth and threatened to drag me across the road. The time, the money – the *effort* that'd been spent on me. It was *all* about to be wasted.

How he'd had to cajole and wet nurse me into pulling my finger from my fucking arse. And how that had been a fucking waste of time. How he'd tried to be patient. Understanding. But this? This was a slap in the face. Didn't I *know* there were people inside *there* who were important in the publishing world? Not to mention the fans, inside and out, who'd been queueing since God knows when, in the pissing rain?

I was selfish. Ungrateful. Could have fucking told him earlier. I was *taking the piss.*

And when I'd finally down-downed him and managed to get a word in edgeways, I told him I was going to do it. Was ready to do it. I *wanted* to do it. And had only just decided.

I was going to write my story.

But all the rest of it – the Susie circus, the interviews, social media – I wanted none of it. Tell them I was ill. Tell them anything. I'd been out of the limelight this long. Just leave me to write *my* story, *my* way, and let the Susie machine rumble on. It'd done alright so far without me. Let it rumble on. And let me fuck off back to Cyprus to write my thing.

Hands on hips, Eddie had wagged his head from side-to-side as he weighed things up.

And when he spoke, it was with eyes filled with pounds signs.

'It'll be brutally honest? Have *everything* in it?'

'Warts and all. There's no other way,' had been my answer. 'Besides, you told me someone else would write it anyway.'

Eddie whistled through his teeth. 'You have *no idea* what's been offered.'

'Then it seems we've reached an agreement.'

The next day, we had a long phone call when Eddie was on the train back to London. Yes – I'd finish the sequel with Vegas first. Yes – I'd come to London to sign the books. Yes – I *really* was going to write my story. As soon as I could. As best as I could. And, no – I wouldn't be calling it 'The Naked Writer'.

That had been the strength of it.

And although Eddie had huffed and puffed about cancelling the events at the two London flagship stores in particular, I allowed him that. I had let everyone down at the last minute and caused a lot of ball ache for a lot of people. He went along with the illness excuse as mitigation. Which would doubtlessly be questioned when my supposed 'ongoing health issues' and silence would result in the sequel and an autobiography. Not to mention, when I'd invariably be spotted out and about in Cyprus. But as Eddie reasoned – who doesn't love a writer hiding out on a Mediterranean island? I could almost see the pound signs in his eyes getting bigger.

I looked at the loose-leaf notes beside my laptop and flicked through them. There was a fistful of stats from Tanya, who had been more than happy to supply me with facts and figures about violence against women. Depressing reading, indeed. And after some online snooping, which threw up a surname and sad headlines, I managed to track down Carol, who had told me about her murdered daughter. I messaged her through Facebook, and we later spoke at length on the phone. Such a lovely woman. So generous to let me cite her terrible story. She hoped it would do some good.

I sighed as I flicked once more through the handwritten notes and Tanya's printouts. It was going to be a big job. A tough job. But one I was determined to do.

For Spencer. For me. For Luke – who would never know he was the trigger for my decision to write this book – and whose story sat within mine. For Carol and Jade. For all the other victims out there. And for the women who might recognise some warning signs and find the courage and strength to reach safety.

It was time to rattle my tambourine.

No sooner had Lunge thrown up his arms in greeting, uncertainty registered on his face when he spotted Luke behind me.

'Mister Sally?' he asked, as he pointed and looked at me quizzically.

I found it hysterical. 'Yes! Mister Sally,' I told him with a laugh, as Luke leaned forward to shake his hand.

Lunge ushered us to an outside table. 'Well, this is rather lovely,' Luke said, once we were settled and he'd looked around.

'It's rustic heaven,' I agreed. I watched Luke as he studied the menu. It was good to see him looking so much fresher after his day of lounging and sleeping poolside. I'd joined him once I'd finished in the office – feeling pleased at the inroads I'd made – and after some al fresco lunch, we got in the pool to cool down.

Both naked, we inevitably ended up having sex, with me wrapped around Luke's waist as we bobbed about in the shallow end. Afterwards, as we stretched out on our loungers, he told me he'd fallen in love with his studio space and its views across the pool, garden, banana groves and the sea beyond.

'And you won't mind shifting to the lounge or my office when Elena and Adam decide to pay a visit?'

'Good Lord, no. I'm just thrilled to have somewhere like that to work in, and can't wait to get started.'

And that's when I told him about Petra's clients.

The expression on his face was priceless. Luke reached over and held my hand. When he spoke, I could hear the tremble of emotion in his voice. 'That's... beyond amazing. I can't thank you and your friend enough. You have *no idea* what it means to me.'

'I think I have a bit of an idea,' I replied with a smile. As I squeezed his hand, I added, 'And I think that studio room... the villa... and Cyprus... will be *good* for us.'

'Me too.'

We chatted about all the places and things we wanted to see and put the Akamas turtles high on the list. And having learned that the water levels could fluctuate at the Baths of Aphrodite, decided to give it the benefit of the doubt and a visit. Then we kicked around the possibility of a hot tub warranting the expense and decided we were undecided.

A short while later, Luke dropped off, face down on his lounger, for an afternoon snooze. I reached for my wrap, spread it over his back and left him to it.

And as I looked at him now – with the beginnings of a tan – he looked rested and extremely handsome.

Lunge took our orders and just as I was telling Luke that the old postcard faces were playing *tavli*, the violins from the telly struck up.

'Quick! Quick! Watch this!' I instructed, as I pointed to the screen.

Just in time, we were rewarded with a shot of the same bejewelled woman I'd seen on my last visit. She stood at the top of a boardroom table, wearing a lilac-coloured power suit, jumbo earrings and too much hairspray. With wild eyes and a finger raised to the ceiling, she hissed at the suited men who sat around the table in cowering attendance. As the nearest one muttered something (seemingly) in defence, she reached for the glass of water in front of her and threw its contents over his face.

A few cheers of approval went up from the postcard faces.

And as the woman's challenging stare went from suit to suit, the violins went berserk as the credits began to roll.

'Fuck me,' said Luke. 'It looks like someone's put a broom up her ass widthways.'

'It gets a lot worse,' I warned him.

Johnny clamped both hands warmly around Luke's offered handshake.

'Welcome! Welcome! Amber's told me about you. You're the painter – right?'

'On a good day,' Luke replied with humour.

Spotting Roger drinking on his own, it was too good an opportunity to resist. I left Luke and Johnny to it and went over. After brief pleasantries, he was most eager to question me; he'd unearthed the 'Naked Writer' interview and was itching to get some juice. I lied and told him nothing could be discussed; a film was being made about me and a secrecy clause was in place.

The lie had been worth it to see his eyes almost pop out on stalks.

Besides, give it a couple of years, I reasoned, and he'd be able to read everything for himself. But he'd have to pay for the privilege. Like anyone else remotely interested.

'Mum's the word,' said Roger, as he pressed a finger to his lips. And as if he was somehow involved. I could already half-imagine the Chinese whispers.

I absently thanked Johnny when he brought my drink over and glanced up to see he'd returned to chat to Luke, who was happily getting stuck into his Keo. From their smiles and easy manners, they already looked like long lost mates.

I turned my attention back to Roger and gave him my pitch with the assistance of my phone. And by the end of it, not only was he impressed with what he'd seen and heard, but visibly excited at the prospect of earning a bit of commission for pushing any work Luke's way – courtesy of his 'high-profile and affluent contacts'.

Roger leaned forward. 'Leave it with me,' he said, before adding, 'you know, I've already got a couple of people in mind.' I thought he was shaping up to tap the side of his nose, but he settled for jutting out his lower lip as he gave me a grave, knowing look.

Only time would tell if he'd come up with anything.

But from the way his eyes greedily glittered, I wouldn't be surprised if he did.

60s nite at Sonny's. And DJ Puny was wearing a Beatles wig, wraparound sunglasses he could have stolen from Pool Man, and a black and white geometric short-sleeved shirt. A quick thumbs up from him as he bent over his decks.

As we perched on our bar stools and waited for Andreas, a couple of the men at the end of the bar disinterestedly glanced our way, while others raised their glasses in greeting.

'Well, this is a lot busier,' Luke said with approval as he looked around.

I cast my eye over the tables and saw only three were empty. 'Yep, it sure looks like things are starting to take off for the season. Yesterday being changeover day and all that.'

Luke leaned in towards me. 'Talking about things taking off... ' he said, as he gave me a small nudge and his chin indicated towards the dance floor.

Spurred on by DJ Puny's abrupt change in tempo, the Dad brigade and their partners were out in force. And as 'I Can't Get No Satisfaction' filled the air, they channelled their inner Mick Jagger and strutted around, hands on hips, with elbows wagged backwards and forwards. Lips were pouted. Heels of hands were clapped together. The words tunelessly bellowed out.

'Well, they may look like a bunch of constipated chickens,' Luke said with a grin, 'but at least they're having fun, right?'

Ah ha! Which reminded me... 'Do you know... I've got a theory about dancing... '

As though on cue, Andreas was there with my drink. 'Please, my friend! Don't listen to her madness!'

There'd been no opportunity to tell Luke my revelation about dancing. And, unluckily for him, I'd be saving that particular gem for another day. Instead, Andreas was eager to get his drink order, and we ended up chatting and laughing as we watched the antics on the dance floor. Palms were dramatically held up for 'Stop! In The Name of Love'. 'Let's Twist Again' saw staggers and stumbles, and one squealing lady landing heavily on her arse. Whilst the chorus of 'I'm a Believer' nearly burst our eardrums. And when the Beatles' 'Twist and Shout' filled the air, and imaginary mopped hair dos were shaken about, and another twist in the heat seemed a twist too far, DJ Puny announced that he was 'slowing things down'.

Luke put his drink on the bar. 'Do you know, it's

been a long time since I've had a dance. Shall we?'

Andreas flapped his hand in the air.

'Amber doesn't dance! All this time – I've never seen her dance!'

With a smile, Luke stood and stretched a hand towards me. 'Well, we'll have to do something about that, won't we?'

Luke beamed at me in encouragement. Andreas cheered, 'Yes!!' and followed it up with a piercing whistle.

How could I say no?

I took Luke's hand and let him lead me to the dance floor. And to the sound of Jackie Wilson's 'Sweetest Feeling', Luke twirled me before entwining his fingers with mine, as we danced at arms' length with smiles. Then he pulled me close. As we moved against each other's body, Luke spoke into my ear.

'You've got no idea what I'm going to do to you when we get back tonight.'

'Well, I hope you're going to be gentle with me,' I replied with a grin he couldn't see.

'Oh, I'm not intending to do that for quite some while.'

'Why, I *do* declare!' I said in my best Wild West Southern drawl.

Luke laughed and spun me away from him. And as he pulled me close once more, we cheesily found ourselves singing the end of the chorus to one another, as Luke rocked our outstretched arms.

'Lovin' yoooo..oooh..oooh.'

Our faces were beaming, and I was filled with the unadulterated joy of a soppy teenager.

We wrapped our arms around each other's waist. And with our bodies pressed tightly together, we gently swayed in rhythm to the song.

After a few moments, Luke spoke. 'By the way, you'll er... be pleased to learn I made a total fool of myself earlier, with your friendly barman at The Red Lion.'

I pulled back and looked up at him with a raised eyebrow. 'Oh? How's that?'

Luke lifted his head and spoke to the star-studded sky. 'Well, here's the thing... I asked him what saggy arse means.'

I pressed my lips together to contain the blurt of laughter trying to escape.

Betrayed by his smiling eyes, Luke pursed his lips in mock seriousness and gave a few small nods of his head. 'Oh yeah,' he said to the night, 'your man was quite tickled by it. In fact, I'd even go as far to say that I made his day. Talk of the village and all that.'

Luke looked down at me with a 'what have you got to say about that?' expression.

I managed to give him a glum-lipped expression.

'Oh dear,' I said with a heavy sigh, as though we were tackling a shared dilemma. 'So... did Johnny enlighten you about your backside?' I enquired lightly.

Luke stopped moving.

'Oh, that he did, alright.'

As Jackie Wilson sang his beautiful words, the desire to laugh disappeared as we stood wrapped in each other's arms.

'So... just for the record,' Luke said softly, as his eyes swept over my face, 'I love you, too.'

For a few moments we were in our own bubble. The small smiles broadening into wide, daft grins.

And like the lovestruck teenagers we'd both become, we softly sang to each other as we slowly began to dance. As we gradually turned, I caught a beaming Andreas giving me a thumbs up.

And when I looked into Luke's eyes and felt my heart melt into his chest, I knew we'd finally found our home.

'*S'agapó*,' I told him.

'*S'agapó*, you dreadful woman.'

And to the last strains of the song, I finally remembered the person I once was.

A Note from the Author

Much like Amber, this is the book I never thought I'd write...

When I finished NUDEY BEACH, I always intended to park things there and leave the ending ambiguous as to whether Amber survived or not. But messages began trickling through, asking if there'd be a sequel. And I noticed some reviewers were wondering the same.

So I scratched my nut. Began to imagine how Amber's story might continue.

And got to work.

However... ill health and choking on life's shit sandwich meant it took far longer than intended.

But here we are. Hopefully, better late than never.

What's next?

Well, I'm dropping the filth and going for a comedy novel – which I'm aiming to get out a whole heap quicker. Please follow me on Amazon or Instagram or Facebook to see how I'm getting along.

And if you enjoyed AMBER STONE, a review on Amazon and/or Goodreads would see me vaulting my lounge furniture in gratitude and thanks!

Take care. And be lucky!

Angie x

Printed in Great Britain
by Amazon

48936808R00212